ICY SILENCE

A Megan Scott/Michael Elliott Mystery

SANDRA NIKOLAI

ICY SILENCE

www.sandranikolai.com

Vemcort Publishing
ISBN: 978-0-9947894-2-6

Cover art and design by Carolyn Nikolai

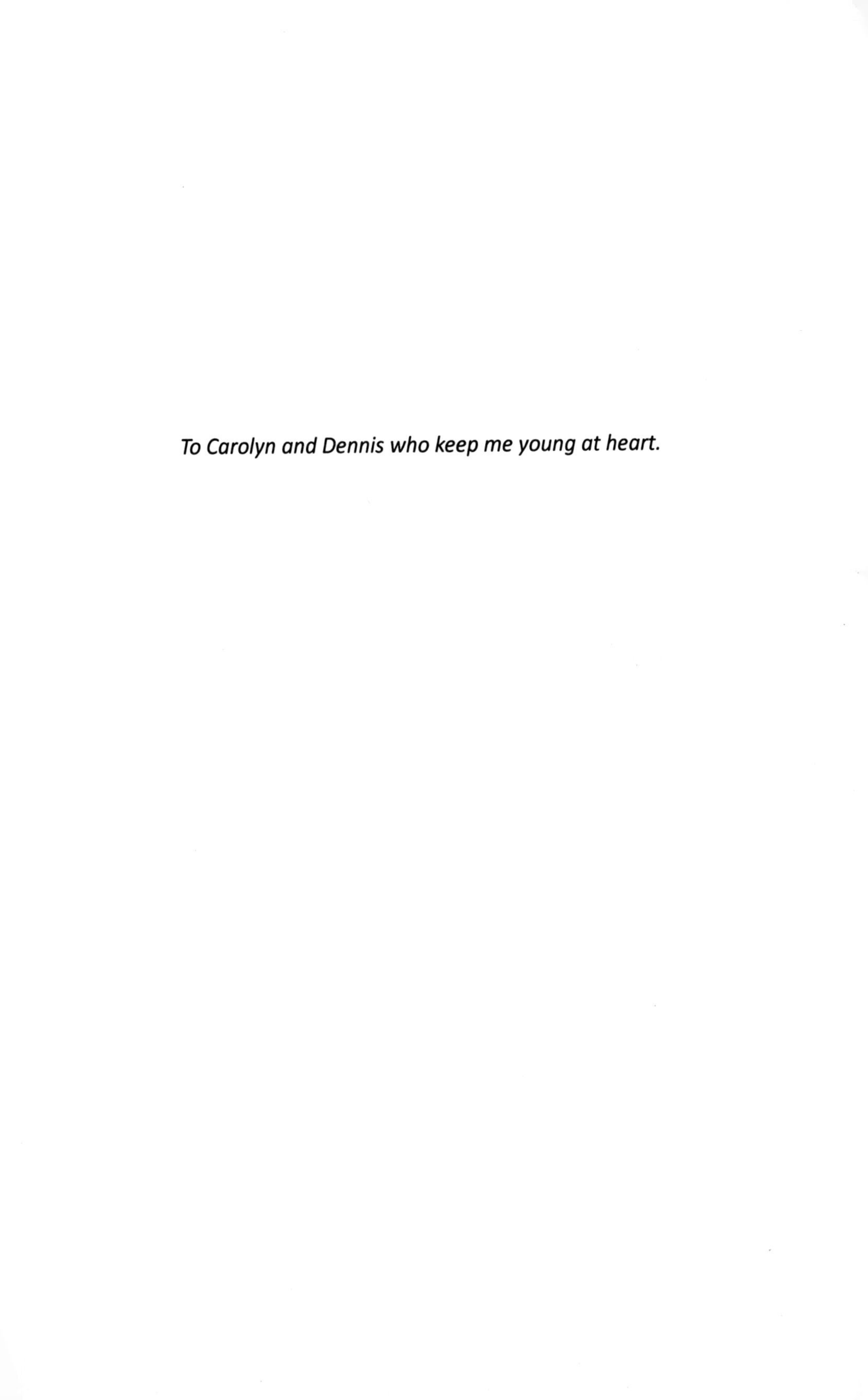

To Carolyn and Dennis who keep me young at heart.

CHAPTER 1

Our windshield wipers were losing the battle in fending off the barrage of ice pellets. The snow that had accompanied us from Montreal to the Eastern Townships had changed to freezing rain halfway through the two-hour trip, delaying our arrival Thursday afternoon at Verdell College School. The elite private boarding school was located in a rural area of the province of Quebec. Surrounded by forests, rivers, and lakes, its isolated location made me wary about how this prep high school might cope with emergency situations. Sherbrooke, the nearest city, was forty miles away.

The weather amplified the hesitation I'd had about taking this trip when Dave called last week to invite Michael and me to Verdell. Although Dave's request to give a presentation on career day came at the last minute, Michael could never refuse to help a close friend. I understood the dilemma, but the timing sucked. I'd been secretly planning a romantic weekend getaway for us for months and had to put my plans on hold—yet again. On a more positive note, we'd finally be spending a weekend together. No newspaper deadlines for him; no ghostwriting projects for me. Tomorrow was our class presentation. Saturday and Sunday, we'd be visiting with Dave and his family in Victoriaville. I planned to make the best of it.

Hands clasping the steering wheel, Michael guided our Subaru Forester along the ice-covered road that cut through the two-hundred-acre campus. To the east, a dense forest of snow-clad evergreens and deciduous trees bordered one side of the school grounds. Closer at hand, clusters of majestic fir trees lined the road, their branches glistening with ice as they huddled against the biting wind. It was a picturesque scene but a threatening one should temperatures plunge and the sudden storm intensify as weather forecasters now predicted. I cringed with the realization that we'd be spending the next two nights here.

"I hope the weather clears up before we head out to Sherbrooke on Saturday," Michael said, reading my thoughts. "Can't wait to check out a lead I got on a member of the Hells Angels."

"When did you find out about this?"

He glanced at me. "A source called me late last night. He said Pierre Favreau is hiding in the Sherbrooke area."

The whereabouts of the escaped killer and member of the Hells Angels was unknown until this latest of Michael's inside scoops. Talk about bad timing.

"What about our plans to spend the weekend with Dave and his family?" I asked.

Michael shrugged. "We can still do that."

"There won't be enough time."

"Sure there will."

"But we'd planned on enjoying this weekend away from work."

"I can't ignore this lead." Michael paused. "You hesitated to accept Dave's invitation. Maybe you would have been happier if you'd stayed home."

I wasn't about to tell him the reason behind my hesitation to come to Verdell and spoil the romantic plans I'd put on hold. "Stayed home alone? And do what? Pace the floors in our condo? Lose sleep every night worrying while you track down a member of the Hells Angels?" Okay, I would have stayed at my mother's place in Montreal, but I'd have probably spent more time chatting on the phone with Michael than with her.

"My job is unpredictable, Megan. You know that. I have to seize every chance I get to investigate a lead."

"Right." There was no changing his mind—for now.

As Michael navigated the car to the left around a small curve, we left the quasi shelter of the trees. The storm let loose and he hunched over the steering wheel to peer through the blast.

We drove by two low-rise brick buildings. Yellow police tape along the side of one of them caught my eye. I pointed it out to

Michael, shouting to be heard above the glacial rain now pelting the car windshield. "Do you know anything about a crime investigation here?"

He shrugged. "It's news to me."

We drove past a chapel, two other edifices, and the three-story main building where we'd be meeting with Dave. The austere gray stone façade of these structures set them decades apart from the contemporary low-rise buildings we'd passed.

Michael turned right onto a side lane that led to the parking lot. Dozens of cars were parked here, but the lot could have accommodated a hundred more.

"We'd better grab our bags," I said. "I don't think we'll want to walk back to the car later."

We stepped out into the freezing rain, our winter boots and goose down parkas preparing us for anything a harsh Canadian winter might blow our way. Laptops and overnight satchels in hand, we maneuvered the icy path back to the front of the prestigious private school.

The words, "Verdell College School (1917) – A solid learning foundation," were inscribed above the entrance to the main building. We climbed the slippery stone steps leading inside.

The dull rays entering the atrium through a skylight and oversized windows created a somber atmosphere in the populated space. Students stood in small groups or sat on red leather divans, their heads bent over cell phones as they read messages and tapped replies. Aged between twelve and eighteen, they were dressed in the school's navy and beige uniforms. Shirts, ties, and blazers. Preppy.

Contrary to the enthusiasm I'd expected to see on their young faces, their expressions displayed sadness. On closer inspection, I noticed some students were crying and hugging one another. Others gave us a guarded look and stopped speaking as we brushed past them.

Then I saw the makeshift memorial.

Along one side of the atrium were flowers, balloons, artwork, framed photos, stuffed animals, and candles in glass jars. Written in fancy lettering on a huge poster were the words, *Nat and Andrew – U will be missed*, encircled by hundreds of initials and signatures. Pasted on the wall was a collage of colorful paper hearts with personal messages. Students stood in front of the memorial, sobbing and wiping their eyes.

Michael met my astonished look and was about to say something when a strong male voice reached us.

"Michael Elliott. You made it."

"You bet." Michael shook the man's hand and introduced me to Dave Pellegrino.

Dave stood several inches shorter than Michael's six-foot frame. Under his parka, a thick neck strained against the collar of his shirt. His dark hair was cut short, and although a receding hairline had begun to form, it didn't detract from his charm.

"Megan Scott, my pleasure." He smiled and gave me a firm handshake. "You know, you're the first ghostwriter I've ever met." His brown eyes reflected sincerity.

"We like to keep a low profile." I smiled.

"Not like you, eh, Michael?" Dave chuckled. "Still chasing the bad guys and writing those award-winning pieces?"

"I try my best."

"As always," Dave said, smiling. "By the way, I read your true crime novel on the drug trade in Canada. Talk about an intensive investigation. You did a terrific job putting it all together."

"Thanks. I had lots of help from an expert ghostwriter." Michael smiled at me.

"There you go. Oh…before I forget, here are your visitor ID cards." Dave handed us each a visitor's pass. "Carry it at all times. School policy." He looked at me. "I don't know if Michael told you, but after our studies in Journalism at Ryerson U, we teamed up on a string of newspaper assignments—mostly crime articles. I sure miss working the news beat at times, but it was risky business."

"Some things never change—even a decade later." Michael shrugged.

Dave nodded. "That's why I gave up my job as investigative reporter after I got married and started a family. I also needed the stability of a nine-to-five job. Now I teach English Lit. Not that it's any safer..." He frowned, dispersing his former breezy manner.

Michael took the cue. "About the memorial and the police tape on campus... What happened here?"

"Two students died this week. It's complicated." Dave surveyed our wet clothes and baggage. "Let's get you both settled in first. Then we'll talk. Follow me." He turned and started to walk away.

Before we took a step forward, Michael leaned over and whispered in my ear, "Something's not quite right here."

We caught up with Dave. He gestured toward a corridor on the right that led out of the atrium. "Through there, you can get to the dining hall, library, and chapel. Those buildings are connected outdoors by covered passageways." He raised a thumb to the left. "You'll find the admin and faculty offices and most of the classrooms down that corridor. Perpendicular corridors from this main building lead north to the infirmary, the gymnasium, and other buildings on campus."

"A veritable maze," I said.

Dave shrugged. "It can be a little confusing at first, but everyone gets used to it. By the way, the two top floors of this main building house almost half of the fifty live-in staff and faculty—including me. They assign the one-bedroom apartments here through a draw every year. I won this year." He smiled. "The rest of the staff and faculty reside in a private building on campus."

"They all live at Verdell?" I asked.

He nodded. "On week days. It's more convenient and it saves a lot of traveling time. The top brass believes we can best serve student needs by being available twenty-four seven. For that reason, Verdell keeps a skeleton staff of twenty-five percent on hand on weekends."

"How does your family feel about your live-in arrangement?" Michael asked.

"Okay, I guess. I go home almost every weekend. Most of the staff and faculty members do too. Many of them come from Montreal and further. It's still quite the drive for me to Victoriaville—about a hundred miles north of here—but Samantha and I love the small-town ambiance there. Great for the kids too."

"Why Verdell?"

Dave lowered his voice. "Why else? It pays the big bucks." He waved us on. "Follow me."

He led us to the back of the atrium and down a staircase into an underground corridor. It spanned the width of a couple of middle-sized cars placed side by side and had a ventilation system. I recalled similar passageways under McGill and other universities in Montreal that linked to a network of city tunnels. Affected by a sudden dose of irony, I contemplated whether the concrete floor and varnished concrete blocks along the walls here symbolized Verdell's promise to provide a solid learning foundation.

"The students nicknamed this underground corridor 'the echo' because they claim you can hear the wind echoing—even howling—here when no one is around," Dave said. "Some of them insist it's haunted." He raised an eyebrow in our direction.

I met his gaze, not sure if he were kidding or not.

Michael chuckled. "Good try, Dave."

Dave looked past me at Michael. "Thought I had you going for a while. I forgot how you could always see right through me." He smiled. "For the record, I've walked through here alone late at night and never heard a thing. Not even the wind."

I noticed the occasional wide slab of concrete built into the walls and asked Dave about them.

"The echo was one of the original passageways in a mine," Dave said. "Pathways from here led to old abandoned mines built more than a hundred years ago. After the school bought the property, it sealed up the pathways with concrete. Major renovations and expansions have taken place on campus since then. The varnished blocks along the echo alone cost a fortune."

"What kind of mines were they?"

"Copper. They were among the oldest mines in the country. Demand from the United States soared for the metal during the Civil War in the 1860s. The Eastern Townships employed fifteen hundred men to work in a complex of local mines to meet their requirements. For decades, the miners toiled, raised families, and established communities and towns until demand for copper dwindled."

"The insignia on the main building indicates Verdell was built in 1917."

"That's right. About a decade after the old mines closed down. Barratt Mining recently resumed operations for copper in the area."

Barratt Mining. The name rang a bell, but I couldn't recall where I'd heard it before. "How long is the echo?"

"I can't give you an accurate measure. I can tell you it runs from the main building and continues to the dining hall, library, chapel, and girls' dorm. A separate staircase goes up to each of those buildings from the echo. The girls love it. It's faster to walk through the echo from the girls' dorm to the classrooms than to wind your way through the buildings and passageways connected at ground level. Both paths are convenient because you don't have to step outdoors. No expense was spared, I can tell you." He smiled.

"What about the boys' dorm?" Michael asked him.

"It's located across the way from the girls' dorm and further down the road. It isn't connected to the echo because the original passageway came to an end under the girls' dorm. There are plans to extend the echo to include the boys, but it's a question of funding. You probably noticed low-rise buildings on campus when you were driving in. They're the boys' dorm and and the private residence I mentioned for the live-in staff—part of the renovations and expansion."

I noted that the students going by were tapping messages on their smartphones. "Are phones allowed in class?"

"Yes, but they have to be turned off," Dave said. "It's one of the guidelines the students have to follow when they reside at Verdell."

"What other guidelines are there?"

"They have to respect dress code, curfew, and private property. They're encouraged to study hard and be on good behavior at all times. Since they're being prepped for admission to the best colleges and universities in the world, Verdell ensures the guidelines are enforced."

"How?"

"Layers of teachers and students supervise every building and dorm on campus to make sure things run smoothly and to handle problems. I'm on the supervisory team with other teachers. We report students who damage school property, cheat on exams, use illegal substances—that sort of thing. In truth, those occurrences are rare here."

"It sounds restrictive compared with public schools." I glimpsed a closed-circuit surveillance camera almost concealed around a bend. "Like Big Brother is watching."

Dave shrugged. "The guidelines come with the territory. When you ask high tuition fees for educating kids from wealthy families, you have to implement strategies to ensure you produce high achievers. Most of our students graduate with high honors and go on to higher-level learning. Granted, it's a no-nonsense environment, but we manage to have fun. There are frequent day trips to Sherbrooke where students and staff can visit art museums and theaters, shop in fancy boutiques, and eat in gourmet restaurants."

"Do any students ever rebel against the stringent system?" I asked.

"No. They know from the start that Verdell has a strict code of standards and what the repercussions are if they don't follow them."

"Speaking of law enforcement," Michael said, "you never did explain the police tape. Does it have anything to do with the two students who died? And how come we didn't hear about it on the news?"

If anything, Michael was persistent.

"It was reported," Dave said, "but for the sake of the families concerned, Verdell and law enforcement officials kept the incident as low key as possible."

"Were the students in any of your classes?"

"Yes. English Lit." Dave choked up.

"My sympathies," I said.

"So sorry for your loss," Michael said. "How did they die?"

Dave frowned. "The police are treating their deaths as an apparent murder-suicide. They wrapped up their investigation this afternoon—just before you arrived." He took in a deep breath. "I was selfish in not letting you know about it beforehand, Michael. Truth is, I desperately need your help before it's too late."

CHAPTER 2

The weather had hampered our weekend trip and now a precarious element had been added to the scenario: two students had died at Verdell under mysterious circumstances. Dave cut short our conversation in the echo because of the growing number of students and staff walking around, so we had yet to find out why he had appealed to Michael for help.

We walked a little further when Dave came to a stop. He motioned toward a staircase on the left. "These stairs go to the girls' residence," he said. "Follow me."

He led us up a steep staircase and into the lobby of the girls' dorm. Classic buttoned leather sofas and armchairs sat on a Persian rug around an English-style stone fireplace.

"Megan, you'll be staying in one of the dorm rooms here," Dave said, handing me a key. "It's a private room—not joined through a shared kitchenette to another room like the other dorm suites are. Michael will be staying in the boys' dorm across the way. We'll head out there next."

"What?" I gaped at him. So that's why he was wearing a parka when he'd greeted us in the atrium.

"Sorry about the separate sleeping arrangements for you two. In view of strict school policy about sexual intimacy, we don't want to set a bad example for our students."

"A bad example? In this day and age?" I rolled my eyes. Who would have thought my live-in relationship with Michael was any of the school's business anyway?

"No problem," Michael said, giving me a quick side-glance. "It's only for a couple of days."

Oh, great! So much for not wanting to sleep alone in our condo. Who would have guessed I'd end up sleeping alone in a school dorm surrounded by people I didn't know? And in the middle of nowhere. Not to mention the lurking of Pierre Favreau and the Hells Angels, heaven knew where.

Dave and Michael left for the boys' residence across the road. The only elevator in the girls' dorm was a freight elevator and it didn't work. I climbed the stairs to my room on the third floor. I removed my parka and boots, convinced I wouldn't need them again tonight, and took a few minutes to unpack. I hung up pieces of clothing in the closet to get the wrinkles out and put my toiletries in the bathroom.

Moments after I'd returned to the lobby, Michael and Dave strode in. They were soaked from their walk outdoors, ice pellets dotting their coats like tiny crystal beads. Luckily, their hoods had afforded a degree of protection from the elements.

Dave didn't speak much as he escorted us back through the echo to the main building. No doubt he had a lot on his mind these days.

After we'd entered Dave's office, the men hung up their coats to dry. With a solemn look on his face, Dave invited us to sit down and briefed us on the recent deaths at the school. "The victims' names are Natalie Dunn and Andrew Boyle. I borrowed their files from admin earlier." He opened two manila folders and slid them across the desk to us.

Inside one folder was a photo of Natalie and personal information about her. The slim girl with the large brown eyes and wavy blond hair looked as innocent as any sixteen-year-old junior student. She was enrolled in the arts and indicated an interest in literature.

"Was she a good student?" I asked Dave.

"A darned good one," he said. "She had an innate aptitude for interpreting Shakespeare. She handed in her assignments on time and never asked me to bend the rules."

"What do you mean?"

"Certain students feel privileged and ask for extensions. Nat never did." He switched his gaze to the other folder.

Andrew's photo depicted a gangly young man with a reddish complexion. His interests were in sports. The seventeen-year-old senior student played basketball and soccer.

"Off the record," Dave said, "Andrew had obtained counseling through the school's doctor to help control a drug addiction problem."

"I thought Verdell had a tough policy on drugs," Michael said. "Why was he still here?"

"Well..." Dave pressed his lips together. "The policy has a gray area when it comes to families who provide financial contributions to the school. Money talks, if you get my drift." He shrugged apologetically, as if he had no choice but to accept the status quo.

"Was Andrew still doing drugs before he died?"

"I don't know," Dave said. "The autopsy results will tell us."

I scanned the rest of the information in both files. The results of the students' midterm exams were unremarkable, which surprised me, considering the high standards expected at the school. I voiced my observations to Dave.

"The final exams alone determine if the student meets the criteria for success and is qualified to move on," he said.

"From what you said earlier, I assumed only the best students were accepted at Verdell," I said.

"That's true, but..." Dave paused, as if he were searching for the right words. "In practice, Verdell adopts a more realistic viewpoint. Since the school needs to fill the classrooms, it doesn't refuse anyone who can afford the hefty fees. More than eighty percent of the students come from affluent families, so money isn't a problem for them. Off the record, Andrew came from an upper middle-class family. Nat came from an average-income family that managed to pay the high admission fees through loans or other means."

"How would you know?"

"Verdell notes the method of payment and brief family profile in the student file."

"What about the protection of personal information?" I asked.

"It's not what you think," Dave said. "The parents sign an agreement form when they provide the information. Admin uses the data to target wealthy families for sponsorship funds, not those who can't afford it. An elite establishment like Verdell needs substantial outside financing to stay in operation."

It was becoming clearer by the minute that Verdell was a money pit, despite the visual indications and glib pronouncements Dave had indulged in earlier. To what extent did administration and staff close their eyes to what was going on here in the name of money?

Michael steered the conversation in another direction. "What happened to them, Dave? How did the students die?"

Dave glanced down, seemed to be putting his thoughts in order. "We found out about the accident two days ago, yet it feels like months. You know what I mean?"

Michael nodded.

"Tuesday morning, I went to get something out of my car. I'd parked my Honda Accord in the lot behind the school. Since I don't drive anywhere during weekdays, it stays in the same spot. But it wasn't there. I walked around the lot looking for it, thinking maybe someone had played a trick on me and moved it to another spot."

"Do people play tricks like that often around here?"

"Sometimes the staff is worse than the kids. Difference is, we don't get caught." Dave grinned. "Anyway, when I couldn't find my car, I told Mrs. Desmond. She's the school dean. That same morning, Nat and Andrew missed their breakfast check-in and didn't show up for class. Their dorm supervisors visited their rooms and reported them missing."

"What did the dean do?"

"First, let me tell you about Mrs. Desmond." He leaned forward and lowered his voice. "She's as tough as nails. Michael, remember our first boss at the newspaper? The one the reporters secretly called *the whip*?"

Michael smiled. "How could I forget? He'd be snapping at us to finish one assignment so we could work on the next."

"Well, she's *the whip #2*. A stickler in enforcing Verdell's guidelines. You don't ever want to get on her bad side, trust me." Dave sat back and took in a deep breath. "About the missing students... Mrs. Desmond sent supervisory personnel to expand the search for them and for my car. It had snowed overnight, and someone noticed tire tracks leading from the campus into the forest."

"*Into* the forest?"

"There's an old dirt trail that runs through the trees. The land is private property and doesn't belong to the school. Staff and students know they're not allowed to drive or even walk on that stretch of land."

"Where does the trail lead?"

"To the Saga River. Needless to say, the dean called the police." Dave winced, as if the memory were too painful to recount. "When they dredged up my missing Honda Accord, they found Andrew behind the wheel and Nat in the trunk."

My breath caught in my throat. "That's horrific!"

"Gruesome," Michael said. "You said the cops think it's a murder-suicide."

Dave shrugged. "So far."

"You sound skeptical."

"Autopsy results will determine what happened."

Memories of my late husband suddenly surfaced. I recalled how I too had to wait for autopsy results, only to find out that he'd been murdered. I swallowed hard. "It must be a nightmare for their families."

"They were devastated," Dave said. "They drove here from out of town the next day. We had a private memorial service in the chapel. The school counselor met with the families and is offering counseling to students and staff on an ongoing basis. Regular classes are canceled this week to allow for a grieving period, though some students prefer to keep busy. Everyone copes in a different way. Until the police investigation is over, no one will rest easy."

"About the car," Michael said. "Was it broken into?"

"No, teachers don't lock their cars here. It was hotwired, though. Samantha got so upset when I told her. Not only about the students but also about the car. It was totaled." Dave fingered loose papers on his desk.

"I have a feeling this situation is a lot more complicated than you're telling me," Michael said. "For starters, you said you needed my help. What's going on?"

Dave looked down, kept fidgeting with the papers. "There are certain things that might be misinterpreted. Things that could cost me my job...not to mention my marriage."

Michael frowned. "What things?"

Dave retrieved a small key from his jacket and unlocked the top drawer of his desk. He took out a sheet of paper. "This is a printout of an email Nat sent me days ago." He placed it before us.

The note read:

"Dear Dave,

My life improved after I came to Verdell. I met a wonderful English Lit teacher—you. I'm so lucky to have you in my life. I enjoy your classes so much, but more than that, I'm forever grateful for the secret bond we have between us, despite our age difference.

Love,
Nat"

"Have you shown this email to anyone?" Michael asked Dave.

"No."

"Not even the police?"

"Especially not them."

"Is Nat's email still on your computer?" Michael gestured to the laptop on Dave's desk.

Dave shook his head. "No, I deleted it...and others. The text messages too."

"Text messages?"

Dave nodded. "Several."

"In this email, she mentions she had a 'secret bond' with you. What do you think she meant?"

"Damned if I know." Dave raised his hands, then let them fall with a thump on his desk.

"Level with me, Dave. A student's infatuation with a teacher is a notion that's as ancient as—"

"Okay, okay. Here's the thing: I make a habit of bolstering class effort by praising my students. Nat was an excellent student and I praised her work."

"Often?"

"Not more than any of the others." Dave paused. "Well…maybe a little more. Sometimes she'd stay after class to ask my opinion or interpretation about specific lines in a poem or story. We'd get into these lengthy discussions. She could have misinterpreted the extra time and attention I gave her. I don't know."

There was an awkward pause.

Dave's eyes flitted across the room before he focused on us. "Look, this is puppy love in its purest form, but I'm afraid it might be misconstrued as something else. I'm happily married and have a four-year-old daughter. I can't risk the scandal." He crumpled up the sheet and tossed it in a wastebasket.

"I understand," Michael said, "but I don't see what that email has to do with Nat's death."

"This is a cloistered school," Dave said. "Gossip travels fast in a community of three hundred people. What if she told a close friend about her emails to me?"

"Did you encourage her to write those emails?"

"No, on the contrary."

"Then you have nothing to worry about."

Dave shrugged. "What if it wasn't a murder-suicide? What if the cops discover someone murdered her?"

"Did you murder her?"

Dave sat upright. "Hell, no! What do you take me for? A lunatic?"

Michael spoke quietly. "I'm trying to show you that you worry too much."

Dave gathered his composure. "I'm justified to be concerned about the emails she sent me. If the police change their minds and think her death is suspicious, it would make me look guilty in their eyes."

They were butting heads. It was time for a change of direction.

"Nat's a pretty girl," I said to Dave. "She must have been popular with the boys. Do you know if she and Andrew were...lovers?"

"Like I mentioned earlier, the school considers sexual intimacy inappropriate. If by fluke such an indiscretion did occur, I'd probably be one of the last people to hear about it." He looked at us. "I apologize again about your separate sleeping quarters."

"On that subject," I said, "do you think Mrs. Desmond might make an exception in our case? After all, we're not students. We're mature adults."

"The dean is quite firm when it comes to these matters. If you two were married, it would have been a different situation." He managed a brief smile.

Michael must have appreciated that comment. He'd wanted to tie the knot for months now, but I'd refused. I ignored his gaze on me and pursued my original topic of interest. "It's my guess that Nat and Andrew slipped out after curfew while everyone else was asleep. If Andrew killed Nat and then killed himself, he must have had a motive."

Dave nodded in agreement but remained silent.

"If we want to get to the truth, we need to find out more about the relationship between Andrew and Nat." Michael leaned forward in a gesture of encouragement.

Dave fidgeted with his papers again and glanced at his watch. "Let's put this on hold for now. We'll have to hurry if we want to get dinner. The cafeteria is closing down soon." He stood up.

Michael slammed his hand on the desk. "For Pete's sake, level with us, Dave. We're here to help you."

Dave sat back down. He passed a trembling hand over his face. "It's my worst nightmare come true."

"Why would you say that?"

"The police seized Nat's computer. What if they question her emails to me? Or check her text messages—if they have her phone. I could be in serious trouble."

"Why the hell did you delete your emails in the first place? The cops might suspect a cover-up."

Dave took in a deep breath. “I didn’t think. I panicked.”

“What aren’t you telling us?” Michael asked.

Dave stared at him. “Nat sent me a text message days ago. She wanted to see me one evening. She said she’d kill herself if I didn’t acknowledge my physical bond to her.”

“Did you meet with her?”

He shook his head. “No way in hell *that* was going to happen.”

“Did you reply to her text message?”

“Yes.” Dave squirmed in his chair. “I threatened her. I said I’d report her to admin on charges of harassment if she didn’t stop. The next day, the police recovered her body from the river.”

CHAPTER 3

At Dave's insistence, we cut short our discussion and headed for the dining hall. It was our good luck the kitchen was still serving meals at eight in the evening.

Entering Verdell's dining hall was like stepping into another era—the 1800s to be precise. Rows of wood tables ran horizontally across a black-and-white checkerboard floor. The seating space could easily accommodate the entire school population. Dark wood beams crisscrossed the ceiling, creating a rustic effect, and large windowpanes overlooked the campus and bordering forest. The school's coat of arms hung above a stone fireplace on the back wall. I had no idea what the various components in the plaque symbolized, though the words engraved along the bottom of the shield displayed Verdell's motto: A solid learning foundation.

Closer at hand, a poster tacked on the wall near the entrance conveyed a clear message. It reminded students that the use of phones and other electronic devices was prohibited in this room, the library, the chapel, the classrooms, and after lights out in the dorms.

I pointed it out to Michael.

He shrugged. "So? We're not students."

I gave him "the look" and made sure our phones were turned off.

We moved to the food station that displayed hot meals in metal containers behind a glass counter. In the interim, Dave grabbed a can of pop and headed to a table.

"So many choices." Michael surveyed the lineup of food bins. "I'll go with the shepherd's pie. Chocolate cake for dessert."

A female server whose nametag read *Glenda* handed him the two plates. He placed them on his tray and joined Dave at the table.

I chose the turkey slices and veggies, but they'd run out of potatoes wedges.

"We can get more from the kitchen," Glenda said, her Irish accent surfacing. She pointed a thumb toward a swing door about twenty feet behind her.

"It's okay," I said. "I can do without."

"No, dear, you wait right here. I'll go ask the cook. It'll only take a moment." She pulled the empty metal container from its slot and turned to a young helper who was tidying up. "Eric, wipe the empty slot, please." She disappeared through the swing door.

Soon a bearded man wearing black-rimmed glasses and a white cook shirt followed her in. He was carrying a metal container in gloved hands. I noticed a scar above his left eye while he rested the steaming receptacle on the counter. As he looked up at me, his small dark eyes registered surprise, and he almost dropped the container. He placed it into the empty slot, stared at me again, and abruptly left.

"Thank you, Paul," Glenda said to his back, then handed me my plate.

I sat down next to Michael but said nothing about the cook's odd behavior. "The staff is so accommodating here. Glenda ran out of potatoes and went to the kitchen to get more from the cook."

"She was only following protocol," Dave said. "They have to make sure the kitchen pantry is well stocked and the serving trays are full. Paul is on kitchen duty tonight. You guys should try his homemade pasta the next time."

"Aren't you hungry?" Michael asked him. "That ginger ale won't get you far."

"With everything that's been happening, I don't have much of an appetite." He lowered his voice. "Look, about the incident here, I promise we'll continue our discussion after tomorrow's class presentation."

Michael shifted in his chair. "I feel awkward about making a presentation about a potential career path to students whose feelings are pretty raw. It might be the last thing they want to hear right now."

"I spoke to my senior English Lit students about it earlier. They're looking forward to hearing your presentations. They need a diversion from their grief. In fact, they're eager for things to get back to normal again. So am I." Dave took a long sip of his drink. "Are you up for it?"

"You bet," Michael said. "What's the schedule?"

"Come to my office at eight tomorrow morning. We'll walk over to the classroom together." He studied Michael's pullover and jeans. "One more thing. Did you bring a jacket and tie like I suggested?"

"Yes."

"Wear them. It meets the protocol." I didn't escape his scrutiny. "Megan, you might want to pull back your hair in a ponytail."

My hands flew to my hair in a protective gesture and I laughed. "Are you kidding me?"

"No." Dave remained serious. "Our girls with shoulder-length hair are encouraged to tie it back when in class. Since you and Michael are young adults, the students will identify with you. I'm sure you want to set a good example."

I was speechless. Fine, I'll play Verdell's ridiculous "rules" game. The upside to this madness: I wouldn't have to spend time trying to tame my frizzy locks every morning while I was a so-called *guest* at the school.

Michael met me downstairs in the girls' dorm lobby the next morning.

"How did you sleep?" I asked him.

"Not well. I was lonely." He gave me a sheepish grin.

"Me too." I smiled. "Did you turn off the lights at curfew?"

"Yes, but I turned on my laptop. I was curious about the abandoned mines Dave mentioned. I went online and researched the industry in the area."

"Sounds boring."

"I wasn't sleepy. I expanded my search and found out which mining projects had been started, which ones had been abandoned... I researched the old mining sites around Verdell too. There are four tunnels running deep under the school. Incredible, eh? And a country road borders the river behind the forest. It leads out to the main road we took to get here."

"Busy night."

"Not the sort of busy I would have liked." His blue eyes twinkled.

I laughed.

We reached Dave's office at eight sharp. We took our seats at his desk while he briefed us once more on the advantages of Verdell's unique environment.

"This school has a reputation for producing high fliers," Dave said, beaming with pride. "Students can be assured that the education they get here will give them a competitive edge in the outside world—no matter what field of higher learning they pursue next."

"Sounds utopian," I said.

He shrugged. "In a way, it is. Because of limited classroom size, Verdell prides itself in honing exceptional achievers in every sense of the word."

"How can you be so sure?" Michael asked. "No matter how prepared these students are when they graduate from university, their exposure to the real career world is limited. It's tough out there and you know it."

"Many of our graduates have been accepted at the best colleges and universities and have attained excellent jobs afterward. The results speak for themselves."

Dave sounded as if he'd been drinking the Kool-Aid again. His refrain on the virtues of a Verdell education was beginning to grate on my nerves. He'd probably given the same formal speech to other presenters before meeting with us because it sounded rehearsed. Or maybe he was pumping himself up before going to class so as to exhibit a more detached attitude.

"Dave, you said the majority of students here come from

privileged families," Michael said. "How many graduates received help from their well-heeled parents to get those jobs? Better yet, how many graduates are working in corporations that their parents own?"

Michael's tone was cynical. Seeing that he'd rebuffed his parents' wealthy lifestyle, his response didn't surprise me.

"It doesn't alter the fact that our students are guaranteed a solid learning base at Verdell and excel with superior results. Let me show you." Dave picked up a couple of files from the tray on his desk and opened the first one. "Take Zack Barratt, for example."

Another person named *Barratt*? Maybe it was a common family name in the area.

"Zack is a senior student with a grade A average. His peers and the faculty have voted him most likely to succeed for the fourth consecutive year. He's also one of Verdell's top athletes." He opened the other file. "Helga Peterson shares the same qualifications—a grade A student and top athlete. These are just two of the all-round achievers Verdell generates. You won't find the same level of competence and success anywhere else. You see what I mean?" He beamed with pride.

Students with Einstein IQs and Schwarzenegger strength. What could I say? Verdell's rules and methodologies were obviously part of Dave's indoctrination, and he enjoyed promoting its success. As my mother would say, live and let live.

Michael gave Dave a nod, conceding and ending the debate. Like me, he hadn't come here to make an issue out of Verdell's student success rate.

"By the way," Dave went on, "if you need anything this weekend, Zack and Helga are your go-to students. I'll introduce them to you when we get to class." He glanced at his watch. "Which is right about now."

As we headed down the corridor, I counted ten empty classrooms along the way. I envisioned how energetic minds might be solving algebraic equations or reading about genetics and evolution during regular classes.

We came to a stop at Dave's English Lit classroom where a man in a dark suit and a young woman holding a notebook stood by the door. They greeted Dave with a friendly "Good Morning." Dave introduced us to Leonard Whitehead, a software developer, and Ann Plourde, an accountant.

"We're scheduled to speak later this morning, but we were wondering if we might sit in on other presentations," Ann said to Dave.

Dave glanced at Michael and me. "Would that be okay with you?"

"Sure," Michael said.

I nodded in agreement.

Dave ushered us into the classroom. True to his word, he introduced Zack and Helga to the four of us, which led me to assume he'd already offered the same spiel about his star pupils to Ann and Leonard.

Tall and fair-haired, Zack exuded charm, confidence, and sophistication—attributes often associated with having been born into a wealthy family. Six pins representing achievements in sports and academic pursuits dotted the lapel of his dark blue blazer.

"Pleased to meet you," Zack said, shaking hands with us.

Helga's wide smile softened the brunette's muscular physique. She stood as straight and tall as Zack and exuded as much poise. She pulled out two business cards from her blazer. "I'm on the supervisory student team for the girls' dorm this week. Here's my number if you need to reach me." She handed Ann and me each a card. "We'd like to invite the four of you to sit in on our basketball practice sessions while you're here. Zack's team players are amazing."

"Oh, we have nothing over Helga's team," Zack said to us. "They're heading for the championships." He smiled at Helga, revealing a set of perfect teeth to top off his athletic form.

The way their gazes lingered on each other implied there was more than student camaraderie between them. Interesting. I wondered how they handled raging hormones under Verdell's archaic polices.

Zack fished out his student cards and offered one to Michael and another to Leonard. "I'm also one of the supervisory students on duty for the boys' dorm this week. You can reach me by email or on my cell. I'll reply ASAP." He pronounced ASAP as *A-sap* rather than spell out the letters.

Dave checked his watch. "We'd better get started." He called the class to attention.

Dave had briefed us about the one-on-one approach Verdell offered their students, so I wasn't surprised the classroom held only fifteen desks. Each girl and boy wore the traditional blue blazer and tie and sat up straight. No face piercings, body tattoos, or pink hair in evidence. Tiny earrings for the girls and clean haircuts for the boys. Except for the color of their hair, their uniform appearance at first glance gave me the impression I was looking at clones.

It was hard to ignore the empty desk—Andrew's. Teary eyes and blotchy faces indicated how deeply his death had affected his peers.

Michael stood at the front of the class and introduced the topic of his presentation. He stated the pros and cons of working as an investigative journalist, provoking polite smiles as he described a few humorous episodes from his earlier days as a rookie reporter. After he finished, he handed the floor to the students. They stood up one at a time and introduced themselves before asking their questions.

At one point, it was Helga's turn. She was direct in her approach. "Did your family support your choice of career? And if not, how did you handle the conflict and still pursue your dream?"

I cringed. Michael's career choice had created a deep rift in his relationship with his parents, and his conversations with them were infrequent and courteous at best. He'd skirted the topic every time I suggested he try to patch things up with them. I'd since given up trying to persuade him and left the next move up to him.

Before Michael could answer, Dave intervened. "Maybe this question is a tad too personal."

"No problem," Michael said, then answered Helga's questions. "Like other parents, my parents had their own idea of a dream career for me. And yes, we went through some rough times when

I told them about my plans. In fact, we're still arguing about it." His smile drew a chuckle. "What convinced me to pursue studies in investigative journalism was the crazy notion that I could make a difference in the world while doing what I loved most. I'd like to believe I'm making progress in achieving that goal. My critics might argue otherwise."

Two more brief questions were raised until the last student stood up.

Zack's six-foot frame drew all eyes upward. "I've read your articles, Mr. Elliott. Your investigations focus on organized crime, like the drug operations of the Hells Angels in Quebec and Ontario. Is confidentiality a problem for you?"

"Confidentiality?"

"I assume that most journalists work with informers to gather evidence."

"Sometimes."

"Do you protect your sources?"

"As much as I can."

"I've read how some informers have lost their lives. Have you ever lost an informer?"

Michael paused, no doubt recalling the recent death of one of his trusted informers who'd been killed by the Hells Angels. Claude Savant had been shot in the head in a gangland-style execution and his body dumped by the side of a road north of Montreal. "I don't discuss matters relating to my informers."

"I apologize," Zack said, palms open. "I didn't mean to be intrusive. Curiosity got the better of me."

"I understand."

Zack had another question. "Do you feel your work has helped the police in reducing criminal operations?"

Michael nodded. "My investigations have helped them make arrests. But like a virus, criminal organizations recruit new members and spread out to new areas. It's a vicious cycle. Unless we destroy their operations, they'll keep on spreading their venom."

"I've read how some criminals get away with light sentences and are released soon afterward. Does this ever discourage you?"

"Never."

"My last question. Do you ever worry that you might get shot or a bomb might go off under your car?"

There was a deafening silence in the classroom.

"Criminals don't make a habit of knocking off reporters," Michael said. "They focus on more significant targets."

"Thank you." Zack sat down.

Dave took over. "Okay, that's all the time we have for this segment. Thanks, Michael. Next up is Megan Scott. She'll tell you all about her job as a ghostwriter."

I smiled and mustered as much positive energy as I could, even though I suspected that my contribution to career day wouldn't draw the same level of curiosity as Michael's had. Working alone behind the scenes as a ghostwriter offered little enticement to a generation of teens who had social media running through their veins. And it wasn't an incentive to high achievers at Verdell aiming for careers in medicine, science, and technology either.

Then again, it could all be in my mind.

I took a deep breath and began. "Clients hire my services as a ghostwriter when they need someone to write material for them anonymously. I've been hired to write non-fiction books, business reports, marketing brochures...that type of end product. I plan every step of my projects: research, writing, schedules, and so on to avoid complications. I work alone from my home office most of the time, but I do get out to meet with clients to discuss their projects. And I've met some pretty interesting clients—from architects to wildlife rescuers."

Aware of the occasional facial tissue surfacing to wipe away a tear or blow a nose, I rolled out the rest of my presentation without delay.

When it was time to take questions, a slender girl in the front row stood up and introduced herself as Sophie Toomey. Her complexion paled against a backdrop of dark brown hair tied back in a ponytail. She wore frameless glasses and read from her notes. "Thank you for coming here today. Do you enjoy working alone at home and why?" She gave me a shy smile, revealing pink and purple braces.

"Yes, there are many reasons why working alone appeals to me. For one, I value my privacy. It's a precious commodity in a world where infringement of personal information happens every day."

Heads nodded in agreement.

"Working from home gives me that privacy and offers the extra benefit of safety. No fear of employers using cameras to spy on employees at the office, no fear of being mugged on the street after working late hours, no fear of being kidnapped..."

Did I say that?

Sophie stared at me. "Kidnapped?"

The girl sitting in the desk next to her rolled her eyes in annoyance. At Sophie? At me?

Oh-oh. Damage control needed here. I forced a smile. "I suppose our fears can sometimes be exaggerated at night when it's dark and we're all alone."

The anxiety in Sophie's eyes intensified and she paled.

Had I traumatized the poor girl?

I waited.

Sophie took my silence as a signal to move on to the next question. "I'd like to know if there's a downside to your work as a ghostwriter. Apart from what you just said."

Oh yes, I had traumatized her. "The downside is that my name never appears as the author. Someone else gets the credit. I'm okay with that. The work is my reward and when it's finished, I let it go."

Sophie had another question. "Do clients ever confide their deep, dark secrets to you?"

"Only if they're writing their deep, dark autobiography." I smiled.

Sophie folded her notes. "Thank you." She sat down.

There were no other questions. I felt proud—and somewhat relieved—that I'd managed to make it through the presentation.

Zack surprised me by standing up at the last moment. "Miss Scott—it is *Miss* Scott, isn't it?"

I tensed up. Whose business was it anyway? Then I assumed he was just trying to be polite. I swallowed my anger. "Yes."

"What would you say are important skills a ghostwriter should have and can you site examples?"

I gave it some thought. "Listening to what the client wants is number one. In the case of a memoir, I also listen to the client so I can capture his voice in words. I sometimes ask their permission to record our meetings for that purpose. In general, I highlight details that capture the essence of the project and try to shape the prose into something interesting—even if the material is *so* boring."

One girl let out a nervous giggle.

"Despite the anonymity of your line of work, have you ever encountered threatening situations?"

His question unnerved me. Months earlier, I'd come close to getting killed after I'd dropped off a client in the Old Port of Montreal. As I was leaving the port, I spotted an escaped convict named Pierre Favreau and followed him, camera in hand. I was kidnapped and threatened at knifepoint, then gagged and bound...

"Miss Scott?"

I snapped back to reality. "Yes—I mean—it can get dangerous in the physical sense."

"From behind a desk?" Zack grinned.

I hesitated, not wanting to reveal my horrid experience. I decided to match Zack's humor instead. "Yes. Paper cuts. See?" I raised a bandaged finger.

"Thank you." He gave me a brief smile and sat down.

Dave moved to the front of the class. "How about a round of applause for our guests," he said, bringing the session to a close. "Okay, everyone. Take a fifteen-minute break before the next class."

A few students headed out. The rest chatted in groups. Presenters Leonard and Ann also went by.

Ann touched Dave's arm and said, "We'll be back in half an hour for our presentations."

"Okay, see you then." Dave turned to Michael. "Why don't you and Megan grab a cup of coffee in the dining hall? Check with the cook to see what's on the menu for lunch and dinner."

Michael was about to answer when a woman's voice reached us.

"Mr. Pellegrino, please excuse the intrusion." A woman wearing a gray jacket over a matching skirt stood in the doorway. She peered at him over her bifocals. "Can I see you for a moment?"

Two uniformed police officers stood behind her in the corridor.

"Oh...okay, Mrs. Desmond." Dave waved Zack over. "Zack, please have the class open their textbooks to Shakespeare's next sonnet in the meantime. My book and notes are on the desk."

"Sure." Zack retrieved them.

The presence of police officers had drawn the students' curiosity. They gawked toward the corridor.

Mrs. Desmond stepped back as Michael and I followed Dave out of the classroom, then closed the door behind us. She fingered her pearl necklace. "We don't want to attract undue attention. Mr. Pellegrino, perhaps you can speak with these officers elsewhere."

"Sorry, ma'am," one of the officers said, "but we were asked to bring Mr. Pellegrino to the station for questioning."

"The station?" Dave asked. "Why?"

"In relation to the incident involving the two deceased students, sir." The officer kept his gaze on Dave.

"I've already spoken with the investigators here this week," Dave said.

The constable stiffened. "We're just following orders, sir."

His demeanor told me there was more to their unannounced arrival at Verdell than we knew. A discreet side-glance from Michael told me he was thinking the same thing.

"I'll get my coat then," Dave said. "It's in my office." He headed down the hall, the constables tagging along.

"This is certainly turning out to be a most peculiar situation." Mrs. Desmond looked at Michael and me. "Excuse my manners. I'm Mrs. Desmond, the dean at Verdell. It's unfortunate that we had to meet under such awkward circumstances." She shook our hands with a firm grasp. "Thank you for making the trip from Montreal. The weather has worsened, so I'm relieved you won't be driving back on these treacherous roads today. I hope you enjoyed your session with our students."

"Yes, it was a change from our usual routine," Michael

said, smiling. "Zack and his classmates kept us busy with lots of questions."

The dean's eyes lit up. "Zack is one of our most successful students. It's wonderful to have seen him mature through the years. He sets a fine example for other students. I couldn't be prouder." Her maternal favoritism for the boy expressed itself in a snooty look of self-satisfaction, as if she based his success on her role in enforcing Verdell's rigorous guidelines.

I took the cue. "We understand that Verdell offers a valuable learning experience," I said, recapping what Dave had told us.

"It's exceptional, actually." She raised her chin. "Mind you, if it weren't for the generous sums Zack's father and other sponsors donated to Verdell every year, none of our students would attain superior levels in intellectual and physical pursuits. Trenton Barratt is a pillar in the community. I was honored to attend many fundraising events with him. Such a lovely man."

Trenton Barratt. The name finally hit home. I recalled coming across it in research material last summer while working on a project for Gary Stilt, an investment dealer who procured funds for mining exploration. He ceased to be my client when the Hells Angels killed him aboard a yacht. "Would Trenton Barratt be affiliated with Barratt Mining?"

"Yes. He owns the company." Mrs. Desmond looked at me over her bifocals. "Do you know him personally?"

"I've never met him. I've heard about his company, though."

"Most people have." She frowned in annoyance.

Footsteps sounded from the other end of the corridor.

We turned to see Dave and the constables heading toward us.

"Mrs. Desmond," Dave said, "My visit to the police station might take some time." He drew in a deep breath. "They want a sample of my DNA."

Mrs. Desmond blinked but otherwise maintained her composure. "Isn't this somewhat drastic?" She eyed the constables.

"Just following procedure, ma'am," one of them said.

"How long will it take?"

"We don't know, ma'am, but we have to leave right now. The

roads are icy. We've seen cars abandoned in ditches."

"Dave, would you like me to go with you?" Michael asked.

"No need," Dave said. "I'll go to the station and set things straight. They'll drive me back." He gestured toward the classroom door. "Mrs. Desmond, two more guests will be arriving soon to make their presentations."

"I'll take care of it and the rest of your schedule for the day," the dean said. "No need to rush back here until you're done."

"Thank you, Mrs. Desmond," Dave said, then shook hands with Michael and me. "Great presentations. Thanks again."

"Our pleasure," Michael said, meeting his gaze.

"I'll catch up with you later." Dave left with the constables.

Mrs. Desmond watched the men move down the corridor, then turned to us. "I assume Mr. Pellegrino informed you about the recent incident involving the demise of two students here."

"Yes," Michael said. "Unfortunate."

"The reason behind their deaths is still a mystery. Now the police want Mr. Pellegrino's DNA. How crude." She grimaced as if she'd swallowed something sour. "Please keep this latest development between us. The least hint of a scandal would absolutely tarnish the school's reputation." Her hand sliced the air to stress the significance of her statement.

"I've known Dave for a long time. He was a topnotch journalist in every way. When it comes to ethics, he'd never compromise his reputation or Verdell's."

Mrs. Desmond's gaze softened. "I didn't mean to cast doubt on Mr. Pellegrino's reputation. I've always held him in high regard." She glanced away for a moment. "If you have some free time this afternoon, I suggest you visit our magnificent library. We have a wonderful selection of classical books."

"Sounds good," I said.

She opened the door to Dave's classroom, then looked back at us. "Oh...we're holding another memorial service for Natalie Dunn and Andrew Boyle this evening in the chapel. Perhaps you'd like to attend. It's a multifaith chapel, by the way."

"Thank you." Raised as a Roman Catholic, I'd never been inside a multifaith chapel.

Students who had left the classroom earlier now returned, slipping by Mrs. Desmond.

“Well, I’d better get to work. Mustn’t keep the students waiting.” The dean followed them into the classroom and shut the door.

Michael had a silly grin on his face and looked as if he were bursting to tell me something.

“What is it?” I asked him.

“Not here,” he whispered. “Let’s go back to your dorm.” He started to move away.

I caught up to him. “You know my room is off limits.”

“Has that ever stopped me?”

“What if someone sees you there?”

“We’ll be careful.”

We entered the atrium and took the stairs down to the echo. Michael hurried along the echo past the staircases that led to the dining room, library, and chapel. I had to run to keep up with him. If he hadn’t raised my curiosity to such a high level, I wouldn’t have been so forgiving.

We climbed the stairs leading to the lobby of the women’s dorm. I made sure no one was looking our way before we slinked out the exit door to the stairs.

We were greeted with the faint scent of disinfectant. The antiseptic scent brought back memories of my earlier school days, as did the stone steps leading to the third floor. I remembered how the janitor would get a head start cleaning the school corridors every afternoon right before school was let out. He’d stand there, mop in hand, instructing us to tiptoe around the wet areas that smelled of bleach. I never understood why he didn’t wait until the students had left the premises before tackling the job. All we did was dirty the floors all over again with our wet boots in the winter—boots that hadn’t had time to dry in our lockers.

I ushered Michael down the corridor and into my room, then locked the door. “Okay, spill the beans.”

He inspected the room. “You know what? My dorm room is larger than yours.”

"Okay, so they gave you preferential treatment. Now tell me your secret."

"Yeah, but your view out the window is so much better. Tall trees, the narrow road cutting through campus... My room is facing a tennis court topped with six feet of snow. It's where they dump the stuff when they clear the paths here."

I couldn't argue. If that were my view from the room, I'd be disheartened too. "Okay. Enough with the chitchat. What's the big news?"

Michael dug out two keys from his jacket. "Dave slipped these into my hand earlier."

I recognized the small key as the one Dave had used to unlock his desk. The larger key would unlock the door to his office. "Talk about a sleight-of-hand trick."

"Did you notice it?"

"No. I doubt anyone did. Why do you think Dave gave them to you?"

"That's what we're going to find out. We'll visit his office later."

"And how do you propose to do that?"

Michael smiled. "We'll make our move after curfew."

CHAPTER 4

Michael and I planned to sneak into Dave's office later Friday evening. We agreed it was risky but nonetheless feasible.

"I hope it isn't a waste of time," I said.

"What do you mean?" Michael stared out the window of my room.

"What if we get caught? We could be charged with theft and who knows what else. Besides, Dave might be coming back soon."

"I doubt it."

"Why so pessimistic? You were raving about his integrity to Mrs. Desmond earlier. Are you having second thoughts?"

"That's not what I meant. Come over here and take a look outside."

I did. A dark sky brooded over the campus as ice pellets bombarded the windowsills. The light from the lampposts reflected off a glossy sheet of ice on the snow like gelatin over a white chocolate mousse.

"We'll be lucky if the power holds up," Michael said. "The overhead lines are already drooping under the weight of the accumulated ice."

As if on cue, the lights in the room flickered.

"Oh-oh," I said. "Can you imagine being stuck here for days?" Images of a drawn-out weekend in this rules-dominated environment depressed me.

"We might have no choice. I checked the weather report a minute ago. There's an extended freezing rain warning for a large part of the province. It could last days—maybe longer." He shook his head. "Looks like my investigation into the Hells Angels is on hold for now."

Thank goodness! I gazed out at the campus grounds, taking in its serene yet ominous beauty. I kept thinking how we could have been spending a romantic weekend in an ice storm instead of spending it cooped up with kids in a boarding school.

As is often the case when my brain is more or less at rest, a memory came to mind. "I need to check something." I opened up my laptop and accessed the client files. "Aha, I knew it."

"What?" Michael walked up to me.

"Information on Trenton Barratt. Mrs. Desmond said Zack's father was a generous sponsor. I knew I'd come across his name before."

"So?"

"Gary Stilt listed Barratt Mining as one of his investors for the pamphlet he wanted me to ghostwrite last—" The memory of that gruesome day hit me again. Two ex-cons had kidnapped me aboard a yacht in the Port of Montreal last summer but I escaped. Minutes later I had to identify the body of Gary Stilt, a client whom I'd met that afternoon at a business meeting in town. He'd been killed aboard the yacht. Months had gone by since my ordeal, but I hadn't yet recovered from the shock. "The police never did find Gary's Prada portfolio aboard the yacht. It contained thousands of dollars for the Hells Angels' drug operations. I heard the ex-cons argue about how they wanted to split up the money before they—" I choked up.

Michael sensed my inner torment. "Let it go, Megan."

"I can't. It's too fresh in my mind." I closed the files, taking a moment to swallow the lump in my throat.

Michael put his arms around me. "I'll never let anything happen to you again. You know that, don't you?"

I looked up at him. "It works both ways."

His lips met mine, setting off butterflies inside me the way his kisses always did. He held me close and whispered, "I'm crazy about you, Megan. Marry me. We'll have a Christmas wedding when we get back home."

Destiny had brought us together years ago. Our frequent encounters with death had strengthened that tie, but I wasn't ready for another long-term commitment. "You know how I feel about marriage. I'm happy with the arrangement we have."

Michael's phone rang. He reached for it and glanced at the screen, perhaps a bit relieved not to look at me after that response. "It's Dave." He took the call. "How are you doing, Dave? What's up?"

I crossed my fingers and hoped everything was okay.

"Yes, she's right here. Hang on." Michael accessed the speakerphone. "Okay, Dave. We're both listening now."

"I'm still at the police station." Dave's voice came through. "They took a sample of my DNA."

"Did you find out why they wanted it?"

A loud sigh at the other end of the line. "They suspect I might be the father of the baby Nat was carrying."

Michael looked as surprised as I felt. "Did they say why they suspect you?"

"Not in so many words, but I think it has to do with the emails and text messages between us."

"When will they have the results of the paternity test?"

Another deep sigh. "Within a day or so. They put a rush on it."

"So you're on your way back here."

"No. The police have closed the roads. Ice everywhere. Multi-car pileups. Too dangerous to travel right now. They offered me a jail cell for the night. Ironic, isn't it?" A chuckle broke the tension in Dave's voice. "I called home, told Samantha not to worry and not to drive to the police station in this weather."

"You're doing fine," Michael said. "Hang in there a while longer."

"There's something else I need to tell you."

"We're listening."

"Forensics found blood spatter on pieces of evidence. The police didn't elaborate except to say the blood didn't belong to either Nat or Andrew. They're comparing my DNA to it." Dave's voice cracked.

"That's plain crazy. They suspect you of murder?"

"They didn't say so, but it's obvious they now think the students' deaths are suspicious. They must have evidence that implicates me somehow. Why else would they bring me in for questioning?"

Michael frowned. "Have you brought Mrs. Desmond up to date?"

"I told her about the paternity test but not about the blood spatter. Having the police suspect me of fathering a child is one thing. Murder is an entirely different issue."

"How did she react?"

"As expected. Her priority is to preserve the school's sterling reputation. She'll move heaven and hell to protect it—no matter what. I could lose my job...my family... This is a freakin' nightmare." Dave choked up.

"There must be something we can do at this end," Michael said.

I noticed he'd included me.

"Use the key to my office," Dave said. "Search my desk for anything that could have been used against me. It's the only room in the school where I had direct interaction with students and staff." There was a commotion in the background and people talking. "I have to go. They want to interview me again. Promise you'll come through for me, Michael."

"I promise."

"I'll call you back when I have more news. Bye."

Michael hung up and stared at me. "We can't wait. We have to make our move now."

We skipped the memorial service. No one would notice our absence. We hurried along the echo, then took the stairs up to the main building. We crossed the atrium into the dimly lit corridor housing the admin and staff offices. Peering at us from framed photos on the walls, the school's athletic teams were silent witnesses to our covert mission.

Since everyone else was at the memorial service, we slipped into Dave's office without a hitch. To be on the safe side, we kept the lights off. We didn't want anyone happening by and finding us here.

Michael retrieved a flashlight from the portfolio he'd brought along. He aimed it at the deep side drawer in the desk and used one of Dave's keys to unlock it. He fingered the folders. "There's nothing much in here."

"We'll take Dave's laptop." It sat on his desk. "He must have a cover for it."

"I'll check." Michael walked over to a cabinet in the corner. He opened the door and pointed his flashlight inside. "This must be it." He handed me a sleeve case bearing an image of Shakespeare against a backdrop of text.

I placed the laptop into it.

Michael searched through the smaller side drawers of Dave's desk. He grabbed an agenda and placed it in his portfolio. He combed through the other drawers but didn't take anything else. "I guess that's it."

"Wait. What about that?" I pointed to a thick book on Dave's desk.

Michael shone the flashlight on it, revealing tattered pages. "It's just an old book."

"He must have kept it on his desk for a reason."

"Fine." Michael added it to our collection. "We'd better go. We have lots of work to do tonight."

"Your place or mine?"

"Oh...yeah. That could be a problem."

Footsteps approached.

Michael clicked off the flashlight.

A tall shadow appeared on the other side of the frosted glass. Someone tried the doorknob. Once. Twice.

I don't remember the last time I'd held my breath for so long. Well...yes. There was one other instance twenty years back. I was a junior in high school and had been called to the principal's office for having ripped a classmate's math assignment. The sneak was a tall boy who sat beside me. Out of the corner of my eye, I'd seen him gawking my way, then scribbling on his paper. He did it several times. I was certain he was copying my answers. When class was over, I grabbed the boy's paper and ripped it. I had to wait half an hour outside the principal's office before I was dismissed with a warning to report cheaters to my teacher in the future. I received an A on my assignment. My classmate, an F. Justice was served.

The footsteps retreated and I exhaled. "I'd give anything to know who that was."

Michael stood up. "Let's get out of here in case they come back with keys. We can check out Dave's laptop in my room."

"Why your room? It's much further and someone might see me."

"Same difference. Someone might see me sneaking into your room."

"Michael, be reasonable," I said. "We can't leave the building—we're not wearing our parkas. At least we don't have to go outdoors to get to the girls' dorm. And if they find out I had a man in my room, I'll accept full responsibility for breaking the rules. Besides, what could Mrs. Desmond do? Ground me? The ice storm has already done that."

He couldn't argue with that kind of logic.

Back in my dorm room, Michael set up Dave's laptop on my desk and scanned his emails. "I have to hand it to Dave. He brought his meticulous skills with him from the newsroom. Everything is filed alphabetically and by topic. Like he said, no emails from Nat. No suspicious emails from anyone else either." He reached for Dave's agenda and began to flip though it.

I was sitting on the bed and paging through the old book we'd retrieved from Dave's desk. It turned out to be a textbook of plays by William Shakespeare. "This is odd. Someone tore out a page."

"Destroying school property is a big no-no here. Guaranteed to strip a privilege or two." Michael stared at me in mock fear.

I smiled. "To bed with no dinner, for sure." I flipped to the index at the back of the book. I discovered that the missing page was from *Romeo and Juliet* and had contained an excerpt from it. I told Michael.

"So?" He looked at me, waiting for an explanation.

"I'll research it." I reached for my laptop and did a quick search of Act V Scene 1 in Shakespeare's famous play. "Here it is. It's the scene where Romeo finds out that Juliet is dead. I'll read it for you."

Well, Juliet, I will lie with thee tonight.
Let's see for means: O mischief, thou art swift
To enter in the thoughts of desperate men!

"I wasn't much into Shakespeare," Michael said. "Do you see a connection to the two student deaths?"

"Hmm... What if Nat and Andrew were secretly dating? What if Nat killed herself when she found out she was pregnant?"

"It's possible. But why would Andrew put Nat's body in the trunk of the car?"

"I don't know. People do strange things when they're distraught. Maybe Andrew was heartbroken over Nat's death and decided to kill himself. He wanted to die by Nat's side—so to speak—like Romeo did with Juliet. In his troubled state of mind, he could have perceived it as a romantic gesture."

"So he drove the car into the lake to end it all." He paused in thought. "Question is: Why did the cops find someone else's blood on the evidence? It leads me to believe that another theory comes into play here. Excuse the pun."

"The blood could be circumstantial."

"True. But I'll bet the cops suspect otherwise."

"That Nat and Andrew were murdered?"

Michael nodded.

"If that's true, what's the motive?" I asked. "And who drove the car into the lake?"

"The cops have to analyze the evidence before they can answer those questions."

"You realize we're talking about a potential killer at Verdell."

"Yes," he said. "One who could be long gone by now."

"Or not. What if the killer is still in the school?"

"Then we have our investigative work cut out for us."

"We?"

Michael shrugged. "Why not? We've worked together on other cases. If the roads are closed and the cops can't get here, I'll need all the help I can get."

"How horrid."

"If you'd rather not—"

"No, it's okay. What I meant was... It would have been so much easier to accept that their deaths were based on a romantic premise."

"Like in *Romeo and Juliet.*"

"Yes."

Michael walked over and sat next to me on the bed. "How about I test a romantic premise of my own?" He leaned over and kissed me on the lips.

Butterflies flew in my stomach, spreading a tingling from head to toe.

"There," he said. "We just broke a rule."

"Rules are made to be broken." I kissed him back.

"Did I ever tell you how much I love your peppermint lip gloss?"

"Every time." I laughed.

Michael's phone rang, interrupting the moment. He glanced at the screen and activated the speakerphone. "Hi, Dave. I have you on speakerphone so Megan can listen in."

"Good. I don't have much time. A police detective interviewed me earlier. When he stepped out of the office to speak with someone, I peeked at the open file on his desk. There was a note in it about Nat. It doesn't make sense to me, but I thought I'd mention it. It said something about a page of text taped across her mouth."

I caught my breath. "Dave, we found an old textbook on your desk. A page is torn out of it."

"What book?"

"The book on Shakespeare's plays."

"Oh...right. It's in the class curriculum this semester. Which page is missing?"

"The one that contains an excerpt from Act V in *Romeo and Juliet*—the scene where Romeo discovers Juliet is dead. Did you tear it out?"

"It's from the school library. I'd never damage school property. You think it's the same page they found on Nat?"

"It's a hypothesis," I said.
"How the hell would it have gotten there?"
There was only one answer.
"The killer put it there," I said.

CHAPTER 5

Dave called us back twenty minutes later. "The detective interviewed me again. He had Nat's laptop and saw the emails she sent me. He asked me once more if I'd had sexual relations with her. I told him nothing happened between us, that Nat loved poetry and had a crush on me. That's all it was. I said I tried to discourage her from sending me 'puppy love' emails. He said he knew because Nat kept every email between us. I think that's why they didn't ask to see my laptop—at least not yet."

"That's good news, isn't it?" Michael asked.

"Yes. Now for the bad news." Dave let out a deep breath. "The cops seized Nat's cell phone from her dorm room too. They saw my last text message to her. They know I threatened to report her."

"The cops can't accuse you of murder based on that text message. Besides, they don't know the cause of death yet."

"I'll tell you this much. She didn't hop into the trunk of the car all by herself. Her hands and feet were bound."

"How'd you get that info?"

"I used to be an investigative reporter. Remember?" Dave's voice had an edge to it.

Michael's jaw twitched—a sign that he understood and shared his friend's duress.

"Sorry," Dave said. "I didn't mean to snap at you."

"No problem. Here's how I see it. The cops suspect you're the father of Nat's baby. They assume you didn't want a scandal on your hands. They imply you had a motive to kill her, but we both know they can't prove it. Their other problem is finding a motive to link you to Andrew's death."

"Maybe you're right." Dave paused. "I have more bad news. You remember the blood spatter I mentioned earlier?"

"Yeah."

"They told me it's on a page taken from a Shakespearean play. Megan, you were right. It's the same page as the one that's missing from the book on my desk."

I drew in a quick breath. "Oh, no!"

"Let's not jump to conclusions," Michael said. "The cops need to compare DNA samples. It might not be your blood."

"They've already put a rush on it," Dave said. "You have to help me. I—I think I'm losing it."

Michael's brow puckered. "Jog your memory, Dave." The urgency in his tone intensified. "Think back. How would your blood have landed on that damn page in the first place?"

A long moment of silence at the other end of the line.

I put myself in Dave's place. He was on the edge and close to breaking down. I recalled how much I'd suffered when the police suspected I was involved in my husband's murder. Even now, it took a load of willpower to push back the ugly memories.

Dave's voice resurfaced. "Okay. I remember now. It happened in one of my English Lit classes. I was showing a student how to trim a poster with an X-Acto knife. I cut my hand. Not a big cut, but a few drops of blood splattered. I must have had the Shakespeare book open on *Romeo and Juliet*. I was preparing questions for my next class."

Relief spread over Michael's face, replaced by concern. "Okay. Next question. Who was around when it happened?"

"My students—all fifteen of them. Are you telling me—"

"We can't discount anyone—student or staff." Michael paused. "One more thing. The cops can't hold you for more than twenty-four hours without charging you."

"I know," Dave said. "The bad news is nothing gets processed on the weekend, so test results could drag till Monday. I don't know how I'd get back to Verdell anyway. It's like hell froze over out here.

The meteorologists are calling it the ice storm of the decade. The police have issued media warnings to the public to avoid traveling and stay off the roads. Tree branches have collapsed under the weight of the ice across main and secondary streets. Live wires are down everywhere."

The lights in my dorm room blinked.

"Dave, the lights are flickering here. I think we're going to lose power soon." Michael checked his watch. "Okay. Here's the plan. Megan and I won't say a word about the missing Shakespeare page and the blood spatter to anyone. You shouldn't either. We're going to meet with Mrs. Desmond to voice our concern about your situation. We'll ask her permission to interview the students and—"

"It's not going to work."

"Why not?"

"Mrs. Desmond is defensive when it comes to anything that threatens the school's reputation. She'll protect her students no matter what."

"What about protecting the staff?"

Dave sighed. "I'm afraid we're dispensable. Money talks where the students are concerned. They're her priority. She won't jeopardize the generous funding she receives from their families."

Michael clenched his jaw. "She needs to know that everyone at Verdell could be in danger."

"All I can say is good luck, my friend. Let me know if you win her over. Talk to you later."

Michael hung up and placed his phone on the desk. "It might be a long shot, but I don't give up that easily."

"You never do." I smiled at him.

There was a knock at the door.

We gaped at each other for a second before Michael rushed to the bathroom, leaving the door slightly ajar.

Who would be visiting at this time of the night? I opened the door.

"Hi, Megan." Helga greeted me with a cheery smile. "I was making the rounds and thought I'd come by to see if everything was okay."

"Everything's fine." I smiled back, keeping my hand on the door to prevent it from opening wide.

She nodded and peered past me, as if she were trying to think of something else to say. "Well, if you need anything, give me a call. Good night."

I shut the door and waited until the sound of her footsteps retreated down the corridor.

Michael came out of the bathroom. "There's nothing like a head count to remind me how much I hated my school days in Montreal. The teachers at the private school I attended watched our every move."

"A private school." I shook my head and feigned sympathy. "Coming from an upper middle-class family certainly has its drawbacks."

Michael smiled. "Okay, point taken, but I'm serious. My father believed the stringent curriculum of a private school would help discipline me. It had the reverse effect."

"And we both know the ending to that story. You broke free from bureaucratic restrictions and did your own thing, like running off to Toronto to study journalism at Ryerson."

"You got it." He winked at me and sat down at my desk.

The item resting near the laptop caught my attention. "Oh, no. Dave's Shakespeare sleeve case. What if Helga noticed it?"

"It's probably a popular design. I wouldn't worry about it."

"I hope you're right."

Michael reached for his phone. "I'll leave a message for Mrs. Desmond. Maybe we'll get lucky and she'll meet with us tomorrow morning."

While he placed the call, I looked out the window. A thick layer of ice had reduced the light from campus lampposts to a soft glow. Even so, I could see the branches on lofty trees drooping from the extra weight. They threatened to crack at any moment. I also noticed a couple of surveillance cameras on poles.

"Done." Michael put his phone on the desk.

"What about the school's surveillance videos?" I asked.

"What about them?"

"We should ask Mrs. Desmond if we could take a look at them."

"Fat chance. You heard what Dave said."

"But the surveillance video of that night could hold important clues. We need to get a copy of it somehow."

"I agree. And I happen to know the right person for the job." Michael scrolled through the contact list on his phone.

I listened as he chatted with one of his contacts in Montreal—a whiz in technology who assisted him with investigative cases. I was stunned when he gave his tech contact details of the school's wireless security system, the make of the car dredged from the river, the approximate time of the incident, and how to send the video clip back to him.

After he'd hung up, I said, "What are you doing, Michael? Hacking into a security system is illegal."

"It's not my problem if people leave their doors open."

"What do you mean?"

"Security system buyers don't often change the manufacturer's default settings. It's easy for hackers to seize control of an unsecured surveillance system and view live or archived footage. Most of the time, the owner isn't even aware the system is being hacked."

"But it's theft. Invasion of privacy. Whatever you want to call it. Don't you feel guilty?"

He shook his head. "Not if I can prove Dave's innocence and catch the real killer."

Who was I to argue? Michael was tackling every obstacle to ensure that justice would be served. I wasn't going to stand in his way.

The call came sooner than I'd expected.

Michael smiled as he spoke with his tech contact. "That's super. Send it right over. Encrypted. Yes, we'll catch up when I get back home. Thanks." He looked at me. "Megan, can I borrow your laptop? I left mine in the dorm, and I don't want to use Dave's to check my email."

"Sure. It's on the ledge by the window."

He removed Dave's laptop from the desk and set mine up in its place. He accessed his email and the encrypted video file. I stood next to him as the video began to play.

A grainy image of the parking lot behind the school came into view. There wasn't much activity until a man wearing a dark jacket with a hood approached a car and entered the driver's side. Soon he stepped out, opened the trunk, and peeked inside. He closed the trunk and entered the driver's side again. The car pulled out and moved at a slow speed across the school grounds.

"It could be Dave's Honda," Michael said.

"I couldn't see the driver's face," I said. "The image is too granular."

Another camera captured the rear of the car as it left the campus grounds and drove into the forest.

"It has to be the killer," I said. "Do you think he was checking on Andrew and Nat in the trunk?"

"If we assume their bodies were in the trunk."

"Where else would they be? He could have put Andrew behind the wheel later to make it look like he'd driven the car."

Michael nodded so-so. "Maybe Andrew isn't in the trunk. Maybe he's sitting in the passenger seat. I can't tell if two people are sitting in the front or if those are the seat headrests."

"I downloaded video enhancement software for a project I worked on. A client had a short video trailer to introduce his book and wanted me to make slight changes to it. Let me try my magic." I nudged him out of the chair. After I played with the software tools, I was able to smooth out the grainy appearance, sharpen the details, and brighten the dark areas.

"Hey, I'm impressed." Michael squeezed my shoulders. "You never told me you could do such technical work."

I smiled. "Oh, I can do lots of stuff." I peered at the screen. "It's still hard to tell if someone's sitting in the passenger seat or not. The coat hood hides the driver's face, so I didn't make any progress there either."

"The image is sharper. I can tell he's on the tall side." Michael pointed to the mystery man on the screen. "He had to be strong enough to overcome Nat and Andrew and place their bodies in the car. With the focus on athletics in this place, I'll bet that premise barely eliminates one percent of the male faculty and students." He shook his head in frustration.

"Maybe, but it eliminates Dave too. He's not that tall." I looked up at Michael.

"Right. He's about five foot nine. This video doesn't prove Dave's alibi, but it can create doubt about him as a suspect." Excitement ran through his voice.

"Let's call Dave and tell him."

"No way. I don't want the police to know how I obtained this video. I could end up in jail—and my tech contact too. We can't tell anyone. Not even Mrs. Desmond. Not yet, anyway. It's a given that certain pieces of evidence unearthed in a murder investigation are best left concealed until the perpetrator is caught."

"Good point." I looked closer at the image on the screen. "Something bugs me. How did our mystery man transport the bodies to the car without detection?"

"He could have had help."

We watched the video another time.

"Michael, your tech contact sent you everything he found based on your instructions, right?"

"Yes. Why?"

"We watched about ten minutes of the video after the car entered the forest and nothing happened. Where's the driver? Why didn't he walk back out?"

"Right. My tech guy included this part of the video for a reason." He paused in thought. "Remember how I discovered a road that runs along the river on the other side of the forest? Maybe someone picked up our mystery man there."

"You mean the killer might be someone from outside Verdell?" I asked.

"Maybe he's not the killer."

"Okay, you lost me."

"Let's assume he's the guy who hotwired the car," Michael said. "What if he popped the trunk to make sure the bodies were in there? What if he's a driver and not the actual killer?"

I shivered as the reality of his theory sunk in. "Are you saying the killer is on campus?"

CHAPTER 6

Michael spent Friday night in his dorm room to ensure a presence there in case Zack checked in on him. We figured we didn't need any strikes against us if we wanted to stay in Mrs. Desmond's good graces.

I snuggled under the bed covers but couldn't fall asleep. I picked up a book I'd noticed earlier on the window ledge: *Great Tales and Poems of Edgar Allan Poe*. I read "The Cask of Amontillado," a story that takes place in nineteenth-century Italy. The story recounted how Montresor believed that his fellow nobleman, Fortunato, had insulted him. He invites Fortunato to his wine cellar for a private tasting and gets him drunk. He lures him into a niche, then chains him to a wall and proceeds to bury him alive behind a stack of stone and mortar.

I slammed the book shut. I'd suffered bouts of claustrophobia since childhood, so I didn't make it to the end to the story. I took a few deep breaths to calm my nerves, then walked over to the window.

A thunderous crash outdoors startled me. I peeked out the window. Branches of a gigantic maple tree had split off and fallen, blocking the road in front of the dorm. Thank goodness no power lines had been snagged in the process. At the rate the ice was accumulating on overhead cable lines, I wouldn't be surprised if more damage was on the agenda.

I slipped under the covers and finally fell asleep to the rhythmic sound of ice pellets hitting the window. Cracking branches woke me up twice during the night until exhaustion overtook me and I fell into a deep sleep.

I met Michael the next morning in the downstairs foyer. Puffy eyes told me he hadn't had much sleep. "Bad night?"

"I had a lousy night," he said. "I heard tree branches snapping like matchsticks. The roads running through campus are cluttered with debris. I almost broke my neck walking here from the boys' dorm. I'll be staying with you from now on. Rules be damned. I brought my stuff with me." He motioned toward his overnight bag and laptop on the floor.

"Good thing there's a bed and a sofa in my dorm room. The sofa's yours." I smiled.

Michael remained serious. "We might have a problem."

"With what?"

"Helga might check in on you to make sure you're not breaking any rules." His eyes twinkled in amusement.

"Rules be damned." I kissed him on the lips, drawing stares from passing students. "Speaking of which… Have you heard back from Mrs. Desmond?"

He nodded. "She agreed to meet with us at ten o'clock."

"Should be interesting."

We climbed the three flights of stairs to my dorm room, catching glances from female students wandering along the corridor. Why weren't they in class? Then I remembered it was Saturday.

Michael deposited his bag and laptop in my room, and I couldn't have been happier. Let Mrs. Desmond try to split us up again with her silly rules. I'll tell her a thing or two.

Michael insisted on having a good breakfast before heading to the dean's office. "I always think better on a full stomach," he said.

We stayed at the ground level, cutting through buildings joined by covered passageways with glass sides. We strolled into the dining hall to find Glenda serving at the counter.

"What's on Paul's dinner menu today?" Michael asked her.

"We're having leftovers—same as yesterday's menu." She shrugged. "Paul never made it back from his grocery run in town yesterday, so we don't have fresh provisions."

"Leftovers." The teenage girl beside me wrinkled her nose. She turned to the girl next to her and said, "I'm sick of this crap. I can't wait to go home for Christmas and eat real food. Our Betsy's the best gourmet cook in Knowlton."

I'd once driven through the upscale village of Knowlton located in the Town of Brome Lake. Sometimes nicknamed *The Knamptons*—a blend of Knowlton and the Hamptons—it was the site of million-dollar mansions.

I glanced at Glenda as she handed me my plate. A shake of her head and a roll of her eyes told me she'd overheard the student's comments.

Michael and I had almost finished breakfast when Ann walked up to our table.

In jeans and a pullover, the career day presenter looked years younger. "Hi. Mind if I join you?"

"Please do," I said. "I thought you'd left Verdell."

Ann placed her tray on the table and sat down beside me. "Leonard took off yesterday right after his presentation. I didn't want to drive back to Sherbrooke in this weather. I'm staying with a friend in her apartment here. It gave me a chance to catch up with her and the others." Noticing my quizzical look, she added, "I used to teach here till about three years ago."

"That's a surprise. What subject?"

"Mathematics. In fact, I attended Verdell before I went on to university. When I heard about a job opening here, I jumped on it. My experience at Verdell had been wonderful, and the salary they offered me was beyond anything I'd expected." She swallowed a scoop of her cereal.

"What made you leave Verdell?" I asked.

She sighed. "The bottom line? Personality conflict. I never thought I'd step foot in this place again. I only accepted to speak here because Dave invited me. We're good friends." She looked at Michael. "He told me you guys are close friends too."

"Yeah," he said. "We go way back to our university days. Speaking of Dave, did you know the police took him to the station for questioning yesterday?"

Ann nodded. "He sent me a text message. I think Verdell is awful about not offering him legal assistance, even as a precautionary measure. But I'm not surprised."

"What do you mean?"

She spoke in a low voice. "Mrs. Desmond always protected the students and Verdell's reputation—no matter what. In Dave's case, it's no different. I think she wants to distance herself from anything that might adversely publicize the two students' deaths." She took a sip of coffee.

"Something tells me you had a falling out with the dean," Michael said to her.

"Am I that obvious?" Ann laughed. "Sorry. It's tough to return to a place where the bad memories top the good ones. Bad, meaning my days as a teacher here, having to cope with the insane rules and regulations. To be honest, teachers were treated as second-class citizens. They still are."

"In what way?"

"Every spare hour we had was allocated to students and their extra-curricular activities. It's a miracle we got the occasional weekend off. Even then, I'd be so exhausted I couldn't enjoy my time off with my husband and family. When I complained to the dean, she said I was dispensable, that there were applicants lined up to replace me at any time. The rest is history."

Michael shrugged. "Dave seems to like it here."

"Money talks." Ann gave us an astute look. "Don't get me wrong. Dave's a great guy, but like other teachers here, he sold out to the big bucks and the private schooling system. I wonder if being a yes-man turned him into a scapegoat."

"A yes-man?" Michael frowned.

"A scapegoat?" I echoed.

"Yes to both," Ann said. "Dave's car gets stolen and two dead students are found inside it. It implies someone took advantage of him and is trying to shed a negative light on him. Depending on how things balance out, the incident might give Mrs. Desmond a viable reason to dismiss him."

We moved through the covered passageway that connected

the dining hall to the main building.

"Funny, I never thought of Dave as a yes-man," Michael said.

"I think Ann was referring to the rules and regulations at Verdell," I said. "Even Dave mentioned that teachers had to follow strict guidelines here."

"Could be."

"Conditions can't be that bad or Dave wouldn't be teaching here," I said, looking at it from another perspective. "Maybe things have changed since Ann taught at Verdell."

"Maybe. Though I don't like the idea that Dave could lose his job if Mrs. Desmond considers him a problem."

"Would firing him on those grounds be legal?"

"I don't know but money talks."

Michael's phone rang. We slid into a niche away from the sporadic flow of students in the atrium and he answered.

"Guess what!" Dave's voice sounded cheerful over the speakerphone. "The police reviewed video footage from Verdell that placed me in the library around the time Nat and Andrew died. I'd forgotten about my late night visit there." He chuckled. "You know how you get memory lapses about small details when something critical is happening in your life?"

"I sure do." Michael smiled.

"The investigators sent a cruiser to Verdell this morning to interview more people, but it collided with a truck and ended up in a ditch. They can't spare another car because they have to handle a string of accidents—some with critical injuries. One officer said that part of the roof in a mall blew off and killed a pedestrian. Lots of electric poles and live wires are down across roads too."

"Yeah, this ice storm is one for the books. Megan and I will have to prolong our visit."

"Good. Better to stay safe indoors. They don't have enough crews to clear the widespread debris and open the roads anyway. The police told me I wouldn't be able to get back to Verdell today. Maybe not even tomorrow."

"It's okay," Michael said. "We're making headway. We have a meeting with Mrs. Desmond in a few minutes."

"That's fantastic. Don't forget to tell her I'm in the clear."

"You bet."

"Oh…one more thing." Dave lowered his voice. "The police have asked for my help in looking at copies of the school's surveillance videos. They're going to ask Mrs. Desmond and her staff to look over the videos too. Believe me, we're going to catch whoever is trying to frame me for murder."

Michael and I waited ten minutes in the outer office while Mrs. Desmond spoke on the phone behind closed doors. Audrey Brock, her admin assistant, had invited us to take a seat when we arrived. The tall forty-something woman with an easy smile struck me as approachable and efficient, though I wondered if she shared the same obsession with Verdell's rules as Mrs. Desmond.

Now seated in bulky armchairs across from the dean's desk, Michael gave her a recap of our discussion with Dave. He mentioned that DNA results for Nat's baby hadn't yet arrived. He voiced police suspicions that Natalie Dunn and Andrew Boyle might have been murdered. He didn't mention Dave's blood spatter or the nature of the evidence the police had obtained, but merely indicated Dave wasn't considered a suspect.

Mrs. Desmond sat in a high-backed chair, her bifocals perched on the bridge of her nose. A sign that she was mulling over the information was an occasional blink. She spoke in a low voice. "I'm glad to hear Mr. Pellegrino is doing well. As for that other matter, if the police share your suspicions, why haven't their investigators contacted me?"

"They're still reviewing evidence," Michael said.

"They've also been busy with emergencies due to the ice storm," I said.

"Yes…I've seen the local news." She gestured toward a large-screen TV next to a bay window that offered a view of ice-laden maple trees. The terrifying thought that these gigantic trees stood so close to the building crossed my mind, but I dismissed it in the next moment.

Michael leaned forward. "Mrs. Desmond, we'd like your cooperation in ensuring that everyone on campus is...safe."

"Safe? What exactly are you asking?"

"Is every staff and student accounted for?"

His question took her by surprise. "If my memory serves me well, most staff and faculty members are away this weekend. With the holidays approaching, all students have forgone a visit home until then. To be sure, I'll verify the current status with Audrey."

She stepped out of the office, leaving the door ajar. She spoke to Audrey, who nodded while her slender fingers flew over the keyboard.

I diverted my attention to the rows of framed pictures on the wall behind the dean's desk. Smiling students holding trophies, plaques, and ribbons were photographed with Mrs. Desmond over the years. Interspersed among the collage were certificates bearing gold seals and inked signatures, and awards endorsing Verdell as one of the world's best prep schools.

What caught my eye was the photo of a more youthful Zack holding a silver trophy. Standing close behind him was a younger Mrs. Desmond, a protective hand on his shoulder. Next to that photo was one of Mrs. Desmond in a shimmering blue gown. She was standing next to a tall, broad-shouldered man in a tuxedo, his gray hair revealing the maturity of his years. Zack, a little older and also wearing a tuxedo, stood between them.

Mrs. Desmond returned, closing the door behind her. "Audrey said most of the staff and faculty left Thursday afternoon for home instead of Friday morning. Many regular classes were canceled owing to career day presentations, but we suspect the bad weather prompted the staff's earlier departure as well. A handful of members have remained at Verdell in accordance with our skeleton staff requirements." She sat down, her brow furrowing as she gazed at us. "What is your real purpose in coming here today?"

"We'd like your permission to interview the staff and students," I said. "We believe someone might have information that would help prove Nat and Andrew were murdered."

She crossed her arms. "I won't risk a scandal based on a theory.

It took everything to keep the media from running amok with their coverage of the incident."

"That's why I'm offering my help, Mrs. Desmond," Michael said. "I know how the media works. I assure you we'll be discreet in our investigation."

"I appreciate your interest, but I can't—and won't—accommodate your request." She stood up, signaling an end to our meeting. "If you'll excuse me, Audrey and I have details to tend to—even if it is the weekend. I hope the weather lets up so that your drive back home will be safe. In the meantime, I suggest you both spend your remaining time here on more worthwhile pursuits."

"But what if we're right?" I blurted, freezing Mrs. Desmond to the spot. "What if there's a murderer on the loose in Verdell?"

"My dear," she said, her voice matching her glare of authority, "I haven't run this school for decades based on what ifs. I won't start doing so today."

I hated for our meeting to end on a negative note. "Mrs. Desmond, I was admiring the photos of the students on the wall behind you."

She turned to glance at them. "Yes, it's quite the collection of school achievers, isn't it? I'm proud of every one of my students. They're like family to me." She smiled.

"I noticed a picture of Zack and you. You're wearing a beautiful long gown. A man in a tuxedo is standing next to you."

Her eyes lit up. "It was taken at a fundraising dinner for Verdell a year or so ago. Trenton Barratt asked me to accompany him and Zack to the event. We had a lovely evening."

I sat on my bed and watched Michael tap away on his laptop. "What are you looking for?"

"The school website for a list of the staff. Here it is."

I strolled over to him and looked at the screen. A brief bio and photo were posted for each of the personnel.

Viewing the staff photos brought back my experience the other day with Paul, the cook. I told Michael about it. "It was so weird. He stared at me and almost dropped the container of food."

"You have that effect on men." He smiled at me.

"Very funny." I tousled his thick brown hair.

He chuckled.

"I'm serious. It was as if he knew me. Wait. Is there a photo of him on that site?"

"Let's see." He scrolled down the page.

Paul's photo came into view. He had no beard and wasn't wearing glasses. There was something about him...

"Can you zoom in?" I asked.

"Sure."

I took another look. Paul's face seemed rounder without the short beard, and the same scar was apparent over his left eye. I gasped. I knew that face. "Oh my God! It can't be. That's Pierre Favreau—the ex-con who kidnapped me!"

Michael studied the photo. "You're right. That's plain crazy. I still have a copy of his mug shot on my phone. We have to show it to Mrs. Desmond. Let's go." He shut his laptop and stood up.

"What about calling the police first?"

"We should let Mrs. Desmond make that call. Besides, we don't know if Favreau made it back to Verdell or not."

Good point.

We walked at a steady pace along the echo and climbed the stairs leading to the main building. The atrium was abuzz. The horrible weather combined with lunch hour had drawn students together this Saturday. The makeshift memorial was a reminder of an overwhelming tragedy, and students gathered in small groups, talking, consoling one another, trying to heal.

We took the corridor to Mrs. Desmond's office and opened the door. The dean was standing next to Audrey, discussing statistics of sorts with her.

Audrey noticed us first and smiled, accentuating her high cheekbones. "Hello. Can I help you with anything?"

The words tumbled out of my mouth. "We apologize for the intrusion. Mrs. Desmond, it's urgent that we speak with you right away."

She hesitated, as if she were preparing a verbal reproach. The panic in my eyes must have caused her to have a change of heart. "Fine." She ushered us into her office.

I waited until she'd sat down. "Mrs. Desmond, we discovered that one of your staff is an imposter. Paul, your cook, is an escaped convict. His real name is Pierre Favreau."

She pressed her lips together. "That's absurd. You must be mistaken."

"I can identify him. I saw him in the dining hall the other night. He was as close to me as you are now." I hadn't recognized him then, but witnesses could vouch that I'd seen him.

"I've been tracking this man," Michael said. "I have a police mug shot of him." He pulled out his phone and showed her the photo.

Mrs. Desmond's expression paled. "I can't believe it. How on earth—"

"What kind of references did he provide when he was hired?" he asked.

"A highly respected sponsor recommended him." She stiffened. "I do all the staff hiring and can assure you that none of my people have criminal backgrounds."

"Do you know where we can find Favreau?"

"I'm not sure. The last I heard was that he went to Sherbrooke for groceries yesterday morning and hasn't returned. He usually calls in when he's running late."

"You didn't mention him earlier when we asked about the staff."

"He's just a cook." Mrs. Desmond twisted her lips. When we didn't react, she said, "His absence slipped my mind. Let me ask Audrey."

She stepped out of the office but remained within view in the open doorway while she spoke with her admin assistant. Audrey picked up the receiver and made a call.

While we waited, I glanced at Mrs. Desmond's desk. Manila folders in a tray. A box of tissues. A square notepad with the initials G.D. at the top. Stylish pens in a marble holder. An empty plastic bag and coffee cup on the right side of her desk confirmed we hadn't interrupted her lunch. Small favors.

Mrs. Desmond hurried in. "Audrey spoke with the kitchen staff. As far as they know, the cook hasn't returned to Verdell. They left several messages on his phone, but he hasn't called back. It's quite unusual. Perhaps he was in a car accident and was taken to a hospital. If we don't hear from him soon, Audrey will start calling the hospitals." She sat down.

"He might have skipped town after he recognized Megan," Michael said.

In reply to Mrs. Desmond's puzzled look, I said, "Pierre Favreau kidnapped me last summer in Montreal."

She stared at me. "My goodness! What happened?"

"I recognized his partner—another ex-con who had escaped with him from jail—and pursued him in the Old Port. They caught me and tied me up on a yacht, but I managed to escape."

"Favreau is wanted on murder charges, along with other criminal offenses," Michael said. "You can understand why we're eager to find him." He dug out his phone and accessed the Internet.

"As are the police," I added.

"The newspaper in Montreal ran a series of articles covering his escape from jail and the ongoing police investigation." Michael handed her his phone.

Mrs. Desmond scrolled through the text. She stopped once in a while to silently read an excerpt.

"Note the mug shot of Favreau," Michael said. "He had no beard then."

"And no scar above his left eye," I said. "Which he probably got when struggling on the yacht with the man he stabbed to death."

"Good Lord!" She stared at me before glancing back at the photo. "Yes, I recognize him now. He looked like that when he first arrived here months ago." She focused on us. "Well, you two are a surprising pair." She handed the phone back to Michael.

He slipped it in his pocket and guided the conversation back on track. "We don't know where Favreau is or if he's linked to the student deaths here. Even if he isn't involved, we'd like to investigate the probability that Nat and Andrew were murdered."

"What are you proposing?" the dean asked.

"We'd like to talk to staff and students who knew them. We promise we'll use discretion." Michael leaned forward. "If the killer is still on campus and we don't attempt to weed him out, someone else might get hurt. Or worse. You might have another murder on your hands."

"You both appear quite confident about this, though I confess I am not." Mrs. Desmond raised her chin. "If you don't mind, I'd like to call the police to enquire about the progress they're making with this case. It's also my duty to report that Pierre Favreau was working here under an alias. I don't want to be accused of harboring a fugitive." Moments later, she was talking to the lead investigator. "Oh... Yes, I understand. Mr. Pellegrino is? Yes, of course. You have my word this will stay between us. Now I'd like to speak with you about another matter—"

The lights went out.

A thunderous clap boomed through the air.

A gigantic maple tree came crashing through the bay window.

Michael snatched me from its path just in time. We both hit the floor as glass shards flew in all directions. Dazed but unhurt, we stood up.

Mrs. Desmond wasn't as lucky.

CHAPTER 7

Michael and I hauled Mrs. Desmond out from under a collapsed desk and broken tree branches while Audrey ran off in search of assistance.

"I'm quite alright," Mrs. Desmond said, blood dripping from a gash on her forehead. "Please help me to my feet." She leaned on Michael for support. "Oh, hell!" She looked down. "It's my right ankle. I think it's sprained."

Michael guided her to an armchair and used a stack of books to keep her ankle elevated.

An icy wind reached me and I shivered. The fallen tree had a diameter of about twenty inches, but the thick branches spread the width of the room. The crash had destroyed the window and now enabled blustery winds to flow in. We'd have to get out of this office soon.

"We need ice," Michael said to me.

I gestured toward the pieces clinging to the tree branches and countless fragments scattered over the floor. "We have lots."

I looked for the plastic bag I'd seen on the desk. It was gone. I scoured the floor and found it by the far wall. I filled it with pieces of ice and placed it on Mrs. Desmond's ankle.

"Thank you." She managed a smile but I could tell she was in pain.

I took several tissues from a box that had remained intact and cleaned the wound on her forehead.

"No need to fuss over me," she said, though she allowed me to continue.

Audrey rushed in, out of breath, her pale complexion flushed. A silver-haired man in a white coat followed right behind her, a black medical bag in his hand. His nametag identified him as *Dr. Ed Finley*. He observed the tree and shook his head, then rushed to Mrs. Desmond. A split second of panic flashed across his face, replaced by concern. It happened so fast, I wondered if I had imagined it. I stepped back but remained close enough to assist if needed.

After examining her, the doctor said, "It's a sprained ankle, Gloria. Keep it elevated and put ice on it for a couple of days. Take painkillers as required." He opened up his medical bag. "This elastic compression bandage should help decrease the swelling. I'll send over a pair of crutches to help you get around."

"I can manage without crutches," Mrs. Desmond said, waving a hand.

"You need to keep pressure off your ankle." He gave her a stern look, then examined the wound on her forehead. "I'd have suggested getting a stitch or two at the hospital in town, but with this icy weather, you're better off staying here." He carefully applied ointment and a small bandage to her forehead. "That should do it."

"Thank you, doctor," Mrs. Desmond said, a half-smile on her lips.

"I'll be in the infirmary if you need me." Dr. Finley gave her nod, then left.

Audrey approached Mrs. Desmond, her hands tucked inside the pockets of her cardigan. "When I watched the news earlier, they were reporting widespread power failures throughout eastern Canada. It was a matter of time before it hit us. Now we have no electricity and no access to phones and computers."

Michael tapped the screen on his phone. "No signal."

"We're in a rural area," Mrs. Desmond said. "The closest cell tower is miles from here. It could be damaged from the ice buildup. I suppose not having access to their phones could turn into a life-shattering dilemma for our students." Her uneven smile stressed the sarcasm in her comment.

Audrey laughed. "It'll be one for the history books."

"Does Verdell have backup power generators?" Michael asked.

Mrs. Desmond shook her head. "No, the school board thought the funds would be better spent in other areas."

"Is the fireplace in the dining hall functional?" I asked her.

"It hasn't been used in years. I strongly advised the staff against lighting it." She let her gaze wander around the room. "First things first. Audrey, grab my handbag and agenda—if you can find them. Oh…and some painkillers too. Michael, please help me get out of this freezing office."

Michael assisted Mrs. Desmond into an armchair in the corner of Audrey's office, going through the same motions as before to elevate and ice her ankle.

I stood by the doorway while Audrey collected Mrs. Desmond's handbag and agenda. The snow on the tree branches was melting and icicles were dropping to the floor. The process was short-lived since the temperature in the room was dipping fast. Due to the power outage, it would be impossible to get someone to come remove the tree and replace the window.

Another gust of frosty wind hit me. Loose papers rose and swirled about the room, creating tiny tornadoes.

"Time to get out of here." Audrey rushed out and deposited the items on her desk. I watched as she went back and locked the door to Mrs. Desmond's office.

The door to the corridor swung open. A short, slender man and two women rushed in. Their ID badges indicated they were supervisory teachers on duty at the various buildings and dorms on campus.

"Students are complaining about not having electricity and access to their computers and electrical devices," the man said, his eyes roaming to the rest of us. "They want to know when service will be restored."

"Mr. Jarvis, for all we know, the blackout could be temporary," Mrs. Desmond said. "Nevertheless, everyone will be notified about proper procedure this afternoon at assembly."

Mr. Jarvis gaped at her foot. "What happened?"

"A minor sprain. Nothing to be concerned about. We'll see you at assembly later."

Placated by the dean's take-charge attitude, he thanked her and the group left.

Mrs. Desmond took a deep breath. "Now. Where were we? Oh, yes. Audrey, call an emergency assembly in the chapel for this afternoon at three o'clock. I want everyone to attend—even the housekeeping staff. Speaking of which, ask the fellow in maintenance to board up the window and chop off the tree branches so I can use my office." She paused. "I'll be announcing plans to relocate the occupants of the boys' dorm and the few remaining staff in the outer residence to safer areas within the connected complex. Heaven forbid we end up having a giant pajama party." She glanced at Audrey. "Don't tell anyone I said that."

"I won't." Audrey smiled and left.

"Please sit down," Mrs. Desmond said to Michael and me, gesturing to two wood chairs opposite Audrey's desk. "The detective told me they're reviewing new evidence that suggests our two students were murdered. He asked me to keep this information confidential until they complete their investigation. He also asked for my help in reviewing the school surveillance videos. It's impossible now, what with the power outage, but perhaps later. The weather put a damper on the investigator's plans to return to Verdell to interview additional witnesses, though I understand Mr. Pellegrino is assisting the police with the case." She looked expectantly at Michael.

"Dave told me they'd requested his help," he said. "He has a good nose for investigative work."

"I don't doubt it." She let her gaze rest on him. "I should have believed you when you first tried to tell me about your suspicions. The integrity of your profession speaks for itself. I owe you an apology."

"No problem."

"It's unfortunate we lost power before I could tell the detective about our elusive cook."

"It's not too late to alert everyone on campus about him," I said to her. "Even though we don't know where Favreau is right now, he might come back here."

She nodded. "I'll have to be diplomatic about it. Let's put our heads together and come up with a plan to keep everyone safe."

High walls, stained glass windows, and timber roof trusses that extended to a vaulted ceiling. I recognized the architecture and ceiling pendants in the Verdell chapel as English Gothic style from a project I'd completed for a Montreal architect.

Like many places of worship, the chapel contained an altar at the front and vertical rows of wood pews on each side. The rest of the floor held horizontal rows of pews separated by an aisle down the middle of the floor. Unlike other places of worship I'd visited, the multifaith chapel lacked statues and paintings of religious icons, and ornate gold carvings, which would explain its designation. The dim light coming through the windows accentuated the austere ambiance. The only sign that a memorial service had recently taken place were six baskets of flowers near the altar.

By three o'clock, Mrs. Desmond was sitting in a chair at the front of the chapel, her bandaged leg extended and resting on a pillow, her crutches on the floor by her side. She flipped through her notes as she prepared to address the students and staff. Audrey sat on a chair next to her, notebook in hand.

While we waited for everyone to be seated, I caught snippets of conversation from the students behind me. Complaints ran the gamut from not being able to text and tweet to having to complete their school projects on paper.

Strange. I'd managed to hand in my homework and graduate from high school without the help of technological gadgets. My teachers had even forbidden the use of calculators in class, and we had to memorize our math tables. They accepted handwritten assignments because "in those days" not everyone owned a personal computer. I supposed today's students would acknowledge my experience as a step up from drawing on cave walls.

Mrs. Desmond addressed the group. "Hello, everyone. As you know by now, this ice storm is not to be taken lightly. The province has declared a state of emergency. We have no power. This translates to no electricity, no heat, and no way to communicate with the outside world. Regarding the latter, please conserve the power in your phones by turning them off. You'll want to call your family to tell them you're okay when the power returns."

Grumbles resonated in the high-ceilinged chapel as students empathized with one another on their mutual loss.

The dean went on. "The ice storm continues to create treacherous situations. Tree branches have littered the campus, blocking lanes. Before we lost power this morning, we'd already learned that roads in the area had been closed due to fallen trees and live wires. In other words, you can't get to Verdell and you can't leave it—even if you wanted to."

There was a general stirring in the room as the audience digested the gravity of her words.

"To safely get around the connected complex after dark, housekeeping will provide tea lights for your dorm rooms and corridors. Here's the big news, so pay attention." She paused until the room was still. "To prevent injury on the icy paths around campus and to ensure your general welfare, occupants of the boys' dorm and male staff in the private residence will be relocated to half of the gymnasium. Female staff in the private residence will be relocated to the Theater Room. It's small but adequate for you ladies."

Low groans of disappointment followed—notably from the boys.

Mrs. Desmond ignored them. "Here are my instructions. Boys, return to your dorm rooms after assembly and fill a knapsack or overnight bag with personal effects for two days. Housekeeping staff will assist and provide other essentials as required. Maintenance will clear a path and park a van in front of your dorm. You are to wrap your mattresses and beddings in the plastic coverings that housekeeping will provide, then help one other to carry the loads to the van for transport to the gymnasium. Maintenance and housekeeping will provide similar services for the female staff in the private residence. To all, please be careful walking on the icy pavement."

My heart went out to the maintenance and housekeeping staff. They had their work cut out for them. I was grateful that Michael had already moved into my dorm room. Since Mrs. Desmond had so many other things to worry about, I hoped we'd stay under the radar and escape her scrutiny.

"We don't know how long this storm will continue," the dean said. "Though our bottled water and food supplies are adequate, they will have to be rationed to be on the safe side. In consequence, smaller portions will be served."

More murmurs of dissatisfaction followed.

"Since our water system functioned on electricity, we no longer have access to running water for our personal requirements." Someone giggled and she looked up. "Yes, I'm referring to toilet flushing." More giggles. "We'll need volunteers to carry buckets of water from a private well located behind the main building. Volunteers will have access to housekeeping carts on every floor for loading and transporting the buckets to the rooms. We'll also need volunteers to break the ice and clear a path to the well so that the people transporting the water buckets don't slip and break their necks. Supervisory staff and students will coordinate the teams. Show of hands for water bucket volunteers, please." Her gaze wandered around the crowd.

About a dozen hands extended upward. Among the students I recognized were Zack and Helga and other classmates.

Mrs. Desmond waited.

Another group of volunteers raised their hands.

Satisfied, she continued. "Unfortunately, I have more bad news. A reliable source has informed me that Paul, the cook, lied about his identity. His real name is Pierre Favreau, and he's an escaped convict and murderer."

Expressions of fear and disbelief surged across the room like a tsunami until a collective roar swelled in the air. The expression on the students' faces mirrored their panic.

Mrs. Desmond raised a hand to quiet the group. "There's no need to be afraid. We have reason to believe that Paul—that is,

Pierre Favreau—did not return to Verdell after his grocery run in town. It's most likely he won't be able to do so under these precarious weather conditions."

The crowd quieted down, though some rumbling continued.

"One last note. We've had guest presenters at Verdell this week. Most have already left, but due to the ice storm, two of our guests have had no choice but to extend their stay here. Some of you have already met them. Investigative reporter Michael Elliott and ghostwriter Megan Scott." She gestured in our direction and we stood up so the students could see us. "They will be interviewing students and staff regarding the demise of Natalie Dunn and Andrew Boyle. As I understand it, the police have not officially closed this case, which means their investigation is ongoing. Our guests will also be interviewing some of you regarding Pierre Favreau. Please come forward with any details you think might be helpful. That's all for now. Any questions?"

Hands sprang upward.

"Were Nat and Andrew murdered?"

"Did the cook kill them?"

"Are Michael and Megan undercover cops?"

"Will we be forced to eat canned goods?"

"Do we still have classes on Monday?"

Mrs. Desmond answered their questions with the utmost diplomacy while assuring everyone that Verdell would continue to keep them safe and look after their needs. She dismissed the assembly and ordered everyone to disperse and tend to their duties.

Michael and I were about to leave when she called us over. "You can begin interviewing students and staff immediately in the meeting room down the corridor from the admin offices. I trust you'll get to the bottom of this sordid ordeal before the power comes back on." She gave us a discerning look.

Her comment inferred that a bigger problem awaited Verdell once all venues of communications were restored. As she'd already implied, she'd do anything to prevent more scandals from reaching the ears of her sponsors. The power outage had worked in her favor so far.

Mrs. Desmond reached for her crutches. "Audrey, let's get our coats and go back to my office to find the investment report that's gone missing."

"Megan and I will go with you," Michael said to her. "We'll need to access information on your staff and students."

"But that's privileged—" Audrey said before Mrs. Desmond cut her off.

"Give them the information, Audrey. They have to find out what the hell is going on in this school!"

CHAPTER 8

Michael and I stopped by the dorm to grab our parkas. I pulled on my boots, wrapped a scarf around my neck, and stuffed a pair of mittens into my pockets. Because of the shattered window in Mrs. Desmond's office, the indoor temperature there promised to be equivalent to the one outside—freezing. I wanted to be dressed for it.

I was relieved to discover that maintenance had mounted a makeshift plywood barrier to replace the broken window in the dean's office. They'd filled the uneven gap around the protruding tree trunk with rags to prevent the wind and wild animals like raccoons from getting in. They'd sawed off branches so we could move around the office. Though resourceful, their efforts did nothing to raise the temperature in the room, and the wind whistling through slits in the barricade made it feel colder yet.

We stood by as Audrey, donned in a winter coat and scarf, retrieved personnel records from the cabinets along the wall in the dean's office. She pulled out folders of students who shared classes with Natalie Dunn and Andrew Boyle and placed them upright in a storage bin. She repeated the process for the teachers' files.

"After ten years at Verdell," she said, "I'm proud to say I've established a hardcopy filing system that rivals no other. Not even the digital one that my five girls in the accounting department prefer. Take this power outage, for example. Where would my staff be now if they had to rely on information stored only in computers and other technical devices?" She shook her head. "Sometimes the old-fashioned way is so much more reliable. Of course, my staff took the weekend off, so they're not here to defend their position." She smiled at us.

"Where is that file?" Mrs. Desmond scanned the floor. "I distinctly remember having it on my desk before the tree crashed through the window. It contains information on all our benefactors. It couldn't have gone far. Are you sure you haven't seen it, Audrey?"

"No, Mrs. Desmond," Audrey said, her fingers gliding over the file tabs.

Mrs. Desmond looked at me and sighed.

"Would you like me to give you a hand?" I offered.

"Well...if it's no trouble."

I proceeded to pick up every sheet of paper in the office—even if it wasn't in the vicinity of her desk. I'd amassed about twenty papers when I bent over to retrieve another. The heading read *Verdell Benefactors* with this year's date next to it. Dozens of sponsors and the amounts they donated were recorded, beginning with the highest dollar amount.

My eye was drawn to the first name on the list: Trenton Barratt.

The name didn't surprise me, but the amount next to it did: a million dollars.

At the bottom of the list was a negative amount for two million dollars underlined in red. The school deficit?

Mrs. Desmond was chatting with Audrey about the mess in the office. I said nothing about my discovery and continued to collect the rest of the stray papers.

When I'd finished, I handed Mrs. Desmond the pile. "All done."

"Thank you." She took the papers and flipped through them.

Audrey placed another six folders into the bin and handed it to Michael. "Here. You're all set. These files cover the students, teachers, and other staff that Nat and Andrew interacted with. The people Pierre Favreau might have had daily dealings with are in here too." She tossed in a lined notepad and a couple of pens, then waved a tiny square envelope. "You'll need this to go back and forth. If there's anything else I can do for you, let me know."

We thanked her and were about to leave when we heard a

commotion in the outer office.

A short man wearing a hairnet and a soiled white apron rushed in, arms waving. "Help! There's black smoke all over the dining hall. It's coming from the fireplace."

Michael and I hurried out after him into the corridor, Audrey following. We raced across the atrium and through the covered passageway to the dining hall.

The smell of smoke hit us well before we saw the black vapors flowing out of the double doors to the dining hall. The incident had already drawn a crowd. Hovering by an adjacent corridor, they watched in horror and seemed at a loss. Two members of the kitchen staff huddled with them, their expressions filled with angst.

Audrey turned to the man who'd led us here. "Charlie, is anyone else in the hall?"

"No, ma'am," he said, splotches of black soot now evident on his face.

"Where's the fire extinguisher?" Michael asked.

Audrey jerked a hand toward the adjacent corridor. "On a side wall around the corner."

People in our path scattered as Michael and I sped around the corner. Michael spotted the recessed cabinet before I did. He pulled on his leather glove and slammed his fist into the breakable glass, shattering it, sending pieces all over the floor. He removed the fire extinguisher and sped back to the dining room.

"Michael, wait," I called after him. I removed my wool scarf. "You need this around your mouth and nose. Protection from the fumes." I wrapped it around him.

"Shut the doors after," he said, then charged into the billowing smoke.

I didn't know how Mrs. Desmond had caught up with us so fast, but there she was, wobbling toward us on her crutches, her face contorted in anger. "I told everyone we couldn't light the fireplace. The chimney hadn't been cleaned in ages. Who's responsible for this?" She eyed Charlie. "Do you know who lit the fireplace?"

"No, Mrs. Desmond," he said, worry lines running along his forehead.

"I'm sure there's a valid explanation and I'd like to hear it." Her expression hardened. "What happened?"

The sharp edge in her tone was distinct, even for her. I supposed the pressure from recent events, not to mention the nuisance of having to get around on crutches, would make anyone grumpy.

"We were preparing meals in the kitchen when I smelled smoke," Charlie said. "I peeked into the hall and saw dark smoke coming from the fireplace. I used the fire extinguisher in the kitchen to put out the flames, but it wasn't enough. I ran back to the kitchen and got everyone out through the rear door." He stretched his diminutive frame in a show of pride. "Then I ran to your office to tell you about the fire."

"You could have used the other fire extinguisher in the corridor too," Mrs. Desmond said.

Charlie lowered his eyes. "I'm sorry. I guess I panicked."

The dean stared at the crowd of onlookers that had since tripled. "Go back to your dorm rooms or wherever you were," she shouted at them. "You shouldn't be here."

The group backed away and scattered.

The sound of breaking glass reached us from inside the dining hall.

I leapt toward the doors, but Audrey grabbed my arm. "Best to wait it out."

Michael soon resurfaced, patches of black soot on his forehead and parka. He shut the doors behind him. He pulled down the scarf around his mouth and caught his breath. "The fire is out. I had to break a few windows. Couldn't get them to open. Needed to clear out the fumes."

"You did what had to be done," Mrs. Desmond said to him. She looked at Audrey. "Ask housekeeping to send a cleaning crew. Get maintenance to bring plywood to patch up the windows. Let's get this hall fixed up for dinner."

Michael washed up in my dorm room. He changed his parka for a pullover and a leather jacket he'd packed in case the weather turned milder. “Can’t wait to get to those files Audrey gave us.”

“That reminds me,” I said, rubbing my cold hands together. “You’ll never guess what I saw in Mrs. Desmond’s office.”

“What?”

“A record of Verdell’s financial sponsors for the year. Trenton Barratt topped the list at a million dollars.”

I got the reaction I expected. Michael stared at me. “You’re kidding.”

“Nope. Not that the donations helped much. The record shows a deficit of two million dollars.”

He let out a low whistle. “Makes me wonder how they’ve managed to keep the school operational all these years. You ready to go?”

“Yes.”

We pocketed small flashlights, a handful of tea lights, and matches that housekeeping had left at our door, then headed for Mrs. Desmond’s office to retrieve our bin of manila folders.

The trip along the echo was dark and dismal. Tea lights randomly placed along both sides of the echo created gaps of darkness and cast weird shadows along the walls. It looked as if housekeeping staff were having a hard time keeping up with Mrs. Desmond’s increasing list of demands and had rushed through this task.

Conditions were no better in the atrium where the icy downpour functioned like a barrier, allowing little daylight to filter through the windows. Boys and girls stood chatting in groups, waiting until dinner would be served. Each student now wore the standard Verdell blue winter coat and matching pants, wool scarf, and tuque, making it easy to spot staff members in their midst.

The temperature in Mrs. Desmond’s office had dropped considerably. It was so cold that our breaths hung in the air. Audrey and the dean hadn’t returned. I figured they were supervising the cleanup in the dining hall.

Michael carried the bin down the corridor to the meeting room. Although this room wasn’t as frigid as Mrs. Desmond’s office, it was nevertheless cold and damp. A glimpse out the window at the freezing rain impelled me to keep my mittens on.

I placed the tea lights on the table and Michael lit them. Looking at the soft glow did nothing to make me feel warmer.

The cold didn't seem to bother Michael as much. As I'd often done, I teased him about it. "You probably have Mediterranean roots and don't know it."

He shrugged. "My ancestors were Scottish and just as hot blooded as your Italian-Irish ancestors, if not more."

We teased each other back and forth until the jokes and laughter warmed my heart and filtered down to my fingers. My hands didn't feel as cold anymore, so I removed my mittens.

With renewed energy, we plodded through the files. We paused only to cite pertinent facts we'd discovered, all the while choosing the people we wanted to interview. I added their names to a growing list.

We'd almost finished our review when I picked up the last folder. It was Pierre Favreau's file. I perused it but found no new information. Other than a handwritten note indicating he was a referral, we had no idea who had recommended him for the job as cook at Verdell.

The final step was deciding the names of people we wanted to interview by order of priority. After I'd transcribed their names to a new sheet of paper, I tucked my hands under me. "Is it my imagination or is it getting colder in here?"

"When did we last eat?" Michael asked. "I'm starving."

Michael often equated feeling cold with the need to refuel. Come to think of it, he equated food with almost anything that broke his concentration from the job at hand.

"I have a package of chocolate almonds." I reached for my handbag.

"Forget it. I need real food. Something heavier." He checked his watch. "Five-thirty. The kitchen should be operating by now. I'll bet a thick slice of ham and beans are on the dinner menu." He stood up.

"Where are you going? We can't leave the files here."

"Yes, we can." He dug out a key from a small envelope. "Audrey gave us a spare. Let's go."

Mrs. Desmond was standing in front of the closed double doors to the dining hall. She was telling students that dinner would be served soon and directed them to form a straight line along the wall. Her expression seemed drained of vitality. I got the impression she'd remained at her post since she first arrived.

She acknowledged us with a nod. "Thank you both for your help. The smoke has cleared and the windows have been boarded."

Audrey stepped out of the dining hall. "The kitchen staff is ready to serve meals now," she said to Mrs. Desmond. She turned to open both doors wide.

The faint bitterness of singed matter lingered in the air. It was all but forgotten as we joined the line and took a serving tray from the pile on the counter. The kitchen staff wore winter coats—a reminder of the dropping temperatures in the building, not to mention an even colder night ahead.

It was a given that the kitchen staff couldn't cook up a hot dinner, so they used their ingenuity to put together a meal that could be served cold. Michael had called it: a slice of ham and a scoop of beans with a biscuit. Dessert included vanilla pudding or a strawberry ice cream milkshake. The biscuit had been thawed from a supply in the freezer because the center was colder than the rest. The pudding was instant and made with milk. Second helpings of the pudding and milkshake were encouraged, which told me the kitchen staff couldn't keep the milk cold or the ice cream frozen for much longer.

Who was I to complain? I finished eating in ten minutes. So did Michael, though he found a new interest in his paper napkin and was folding and unfolding it in different ways.

Tea lights lit up the faces of students sitting at the table across from us. They spoke in hushed tones, as if sharing secrets. I noticed two students poking at their food. One girl grimaced and put her fork down. Another girl handed her plate over to the boy sitting next to her.

I whispered to Michael, "Some of these kids aren't eating."

He whispered back, "Yeah, I know."

"How are they going to survive over the next few days if they're so picky?"

"Give me a minute." He winked at me.

He'd roused my curiosity, but the resolute look on his face confirmed the topic was closed. At least until he'd finished playing with his napkin.

I looked around. Tea lights cast silent shadows over the walls and ceiling and added to the hushed atmosphere. The occasional crack and tumble of a tree branch was the only sound that prompted louder bursts of conversation in the room, but then the din returned to its former muted level.

As the students vacated the tables, I turned to Michael. "Can we go now?"

"Sure."

"So what's up?"

"Wait till we get to the meeting room," he whispered.

We crossed the covered passageway to the main building and cut through the atrium where students had regrouped, many holding tea lights in glass jars. From the extra number of tea lights lining the corridor, I assumed either Verdell had been stashing supplies or someone with excellent foresight in housekeeping had taken advantage of pre-Christmas sales.

By the time Michael unlocked the door to the meeting room, I'd run out of patience. "For heaven's sake, what's so top secret?" I dug out my flashlight and aimed it inside the room.

He closed the door behind us and spoke in a low voice. "Students are taking drugs here." He lit the tea lights on the table.

"Here? In this excuse for a monastery? Are you sure?" I turned off my flashlight and put it in my pocket.

He nodded. "I saw an exchange under the table between two boys. That's why I was stalling to leave. They had their backs to us and I wanted to see their faces."

"Did you?"

"Yes."

"So you'd be able to identify them?"

"I think I saw one of them in this pile." He motioned to the folders on the table.

"Are you going to tell Mrs. Desmond?"

"Not until I find out—"

There was a light knock at the door.

I opened it to find a young student whom I recognized from my career presentation in Dave's class.

"Hi, I'm Sophie Toomey." She glanced up and down the corridor, panic in her eyes. "I have to talk to you. It's urgent."

CHAPTER 9

Sophie remained standing until I indicated a chair. "I wanted to talk to you about Natalie Dunn," she said. "We shared the same dorm suite."

I sat down facing her. "I remember you from our class presentation, Sophie. You're a senior and Nat was a junior. I thought Verdell housed juniors in the same suite."

"We were among the last students to get accepted at Verdell this year," she said. "No other dorm room had a free bed for a junior student, so they put Nat in my suite."

"What did you want to tell us?"

"Some things went on in Nat's room that might be important." She glanced in Michael's direction, then kept her eyes downcast.

"What kind of things?" I asked.

Out of the corner of my eye, I noticed Michael had gathered the files and placed them at the other end of the table. His remoteness would make Sophie feel more at ease and facilitate my one-on-one talk with her.

Sophie fidgeted with the zipper pull of her jacket. "Someone got into Nat's room late one night last week. Whoever it was must've had a key."

"Did you see this person?"

"No. The door to my room was closed. I heard someone moving around, though."

"Do you know if anything was stolen?"

"No. I mean—I don't think so."

I waited. She clearly needed time to gather her thoughts.

Sophie adjusted her glasses. "I left my room and tiptoed into the kitchenette that Nat and I shared. I looked below the door to her room. It was dark. Nat always turned on the lights when she was in her room."

"Maybe she went straight to bed," I said.

She shook her head. "Nat would have turned on the lights anyway. I'm sure someone else was in her room."

"Did you hear any noise coming from her room? Music?"

"I heard the sliding door to her closet open and close. The drawers in her desk too. Oh…I heard a laugh."

"Male or female?"

"I don't know. It was a short laugh. Not at all like Nat's giggles."

"Then what happened?"

Sophie glanced down. "I got closer to the door and listened. Whoever was in there used her laptop."

"Are you sure?" I asked.

"Yes. It plays a little tune whenever Nat clicks it on."

"You think somebody was trying to hack into her computer?"

"Oh, for sure. Someone got into her email and sent one out."

"How do you know this?"

"I heard the little notes play. You know, the sound it makes when you send an email."

"What happened next?"

"I heard movement," Sophie said. "I rushed back to my room and closed the door."

"So you didn't see anyone leave," I said.

"No."

I threw Michael a side-glance, thinking he might want to question her, but all he did was nod in my direction—a sign that I was doing okay without him.

"Did you mention the intrusion to Nat later on?" I asked Sophie.

Her eyes stated to mist. "I couldn't. She'd gone out that night and never came back. The next day, I found out she was dead." She started to cry. "I lost my best friend."

I was stunned. These girls had clearly shared a lot more than a dorm suite.

"I'm so sorry for your loss, Sophie."

Even though more than a decade had passed since I'd graduated from high school, I could still recall the solidarity and support that meant so much between friends. I felt her pain and waited while she dug out a tissue from her pocket and dabbed at her eyes. "As best friends, you and Nat must have shared lots of stuff."

Sophie nodded. "Everything—clothes, makeup, music..."

"Even secrets?"

The color rose on her face. "Sometimes."

A gut feeling told me she knew about Nat's pregnancy. I had to choose my next words with care if I wanted to gain her confidence. "Were Nat and Andrew close?"

"You mean 'tight'?"

A new interpretation to add to my lingo. "Yes, tight."

"No. Don't believe the rumors."

"What rumors?"

"That they were in love. That it was a 'boyfriend-kills-girlfriend-then-kills-himself' thing." Sophie emphasized the phrase with quotes in the air.

"Someone must have started the rumors about them," I said.

"It was Andrew. What a loser." She rolled her eyes. "He had a thing for Nat. It started after she tried to get him off drugs. He kept telling everyone he'd hooked up with Nat. Word got around they were a couple."

"Andrew was using?"

She fidgeted with her zipper pull again. "Everyone knew he'd gone to rehab to try to break the habit. Nat thought he was a little off—even up to a few weeks ago." She shrugged. "Maybe he was still using."

"How did Nat react when she heard Andrew was spreading rumors about her?"

"She got angry at first, then she let it go. She didn't want to ruin how she felt about her real boyfriend. Oh, crap." Her hand flew to her mouth.

"It's okay, Sophie. Whatever you say won't leave this room. I promise."

She relaxed a little.

"So Nat was seeing someone," I said. "At Verdell?"

"Yes." She smiled, exposing her pink and purple braces. "She was real excited every time she spoke about him. She never mentioned him by name, though. She was so secretive about it."

"How long had she been seeing him?"

"Since September."

"Was she still seeing him…till the end?"

"I think so," Sophie said.

"When was the last time you saw Nat alive?"

"The same evening she…after we returned from dinner. She invited me to her room. She said she had a secret to tell me. I thought it might be about her boyfriend. I was real excited to find out." She took in a deep breath. "That was when she told me she was pregnant. Three months." The color rose on her face again.

"How did she feel about it?"

She smiled. "She was real happy."

"Did she say who the father was?"

"No." Sophie frowned. "We often had fights about that. I was her best friend, but she didn't trust me enough to tell me his name. That last night, I got so angry. I couldn't help it. I said things to her that were mean. Now I feel so bad." She dabbed at new tears flowing down her cheeks.

"Was Nat planning to tell her boyfriend about the pregnancy?"

"I think she already had. She was meeting him after curfew that night to talk about their future plans together."

"Did she say where?"

"No, but it must've been on campus. Someplace secret."

Trying to get more information from her was like trudging through mud up to my knees. I took a deep breath and waited.

Sophie interpreted my sigh as a sign of frustration because she stared at me, her eyes widening behind thick glasses. "Okay, I'll tell you. I don't know if it exists, but I've heard talk about a secret place on campus. It's an underground passageway with trapdoors. I heard students say it's haunted with the ghosts of men who used to work in the old mines. They even heard ghosts wailing through the walls late at night."

Was this girl delusional or was she that gullible? At the least, she was squeezing the last ounce of patience out of me. "You don't believe those old tales, do you?"

"I don't know, but trust me, I wouldn't want to find out." She let out a nervous giggle.

Maybe not.

"Anyway," she said, "I was thinking maybe Nat met up with her boyfriend there."

"How does one get into this passageway?"

Sophie glanced at Michael. "I could get in big trouble if I tell you and someone finds out."

Michael said to her, "I always protect my sources."

His sincerity convinced her. "You have to be a member of a secret society," she said. "The underground society, I think they call it."

"Was Nat a member?" he asked.

"I don't think so."

"Then her boyfriend was a member."

"I guess so."

"How do you become a member?"

"You have to know the right people. It's by referral only." She sounded quite sure about this.

Michael probed further. "Do you know anything else about this secret society? What's their purpose?"

Sophie shook her head. "I don't know. I asked Nat about it after she'd visited the secret place the first time. She said she was sworn to secrecy and refused to talk about it."

"Do you know any other students who are members of this secret society?"

"No."

We'd exhausted the subject. I backtracked to our original topic of discussion. "Sophie, about what you said earlier about hearing the intruder in Nat's room. You're sure someone sent an email from her computer?"

She lifted her chin. "Yes, and I know who it went to."

"Who?"

"Mr. Pellegrino."

She blew me away. "How do you know that?"

"Because I saw it on Nat's laptop."

"How did you get into her room?"

"She gave me a spare key."

"And the password to her laptop too?" I asked.

"Yes. Like I said, we shared everything." Sophie paused. "Except her diary."

"Excuse me?"

"Nat never showed me her diary."

"The police must have seized it as evidence," I said, thinking out loud.

"No, they didn't," she said. "Nat lost her diary two weeks ago. She thought I'd used the spare key to get into her room and taken the diary as a joke, but I hadn't. I got real angry with her when she accused me." Her cheeks flushed pink.

"Did you report what you've told me to your dorm supervisor or the admin staff?"

Sophie shook her head. "No."

"Why not?"

She looked down. "I didn't want to get in trouble."

"I'm not following you. How could you get in trouble?"

"I used Nat's computer sometimes."

"So?"

She raised her voice. "So the police might think I was the one who sent the email to Mr. Pellegrino." Her eyes reflected fear.

"Did the police seize Nat's laptop?" I asked.

"I think so. Why?"

"If the police seized her laptop, they'll examine it for prints."

"Oh, crap." Sophie put a hand to her mouth. "I forgot about that."

"It doesn't matter. Friends share computers, right?" My response pacified her and she nodded. I already knew the answer to my next question, but I had to ask. "What did you do after the intruder left?"

"I was so afraid. I waited a long time to make sure no one was around. Then I went into Nat's room. I logged onto her laptop. I saw the email and the timestamp that showed it had been sent an hour earlier. I printed a copy." She reached into her pocket for a sheet of paper and unfolded it.

Michael walked over and sat next to me. The sheet Sophie handed us was a duplicate of the "puppy love" email Dave had shown us in his office.

"Did you share this with anyone else?" Michael asked her.

Sophie shook her head. "Oh, no, I didn't tell anyone."

"The police?"

"No."

"Did you tell them you heard someone going into Nat's room?"

"No, I was too scared. I've been thinking about telling Helga, my dorm supervisor, though. Not about the email, because I don't know who sent it." Her eyes flitted about the room, as if she were deciding whether or not to divulge more information. She steadied her gaze on the letter in my hands. "That's not the only email to Mr. Pellegrino. I saw more in Nat's outgoing box."

"Did you read them?" I asked her.

Sophie blinked. "Some of them. They weren't as personal as this one."

"Did Nat ever talk to you about Mr. Pellegrino?"

She smiled. "Oh, all the time. She said he was one of the best Lit teachers she'd ever had. She loved to sit in his class and listen to him talk about the great writers. I like his classes a lot too, except that..."

"What?"

She shrugged. "I guess I'm not as passionate as Nat is. Was."

"From her emails, did you get the impression that Nat and Mr. Pellegrino were somehow involved?"

"No way!" Sophie scowled. "Nat wouldn't—I mean—he's much too old for her."

I could feel Michael's eyes on me. It was time for a change of topic.

He leaned forward. "Sophie, would you lend me the key to Nat's room?"

Her expression changed to alarm. "What for?"

He spoke softly. "I'd like to take a look around. I might find a clue that would explain what happened. Something vague or insignificant the investigators might have missed."

"Oh...okay." She dug into her pocket and took out a set of keys. She pulled two keys off the ring and offered them to him. "One for the outside door, the other for the room."

"Thanks." Michael took them and moved back to his spot at the end of the table.

We'd gone full circle from the moment Sophie had knocked at the door. I thought about Nat and Andrew again. It would have been easy for a romantic to believe the sordid car incident was the result of spurned love gone wrong and of a young man's inability to deal with the despair that often accompanies flagrant rejections. But Dave's comments and the school video we'd seen proved otherwise.

"Did Nat or Andrew have any enemies that you know of?" I asked Sophie.

"I don't know," she said.

"Is there anything else you'd like to tell us about Nat or Andrew?"

She looked at me, her dark eyes widening. "Sometimes at night, I start thinking that maybe someone murdered them. I think, what a freaky thing to do at an exclusive school like this. Then I get real scared the killer will come after me next. I can't talk to anyone about it. They'll think I'm just trying to get attention."

"We don't know for certain that Nat and Andrew were murdered."

"Mrs. Desmond said there was an escaped convict on the loose."

I tried to allay her fears. "He could be miles away from here."

Sophie fidgeted, glanced at her watch, and jumped out of her chair. "I've told you everything I know. I have to get back to my room before lights out." She caught herself and smiled. "Oh, that's right. There are no lights." She opened the door.

"Thanks for your help, Sophie," I said.

"You're welcome." She surveyed both sides of the corridor, then dashed out.

I closed the door and sat down to discuss our findings. Sophie's revelations had added pieces to an ever-growing puzzle, but Michael wasn't buying all of it.

"The secret society is worth looking into," he said. "Could be a connection to drug activities. But ghosts? A haunted passageway?" He grimaced. "Let's get real."

"What's real is the father of Nat's baby," I said. "Who is he? And why hasn't he come forward?"

"Not to mention the late-night prowler in Nat's room the night she died." Michael shook his head. "Too many questions, not enough answers. Let's call it a night. We'll interview the next people on our list first thing tomorrow morning."

"Maybe someone else will surprise us and come forward."

"Yeah. This place is full of surprises." He held up the keys to Nat's dorm. "Who knows what we'll find next."

We made our way along the cold, dimly lit echo. A trickle of girls rushed by us to get to their sleeping quarters before curfew. Verdell's rules and regulations had their grasp on students, even during a state of emergency.

In front of every dorm suite on our floor was a bucket of water. Also deposited at the door was a plastic bag that contained a small battery-powered flashlight, an extra blanket, paper cups, and toiletries.

"How considerate," I said. "And practical."

"Money talks," Michael said.

I turned on my flashlight and unlocked the door, holding it open for Michael who scooped up the items and carried them inside. As I shut the door behind us, I felt something underfoot. I picked up a piece of paper, thinking it might have been a note left with the items. I shone my flashlight on it. "Oh, no! Look at this, Michael."

The pasted letters on the note read: "*Go home or be prepared to die!*"

The message was threatening, but the stationary itself held a surprise: The monogram in the upper left corner was GD.

Gloria Desmond?

CHAPTER 10

The threatening note kept me awake all night. Fears of a potential intruder activated my imagination and prompted me to check the lock on the door several times.

Michael slept well. I envied his ability to turn off all thoughts the moment his head hit the pillow. If it hadn't been for the sound of splintering branches crashing to the ground in the early morning hours, I'd have slept in, but the third resounding rumpus dashed any hope of that happening.

I gazed out the window to survey the damage. The icy silence on campus was deceiving. Tree branches had expanded with ice overnight and intertwined their frosty tentacles with those of neighboring trees. Sheets of ice had slid off rooftops and shattered into jagged shards on impact. The campus was strewn with broken branches and debris, a testament to the damage such a storm can inflict and to the challenges facing the school in days ahead. Even in the aftermath of a destructive path, the tempest showed no sign of abandoning its hold.

I shivered at the thought of discarding the three blankets that had kept me warm all night, but I had to get dressed. I grabbed the clothes I'd left on the chair the night before. They felt cold and stiff. I slipped into them as fast as I could, hoping my body temperature would soften the fabric and make the clothes feel wearable again.

Michael stepped out of the bathroom, dressed but unshaven. I assumed the battery in his electric razor had died. "Are you ready?"

I checked my watch. "It's only seven o'clock."

"I'll bet Mrs. Desmond is up."

"It's Sunday morning."

"So?"

"Most people sleep in on Sunday."

Michael gestured toward the window. "Not if they heard the commotion outside last night."

"Touché. Give me a minute."

I slipped into the bathroom, brushed my hair, and put an elastic band around my ponytail. I used some of the bottled water to rinse my face, then gargled with mouthwash. I applied a layer of peppermint lip gloss—my daily routine for preventing chapped lips. Another day without a shower was something I'd never get used to, though.

I shrugged into my parka, pulled on my boots, and grabbed my wool hat and mittens. "Okay, I'm ready."

Michael tucked the threatening note inside his leather jacket. He reached for his wool cap and slipped it on. "Glad I brought this cap. Let's go for breakfast first."

"What I wouldn't give for a cup of hot coffee right now."

"Don't even mention it." He locked the door behind us.

Attendance in the dining hall was what I'd expected: nil, except for a handful of students sitting at a table on one side of the room. I wondered how they'd managed to sleep through the commotion last night and look so perky this morning. Then again, it had more to do with their youthfulness. I did the math and concluded I was almost twice their age. All of a sudden I felt so old.

Mrs. Desmond and Audrey occupied another table at the opposite end of the hall. Like everyone else, they were bundled in coats and hats.

Audrey waved us over. "Get your breakfast—whatever is available—and come join us."

I understood her remark when we placed our orders.

"What would you like this morning?" Charlie beamed at us from the other side of the counter. His demeanor nullified the terror of yesterday's encounter with a smoke-filled dining hall.

"I'll have cereal, an apple, and a muffin," Michael said.

"Sorry, no muffins today." Charlie shook his head, his thickset neck no longer visible behind the collar of a winter coat.

"Okay, I'll have a bagel instead."

"No bagels either."

"How come?"

He leaned forward and said in a low voice, "We were robbed."

"Robbed?" Michael stared at him.

"Yes, sir. Best you talk to Mrs. Desmond. She knows the whole story." Charlie gestured with his chin in her direction, then added soda crackers and a jam packet to Michael's order.

With not much more to choose from, I ordered the same breakfast and we headed for the table.

Mrs. Desmond examined our trays. "I gather you've heard about the latest quandary to hit Verdell."

"We're hoping you can fill in the details." Michael sat next to me.

The dean looked on as the students at the other table walked out. "We believe whoever lit the fireplace yesterday was looking to create a distraction." She frowned. "It worked. They ransacked the kitchen pantry and stole whatever they could carry."

"Where is the pantry located?" I asked.

"Down the corridor from the kitchen."

"Is it locked at all times?"

Mrs. Desmond turned to Audrey. "Is it?"

"No," Audrey said. "The kitchen staff often goes back and forth for supplies, so it's convenient to leave the door unlocked. No one else walks along that corridor anyway."

"It's fortunate no supplies were purchased on Friday," Mrs. Desmond said. "They would have been stolen with the rest."

Her subtle hint at Farveau's vanishing act didn't go unnoticed.

"We scarcely have enough food to provide breakfast for the next few days," Audrey said. "Supplies are low for lunch and dinner meals too. We don't want to alarm the students and staff, but word gets around. We might have a bigger problem on our hands once they realize we can't feed them anymore."

"Now Audrey, the shortage is a problem, but I don't think it'll lead to an uprising." Mrs. Desmond pursed her lips. "Our students come from affluent families and know how to behave, though it's hard to believe any of my boys and girls were responsible for the theft."

"Are you insinuating the staff did it?" Audrey gave her a side-glance.

Mrs. Desmond grinned. "Maybe our guests can find out."

"We'd be glad to help," Michael said, "but I think we've already overstayed our welcome." He pulled out the threatening note and handed it to Mrs. Desmond.

Audrey peered over and read it out loud. "*'Go home or be prepared to die!'*" She gaped at Michael and me. "Is this someone's idea of a sick joke?"

"And on my monogrammed paper too!" Mrs. Desmond's gaze hardened. "Joke or not, we'll look into it. Audrey, call a general assembly for one o'clock this afternoon. We'll need everyone's help if we want to find out who's responsible for lighting the fireplace and now this latest prank."

"We should tell them about the food shortage too," Audrey said.

"Yes, of course." Mrs. Desmond looked at us. "I'd like you to attend the assembly as well. I don't expect you to take part in the search I'm organizing for the missing food supplies. You have enough to handle as it is. However, I'd like you to be present in case anyone decides to come forward with information."

"We'll be there," I said.

"Good morning, everyone," a female voice rang out. I turned to see Ann standing next to me, a glass of juice in her hand. "I hope everyone slept well."

"With what's been going on in this place, how could anyone sleep well?" Mrs. Desmond frowned. "I thought you left Verdell."

Was she referring to Ann leaving her job as a teacher or leaving after her presentation on Friday?

"A friend invited me to stay over," Ann said, interpreting the question as she saw fit.

Mrs. Desmond lifted her chin. "It's against the rules for staff to have an overnight guest."

Ann smiled. "I didn't have a choice, Mrs. Desmond. Didn't you say at assembly the other day that no one can leave Verdell, even if they wanted to, because of the icy road conditions?"

If looks could kill, the dean would have struck Ann down with one fatal glare. "You always did have an excellent memory." She forced a smile.

Ann switched her gaze to Michael and me. "I wish the power would return so we could get more news from Dave. Everyone's so concerned about him."

"If *everyone* at Verdell locked their car doors according to the rules, none of this would have happened, and the police wouldn't have had to drag Mr. Pellegrino to the station for questioning." Mrs. Desmond's tone was as biting as her words. She pushed herself out of her chair. "Come, Audrey. It's time we go tend to our duties."

The two women walked out.

Ann sat down next to me. "One more second and I'd have regretted my next words to that woman."

"Makes two of us," Michael said.

She took a few sips of her juice. "I came over to offer you my help in your investigation into the students' deaths. If there's anything I can do to help prove Dave's innocence, please let me know."

"Thanks," he said.

"I have a question for you," I said to Ann. "It's about Verdell sponsors."

I was about to divulge private information, but at this point, I had to trust Ann. I mentioned how I'd come across records in Mrs. Desmond's office that indicated the school was in a financial deficit position.

"It doesn't surprise me," Ann said. "When I worked here, a friend in accounting confided how Verdell was gradually selling off portions of land surrounding the campus. A lot of money went into renovations and new buildings to attract more students and their wealthy investor parents."

"Doesn't Mrs. Desmond need school board approval for selling off land and initiating major projects?" Michael asked.

"Since she's known many of the board members for years, she

has a lot of influence on them. She's well positioned to get what she wants, as they say in the business world. About Verdell's deficit position? I heard she overdid it with the renovations. It certainly wasn't spent on anything extra for the teachers."

"Thanks for sharing," I said.

"You're welcome." She stood up. "I'm heading for the library. I need to read something cheerful. Have a good day, you two." She walked out.

"I feel as if I'm spinning my wheels," Michael said.

"What do you mean?"

"We have a list of people to interview, but other crazy stuff keeps happening."

I checked my watch, more from habit than anything else. "We have the whole morning. Let's talk to Charlie and the other kitchen staff about Favreau while we're here."

"Exactly what I had in mind. We can do double duty and ask them what they know about the pantry robbery."

The incoming flow of breakfast traffic wasn't more than a trickle. It enabled us to interview members of the kitchen staff one by one.

First up was Glenda. The woman strolled over to our table. Donned in winter gear like the other kitchen staff, she sat down opposite us.

"Tell us about your experience working with Pierre Favreau," Michael asked her. "What did he talk about?"

"Whatever his name is—Paul or Pierre—he was a real sweetheart to me," Glenda said, her Irish accent coming to the fore. "I helped him with the food preparation. He didn't talk much except to teach me about spices and herbs. And he never spoke down to me like other chefs I've worked with." She leaned over and whispered, "Not like the spoiled young rascals here either. Imagine complaining about Verdell's select menu and expecting filet mignon and caviar instead?" She twisted her lips in frustration. "They'd mind their manners better after a good old-fashioned spanking, if you ask me."

"Do you have any idea who might have stolen the supplies from the kitchen pantry?" I asked.

Her brow creased. "None whatsoever. It's shocking, that's what it is. And to think we have to keep mum and not tell the poor little rich kids the cupboard is practically bare." She grimaced and rolled her eyes.

The next staff member to join us was Eric, a young kitchen helper. Slim and long-legged, he sat at the table and relaxed an arm on the back of his chair.

When Michael asked him about his kitchen duties, he showed pride in his job. "I'm in charge of making sure all equipment, utensils, and workstations are clean. I unload deliveries. I assist the cooks by washing and peeling all veggies."

"How did you get along with Pierre Favreau?"

Eric shrugged. "Okay, I guess."

"Did you guys ever talk about stuff?"

"Like when we weren't working, you mean?"

Michael nodded.

Eric scratched his head and grinned. "He asked me once if I had any liquor in my room. I told him I was eighteen years old and didn't drink."

"Did you talk about anything else?"

"No. He didn't talk much and I was okay with that. The guy creeped me out."

"How?"

"I don't know. The way he was always looking at what everyone else in the kitchen was doing."

"Any idea who stole the supplies from the pantry?" Michael asked.

"No," Eric said. "Whoever it was had to know where to go."

"What do you mean?"

"A lot of students think the pantry is in the kitchen and that you could only get to it through that swinging door." He stuck out a thumb toward it. "They might be rich but they're not as smart as I thought."

"What do you do in your spare time, Eric?" I asked.

"I'm taking night courses in business admin. Sometimes I go to the library to study. It makes me feel like I'm one of the students here. I even made a couple of friends." He grinned. "Not with any rich kids. They hang out with their own kind."

We wished Eric well with his studies and waited for Charlie to arrive.

Because the kitchen was running on a skeleton staff too this weekend, Charlie was our last member to be interviewed. The cook who had worked alternate shifts with Favreau sat with us at the table, his coat zipped up to the top, putting the emphasis on his puffy cheeks.

"How do you suppose someone took off with so many supplies from the food pantry?" Michael asked him.

"There had to be more than one thief," Charlie said, speaking with certainty. "They filched it all within minutes. They must've had a cart or something that they stocked with food and wheeled away. Bread, desserts, tins of salmon and tuna, cans of soup, peanut butter—you name it."

"Even so, they would have had to wheel it from the pantry and down the corridor to get it out the front door. Someone would have noticed."

"With all that black smoke coming out of the dining hall and the crowd gawking at it?" Charlie grinned. "They could have driven a truck by there and no one would have seen it."

If the flicker in Michael's eyes was anything to go by, he wasn't taking Charlie's comment to heart. "Tell me what you know about Pierre Favreau."

"You mean Paul." He smiled. "Boy, oh boy, did that guy pull the wool over my eyes. I have to admit he was a damned good cook."

"He worked as a cook when he did time in jail."

"That explains it. Those guys don't suffer from food depravation, that's for sure." Charlie chuckled.

"Did he ever talk about his private life? Friends?"

"Never. He was a loner. I asked him to go have a drink at a pub in town a couple of times, but he always refused. Now I know why. He was afraid someone would recognize him."

"Members of the kitchen staff are away this weekend. Do you know if Favreau chatted or socialized with them?"

Charlie shook his head. "He kept to himself. I don't think he ever left Verdell except to go get groceries every Friday."

"About this past Friday..." Michael leaned forward. "Did you see him leave?"

"Nope. I'm either busy in the kitchen or serving at the counter when he's not on duty."

"How does he get to town?"

"A friend picks him up and drives him back."

"What's his friend's name?"

"I'd tell you if I knew."

"Can you describe the car his friend drives?"

"Sorry. Can't help you there either." Charlie grinned. "Would you like to see his room?"

He didn't have to ask us twice.

CHAPTER 11

Charlie accompanied us to the main building and up a flight of stairs to the staff apartments. He stopped to point out a spacious sitting room with sofas and end tables. "You'll find a sitting room like this on the other floor too. Staff uses them for informal get-togethers."

We followed him around a corner and down a long narrow corridor to the last door. We waited while he pulled out his keys.

Michael asked, "How did you manage to get a key to Favreau's room?"

"It used to be my room," Charlie said. "Months ago, Mrs. Desmond told me I had to give it up to the new cook and move to a smaller room. I kept the spare key."

"Did she say why you had to move?"

"Something about the guy needing his privacy. What a joke." He smirked. "After he took it over, I'd never want my old room back again. Who'd want to sleep in this pigsty?" He opened the door to a room that an escaped killer had inhabited.

The putrid smell hit me first—a mix of urine and beer.

Michael flapped a hand in the air. "Whew! This place reeks."

I looked around and shuddered. Pigsty was an understatement. The grimy windows and dusty furniture meant the room hadn't been cleaned in weeks—maybe longer. I glanced through the open bathroom door. Filthy! I tucked my hands in my pockets. "I thought the housekeeping staff cleaned all the rooms here," I said to Charlie.

He nodded. "They're supposed to." He lowered his voice. "I

heard Favreau bribed them to stay away. I guess he didn't want to share the décor." He gestured toward posters of nude women taped to the wall over the headboard and girlie magazines littering the floor on either side of the bed. "Stay as long as you want. When you're done, shut the door. It locks by itself." He left.

Aside from the stench and dirt, Favreau's negative energy had engrained itself in other aspects of the room. Dark red curtains hung from ceiling to floor, creating a heavy, oppressive mood. Empty beer bottles stacked hodge-podge in a case by the window threatened to spill over. Stains on the carpet indicated they already had. The bed sheets were dingy and soiled.

Michael snapped on vinyl gloves and wasted no time in going through Favreau's dresser. When he didn't find anything significant, he pulled out the three drawers. He bent over and passed a hand inside the wood frame, eager to find something that would link Favreau to the drug scene or the murders at Verdell.

He straightened up, frowning. "Nothing."

"What about the closet?" I gestured toward the door but hesitated to touch it. "Maybe we'll find my client's Prada portfolio. I'm sure Favreau stole it from Gary Stilt's yacht."

He opened the door and aimed his flashlight inside the small space. "There's nothing much in here except some clothing, an old pair of shoes, and an overnight bag." He unzipped the bag. "Empty. I guess he traveled light."

"He got rid of the portfolio. There was no sense in lugging it around after he handed over the money to his boss."

"Could be." Michael put away his flashlight and scanned the room. His gaze fell on the bed. He leaned over and searched under the mattress.

I cringed. Good thing he was wearing vinyl gloves. I crossed my fingers he wouldn't want to extend his search to the bathroom.

"Not a thing, dammit." He turned around and headed for the window. He grasped the hem of the curtains. "Feels a little lumpy to me." He reached in his pocket, pulled out a Swiss army knife, and slit the stitches along the hem. He removed a handful of small plastic packets filled with white pills.

"What are they?"

"Ecstasy," he said. "Another term for the drug methamphetamine or MDMA. It's been around for decades. Often comes in tiny pills stamped with words or logos like these." He showed me the pills. Smiley faces adorned their surface.

"Where are they manufactured?"

"Mainly in covert labs. They're easy to produce and distribute and even easier to obtain. Often found in clubs and party scenes and popular among teens."

I'd married young, so I'd avoided the whole drug scene. It was ironic, though, that my husband had died from having accidentally ingested a poisonous substance. "What are the effects of ecstasy?"

"A sense of euphoria that lasts a few hours," Michael said. "Heightened sensory perception. Unusual levels of energy."

"Any adverse symptoms?"

"Anxiety, dizziness, nausea, chills, among others. It can even lead to death."

"But the students here look so healthy. What makes you think they're taking drugs?"

He shrugged. "Not all of them are doing drugs, but Favreau is sure selling them. I'll bet he's getting his supplies from the Hells Angels or one of their puppet clubs listed under other names. I have to find the source."

"It's hard to believe nobody else at Verdell knows about this."

"Could be someone high up on the food chain here is protecting Favreau."

"High up? Like in administration?"

"That's what we're going to find out." Michael tucked the packets back inside the curtain hem.

"Wait," I said. "Don't you want to hand those pills over to Mrs. Desmond?"

"No. If Favreau is selling drugs at Verdell, someone's buying them from him and either using or reselling them at a profit. I don't want to disturb the flow."

He had a good point.

"Okay, we're done here." He tore a small strip of paper from a magazine. "This is a foolproof way to know if someone visits the room later." He tucked the paper in the doorjamb and closed the door behind us. "Let's go downstairs to the meeting room and scan the personnel files. I didn't get a chance yet to look for the student I saw passing the drugs."

"You know, Michael, we could have hidden Favreau's pills in our dorm room," I said, following him down the flight of stairs.

"Like where? The dresser drawers have no locks. Neither does our luggage. And forget the bathroom cabinet."

He was right. It would have proven more difficult to find a good hiding place than I'd imagined. Then again...

"Under the mattress," I said.

"Not the best idea," Michael said. "What if housekeeping staff came in to change the sheets?"

"I doubt it. Why would they change the sheets if they can't wash them?"

"Right. No clean water. I think our decision to leave the drugs in Favreau's room is the safer option."

"For us."

"You got it."

"By the way, I thought of other people we can add to our interview list."

"Who?"

"The housekeeping staff. They might have information about Favreau."

Before heading to the meeting room, we stopped by Audrey's office. Large candles on her filing cabinets and desk emitted enough light to reveal the names on the manila folders she was holding.

"Hello, you two." Audrey placed the folders into a bankers' box on the floor by her desk. "I decided to move some of Mrs. Desmond's files into this area. She can't use her desk until it's repaired, and it's much too cold to work in that office anyway."

Since our last visit, the doorframe to Mrs. Desmond's office had been sealed with masking tape. It wouldn't keep the cold out, but at least it prevented the frigid air on the other side from flowing into Audrey's office.

"We've set the school assembly for one o'clock this afternoon in the chapel. You'll be there, won't you?" She eyed us.

"Yes," I said. "Audrey, would you have a list of the housekeeping staff?"

My request drew a wide-eyed stare. "Whatever for?"

"We need to interview them."

"Talk about thorough. You two aren't sparing anyone, are you?" She winked at us, then moved to one of the cabinets and pulled out a thick folder. "You'll find everything you need in here." She handed it to me without hesitation, confirming her compliance with Mrs. Desmond's orders to provide whatever information we needed.

Our next stop was the meeting room. Despite the subdued glow from the tea lights, it didn't take Michael long to look through the pile of student files and identify the boy he'd seen passing drugs in the dining hall the other evening.

Greg Talbot was seventeen years old, played on the basketball team, and maintained good marks at Verdell. A senior at the school, the lanky youth with light brown hair could be described as ordinary, though there was a distinct flicker in his eyes that hinted at a humorous side to him.

"The boys were transferred from the outer dorm to the gymnasium," I said. "It's off limits to me. You'll have to interview him alone."

"It's Sunday morning. I'll bet he's shooting hoops."

I smiled at him. "You're so smart."

"It's common sense."

"I love your common sense." I put a hand around his neck and kissed him on the lips.

"Now you did it. My common sense just flew out the door." He chuckled.

"Maybe we should fly out the door too before we get into trouble."

He pulled me closer and kissed me again. "Are you sure?"

"Mmm...quite sure. Your proposition is tempting, but you

never know who might come knocking at any moment."

"You're right." He put distance between us. "Let's go."

The curtain cut across the center of the gymnasium and offered privacy to the boys who had relocated here from their dorm rooms. The other half of the space remained available for sports-related activities.

As Michael had predicted, Greg was shooting hoops with Zack and other boys who shared a similar height advantage. I was surprised to see they were only wearing the standard jerseys and shorts in a building where the room temperature was below the freezing mark. Then again, I couldn't think of a better way to ward off the cold than running around the gymnasium for an hour or so.

About forty students sat in the bleachers. Dressed in Verdell's blue winter gear, they watched the boys play with fresh-faced enthusiasm. I recognized Helga Peterson among them. She saw me, then leaned over to talk to a girlfriend. They both looked my way.

We chose a spot away from the crowd so they couldn't overhear our conversation. I took a seat while Michael made eye contact with Greg and waved him over.

Greg said a few words to Zack, then sprinted toward us.

Zack dribbled the ball, leaped in the air, then tossed it. It soared to a high arc and fell through the basket, earning a round of applause and cheers from his fans in the bleachers.

I turned and happened to see Helga blow a kiss. To Zack?

Zack waved and smiled in the general direction of the group, not acknowledging the kiss or Helga. Clever.

"Hey, guys." Greg had reached us.

"Sorry to interrupt your practice," Michael said to him. "Do you have a few minutes?"

"Anything for Pellegrino's guests." He gave us a cocky smile. "What's up?" He grabbed a towel, then sat on one of the bleachers and stretched his six-foot-plus frame.

"We'd like to talk to you about Andrew Boyle."

Greg wiped his face with the towel. "What about him?"

"We heard you two used to hang out," Michael said, testing him.

"Who told you that? We were in some of the same classes. That's all."

Michael waited.

"Hey, the guy was a loser. I mean—I feel sorry about what happened to him. You know, with Nat and everything."

"I heard they were a couple," I said.

"A couple?" Greg laughed. "No way. The guy was a tool. Nat was too sick for him."

"Sick?" I repeated.

"She was awesome," Greg said, grinning, letting his gaze ride over me.

Michael pulled him back into the conversation. "When was the last time you saw Andrew?"

"In class."

"When?"

"I don't remember. Maybe the same day as...you know. Whatever." Greg raised both hands. "Hey, don't get me wrong. What happened here was bad news."

"Yeah." Michael spoke in a low voice. "This whole place is bad news. We were supposed to be gone by now. Instead we're stuck here. Stressed out big time. Would give anything to be partying with Molly." He gave him a measured look.

Greg narrowed his eyes. "Your speech in class... I thought you were fighting a private war against drugs."

"Between you and me, I need a little something to ease up once in a while. It's not like we're dealing on the street, right?" He grinned.

Greg shrugged, his eyes straying to his friends shooting hoops. "I might know someone."

"Can you drop it off tonight? Say, seven o'clock." Michael told him our dorm room number.

"I'll see what I can do." Greg dropped his towel on the bench. "Gotta go."

"What's Molly?" I asked Michael after we'd left the gymnasium.

"MDMA, better known as ecstasy or E in pill form," he said. "I hadn't mentioned it earlier, but it could be cut with other additives. People often don't know what they're ingesting or how their body is going to react to it until it's too late. With fatal results."

"I can't wait to see if Greg delivers. What makes you think he can get into Favreau's room to get the pills?"

"The main building was built decades ago. The old system of locks and keys is still the rule of the land for the doors to the staff apartments."

"So?"

"I wouldn't be surprised if more than one person in this place has a set of duplicate keys. Even if Greg doesn't have a key, these locks are pretty easy to pick."

I'd seen Michael pick a lock before. With the right tools and a bit of patience, he'd opened locks far more intricate than the ones at Verdell.

"If Greg shows up with the drugs," he said, "it's possible he got them from the supply in Favreau's room. We'll go back there afterward to check the curtain hem."

"Right." My mind went off on a tangent. "That underground passageway Sophie mentioned could be a meeting place for drug exchanges. I think the notion of a haunted passageway is so mysterious. Don't you?"

"If it exists."

"Why would she lie about it?"

"She's a drama queen," Michael said. "The way she examined the corridor before she walked out of the room. Give me a break." He chuckled.

"She's afraid. Can you blame her? In any case, I'm dying to find out how the rumors about the passageway started."

He gave me a side-glance. "Promise me you won't go looking for it without me. Okay?"

I knew he was speaking out of concern. I was about to answer when someone called out our names. We turned to see Helga reaching us in three strides.

"Do you have a moment?" she asked. "I hate to add to your problems, but I think we might have a robbery on our hands."

"We already know about the food that was stolen from the kitchen pantry," I said.

"I don't mean that robbery. I'm referring to the person who got into Natalie Dunn's room the night she died."

CHAPTER 12

Michael and I sat across from Helga in the meeting room. The tea lights flickered on the table every time one of us spoke or moved.

"Sophie said she told you about someone breaking into Nat's room," Helga said.

"A break-in?" I repeated.

"My bad." She raised a hand twice the size of mine. "Not a break-in. Whoever it was must have used a key. I don't know who the intruder was, but I think I know who might have supplied the key."

"Who?"

"Me." She leaned back. "Here's what happened. I was watching the guys practice basketball one night. I'm on the girl's basketball team, so I like to watch the guys sometimes. They have awesome moves."

"Like Zack?" I asked.

Helga's face lit up. "Isn't he a cool player?" She smiled and continued. "Thing is, I'm a supervisor of the girls' dorm, so I have a spare set of keys for each room. I'm sure I had the keys with me the same night Sophie mentioned. Anyway, after the practice, I couldn't find them. I looked everywhere. Then I found them in my locker."

"What night are we talking about again?" I had to be sure.

"The night of the accident—when Nat and Andrew went missing."

I noticed the discretion in her choice of words. "I've misplaced things sometimes. Is it possible you'd left the keys in your locker to begin with?"

Helga shook her head. "No way. I keep the keys in one blazer pocket and my phone in the other. Always have. They're part of my daily wardrobe."

"How would the keys have ended up in your locker? Isn't it locked?"

"No. Verdell believes in the honor system where our lockers are concerned. I don't mean to be crude or snooty, but most of the students here don't need to steal from one another."

The message came through loud and clear. "You implied earlier that someone took your keys to get into Nat's room."

"That's right. The timing fits. My keys went missing that night and showed up in my locker the next morning. Since it was the second time it happened, I'm one hundred percent certain that somebody borrowed them from me—again."

"The second time?" I asked.

Helga nodded. "About two weeks ago. I think it was in science class. I checked my pocket and the keys were gone. I found them in my locker."

"Think back," Michael said to her. "In both instances, who was standing or sitting near you?"

"My friends. Classmates. That's what I find so bizarre. We've known one another for years. I can't point to anyone who'd do such a thing." She shook her head.

I offered a plausible alternative. "Maybe someone wanted to play a trick on you and they hid them."

Helga narrowed her eyes. "If you're right, they're in big trouble once I get my hands on them."

I didn't doubt it for a moment.

"Anyway, I solved the problem." She unzipped her jacket and showed us a set of keys suspended on a silver chain around her neck. "It won't happen a third time."

"Is there anything else you wanted to tell us?" I asked.

"No. That covers it." She stood up. "You going to the assembly?"

"Yes…for sure." I'd almost forgotten about the school gathering at one o'clock this afternoon.

"See you there." Helga left, shutting the door behind her.

I sat next to Michael. "Any thoughts?"

"I'd hate to think the thief—or killer—might be one of these guys." He gestured toward the pile of student folders on the table. "Plain crazy, isn't it?"

"The timing of Helga's missing keys is interesting," I said. "Didn't Sophie say Nat's diary disappeared about two weeks ago?"

"Yeah. First our suspect steals Nat's diary two weeks ago, then sends one last incriminating email to Dave from her computer the night she disappears."

Something nagged at me. "If Nat's computer was password protected, it means the thief found her password somehow. Maybe she wrote it in her diary."

"If you're right, the girl was naïve."

"Lots of people record their passwords in plain sight. They don't stop to think of the risks."

Michael grew pensive. "I'd like to know the motive behind the two visits to Nat's room. Whoever it was is not only a thief but also an opportunist who had a lot to lose. Killing Nat and Andrew was their way out."

"Okay, let's look at a hypothetical scenario," I said. "Let's assume the killer is a male student or staff at Verdell who wasn't prepared to be the father of Nat's baby. I can see how her pregnancy could have complicated his life. What I don't understand is Andrew's death in all of this. Why kill him?"

"Beats me." He ran a hand through his hair.

"And what about Favreau? Let's not lose sight of the fact he's an escaped murderer. Maybe he killed Nat and Andrew. Same question: Why?"

"The weakest theory is that the killer wanted to make their deaths look like a murder-suicide."

I nodded. "We've already debunked that one."

"Right," Michael said. "So here's my take on it. In case the murder-suicide theory didn't pan out, the killer added a layer of protection around himself. He threw in another angle by trying to incriminate Dave."

"Why target Dave?"

"Because the perpetrator thought he was a viable target. Right now, we don't have enough evidence to formulate more theories." He checked his watch. "Eleven o'clock. What do you want to do next?"

"Let's go through the housekeeping files."

We perused the files of thirteen people responsible for keeping Verdell clean. Their duties included the washing and distribution of bed linens and bath towels, vacuuming of rooms, washing of stairs and corridors, restocking carts with supplies for the dorms, and emptying the trash.

Patricia Hubert, the staff supervisor, was responsible for coordinating housekeeping schedules and holding training sessions. Michael and I took a chance she'd be in and knocked at her door on the second floor of the main building.

The petite brunette welcomed us into her one-room apartment but had a time restriction. "I can give you ten minutes," she said, her pronunciation denoting a French-Canadian accent.

"Good enough," Michael said.

"Please sit down." Patricia gestured toward a loveseat in a blue floral print. She sat in a matching armchair adjacent to us, her winter coat scrunching up over her jeans. "My staff starts their shift at noon. I have to give them new instructions. Some students have caught the flu, so we have to take extra precautions. How can I help you?"

"We'll get right to the point," Michael said. "Can you tell us anything about Pierre Favreau that might help us locate him?"

The calm expression on her face changed to anger. "*Le cave!*"

"The idiot," I said, translating for Michael.

She stared at me. "You speak French? Well, let me tell you about Pierre in my best Sunday French." She waved her arms and rambled on about what a *"personne horrible"* he was, how he'd threatened her and her staff to stay out of his apartment, and how relieved she was to hear he hadn't returned to Verdell. She peppered her derogatory descriptions of *"le déviant sexuel"* with swear words that would make a prostitute blush.

I didn't have to translate for Michael. From the astounded look on his face, it was clear he'd grasped the message.

Patricia finished her rant in English with, "I hope he rots in hell."

"Did you complain about him to Mrs. Desmond?" Michael asked her.

"Yes. She spoke with him, but nothing changed." She folded her arms. "I instructed my employees—I have many young women on staff—to stop cleaning his apartment. The pig deserved to live in his own filth."

"We heard he bribed the cleaning staff to stay away," I said.

"I know," Patricia said. "I had already told my employees to stop cleaning his room. They took his money anyway." She laughed.

"Looks like Mrs. Desmond's recollection of Favreau is somewhat lacking." I gave Michael a wry smile on our way to the main floor.

He caught my sarcasm and nodded. "Odd that she'd be covering up for him."

"We'll jog her memory about Patricia's complaints the next time we see her. Who do we interview next?"

"Dave and Sophie mentioned Andrew and his drug problem. Maybe Dr. Finley can enlighten us more."

"It's Sunday. Do you think he's working?"

"From what I've seen at Verdell since the storm hit, not many people have taken time off. I'll bet the doctor is in."

Large glass windows in the infirmary let in the daylight and eliminated the need for tea lights until evening. In contrast to the century-old stone architecture of other buildings on campus, the infirmary was modern and appeared to have been constructed as an afterthought. Walls were painted in light pastel colors and adorned with artwork depicting vibrant landscapes. The mood was uplifting and a welcome break from the drabness of the meeting room.

Michael and I sat waiting while Dr. Finley tended to a student who'd injured her wrist. As he led her out, he advised her to avoid doing cartwheels and to return for a follow-up visit next week.

He spoke in a low voice with the medical receptionist. After he'd fingered several files in a stand on her desk, he looked our way. "Please come in."

I surveyed his winter coat. Even doctors weren't immune to the cold.

"Have a seat." He indicated two chairs opposite his desk. "You wanted to see me?"

"As you know, we're conducting an investigation into the deaths of the two students here," Michael said. "We're hoping you could answer a few questions."

"If you make it brief. I have patients in the other rooms."

"Tell us about the physical health of Natalie Dunn and Andrew Boyle."

The doctor bristled. "Those records are confidential."

"I'm sure Mrs. Desmond would have no problem in authorizing our request." Michael made a move to get up. "Maybe we should have asked her for a note before we—"

"That won't be necessary." Dr. Finley rose and moved toward the door. He asked the receptionist to pull out the files. He returned with them and sat down. "If my memory serves me well," he said, peering at the first file over his glasses, "Andrew had a bit of a problem a few years back. Ah, yes, here it is. A drug problem, to be exact. He attended therapy sessions and was given a clean bill of health."

"What kind of drug?"

Dr. Finley scanned the file. "MDMA." He closed the folder, then glanced at us. "Do you want me to explain what it is?"

"No," Michael said. "We know what it is."

The doctor opened the next file. "Natalie came to see me two months ago. She was complaining about stomach cramps and a missed menstrual period. I told her to give it another week and come back to see me if the situation didn't change." He looked up at us. "She never came back."

"Did she say anything else about her missed period?" I asked him.

He studied me. "You mean, did she wonder if she might be pregnant?"

"Yes."

"Like many young girls with irregular periods, perhaps she was concerned. But pregnant?" His expression reflected skepticism. "Due to the strict code of conduct here at Verdell, students understand that sexual intimacy is inappropriate and can result in suspension. I don't think Natalie would have raised the subject and cast doubts upon her integrity."

Obviously Mrs. Desmond hadn't shared the news of Nat's pregnancy with him.

Without any prodding, the doctor elaborated. "Stress is often a factor. The expectation that one has to perform to high standards often leads to stress disorders, panic attacks, and the like. In such circumstances, I prescribe physical therapy and relaxation techniques."

A lot of good that would have done Natalie.

Michael leaned forward. "Doctor, without going into specifics, can you tell me if you've ever suspected a drug problem at Verdell?"

The doctor removed his glasses and placed them on the desk. He took his time to answer, no doubt weighing the repercussions of his response. "Over the last twenty-five years, I've worked at schools and colleges across the country. I can tell you none are drug free. I've concluded that drug problems exist in our schools and perhaps always will. What we do as health practitioners is offer students appropriate help. We hope they'll find the strength to kick the habit, but not all of them do. Does that answer all your questions?"

"Yes, Doctor." Michael met his gaze.

"Good. Now if you'll excuse me, I have to tend to more students who I suspect have come down with the flu. With just three medical staff available this weekend, we have our hands full."

We thanked him and left. The waiting room was empty, which meant the patients with the flu had already been placed in the other rooms before we arrived. Small favors.

As we walked back to the main building along the covered passageway, I said to Michael, "To use an oxymoron, Dr. Finley speaks with clear ambiguity."

"No kidding," he said. "Weird how he managed to reveal so much without saying anything specific."

"What bothers me was his reaction to Nat's problem. Some people only see what they want to see."

Lunch was an unremarkable sardine salad with pickles on the side. Charlie winked as he added an extra cookie to our plates. We gulped the meal down, then headed to our next destination.

Mrs. Desmond was sitting at the front of the chapel, her foot elevated on a footrest. She'd raised the fur-trimmed hood of her dark gray coat over her head. A chunky candle on a table next to her shed a soft glow over her motionless form so that it appeared as if she were sleeping rather than reviewing her notes. Looks were deceiving since everyone at Verdell knew that an assembly in the chapel these days could only mean more bad news.

Students and staff sat in the pews, waiting, the occasional cough breaking the hush. The stained glass windows prevented even the dull daylight from filtering through, such that a bleak ambiance amplified the quiet unrest in the air.

Michael and I slid into a pew at the rear moments before the dean began her speech. She spoke about the fire and the theft in the kitchen pantry. She mentioned the threatening note that Michael and I had received. She spoke louder, her words reverberating like a repetitive warning. "I promise you that the perpetrator—or perpetrators—will face immediate expulsion from the school once they are discovered."

The crowd squirmed and murmurs echoed up to the high-domed ceiling as attendees absorbed the impact of the dean's warning.

Mrs. Desmond continued. "Verdell is not a place for criminals. We take pride in the achievements of our students. Crime is not in the curriculum. Therefore, Verdell is launching a search of the entire school complex immediately. I expect each of you to do your part and volunteer to search for the missing food supplies. You can meet with your student supervisors right after assembly to schedule your participation." Her eyes scoured the floor. She spit out the words while pointing an accusatory forefinger at the group. "I assure the offenders—and we know you are among us—you will be dealt with most harshly."

Mrs. Desmond ended her presentation, refused to answer questions, and dismissed the group. She rose from her chair and gathered her crutches. She waited until the chapel had almost emptied before she slogged down the aisle.

Michael and I approached her.

"Mrs. Desmond, we learned the housekeeping staff lodged complaints against Pierre Favreau," Michael said. "Can you tell us more?"

She frowned. "I spoke with him about it a couple of times. I assumed the matter was resolved because housekeeping hadn't mentioned it since then."

"We believe it was never resolved," I said.

She pressed her lips together. "Since the man is nowhere to be found and will no longer step foot in Verdell, why bring up the subject again?"

She had a point.

Mrs. Desmond accompanied us out of the chapel and through a covered passageway to the library. "If you have any more questions, I'll be in here."

Michael and I continued to the main building.

"What's next on the agenda?" I asked him.

Someone behind us said, "Excuse me."

We turned to see a man whose ID badge read *Mr. J. Jarvis.* I remembered the short, slender man from Mrs. Desmond's office when he and two other teachers had come in to enquire about the power failure.

"Can I have a word with you in private?" he whispered, his voice raspy. "It's about the stolen food supplies."

We invited him to the meeting room, where we'd spent more time lately than in our dorm room.

Michael asked the inevitable question. "What's on your mind, Mr. Jarvis?"

The teacher joined his hands, his bony knuckles almost hidden inside the cuffs of his winter coat. I had the impression he'd been caught off guard by the ice storm and had borrowed the coat from someone who was two sizes larger. "Well, I don't know how to say this without implicating… That is, it's a touchy subject. I've worked here for fifteen years, and I don't want to lose my job. Could you consider me as an anonymous informer?" His brown eyes bulged in anticipation of Michael's answer.

Michael tried to put him at ease. "You have our word that nothing you say will leave this room."

"Thank you." The teacher paused. "I think I know what happened to the food supplies that were stolen from the kitchen."

"You know where the supplies are?"

"Not exactly. Let me explain." Mr. Jarvis let his gaze rest on the tabletop. "The night of the fire, I was hurrying back from the library. I saw three boys walking ahead of me in the covered passageway between the dining hall and the main building. It was after curfew. I didn't want to get them in trouble, so I slowed down and kept my distance. I'm sure they didn't notice me. They were laughing and talking loud. I overheard them joke about having so much food and how they wouldn't have to worry about starving like the other suckers. At first I thought they were referring to hoarding food in their dorm kitchenettes. Many students do that. Now I'm not so sure."

"Why not?"

"They mentioned full shelves…a storage room…"

"Do you know who they were?"

"No, that's the problem. It was dark. Only a few tea lights were lit. The boys wore the same jackets and tuques, so I couldn't even tell you what color their hair was."

Michael asked, "What about their voices? Did you recognize any of them?"

Mr. Jarvis extended his small hands. "Like I said, they were laughing and jostling one another. If I didn't know any better, I'd say they were drunk—or stoned. I picked up words here and there, but I didn't recognize their voices. I couldn't even tell you whether or not they were students in any of my classes."

"Do you know if they were junior or senior students?"

"No. Since all male students have relocated to the gymnasium, the boys I saw could have been either."

"What happened after?"

"Nothing. They crossed the atrium, took a right, and continued along the corridor to the gymnasium. I took the stairs up to my living quarters."

"Mr. Jarvis, you mentioned you were in the library that night," I said to him. "Do you remember having seen those students there?"

"No, I don't," he said. "I'm a devoted reader. I become immersed in whatever I'm reading. They practically have to throw me out of there every time." He shrugged apologetically.

"Did you encounter other instances of unusual behavior in the echo or anywhere else on campus?" Michael asked him.

"With students?"

"Anyone."

"Unusual behavior." Mr. Jarvis thought about it. "I suppose so. It was last week. Tuesday night, I think. Yes, the night the two students..." He hesitated. "I was going to the library late that night when I saw Dave Pellegrino in the echo. I caught up to him and we started chatting. He said he was on supervisory duty and had received text messages about a disturbance in the boys' dorm. He was on his way there."

"Do you know what happened?"

"No," the teacher said. "If it were serious, I'm sure we would have heard about it from Mrs. Desmond the next day."

"Did Dave seem concerned?" Michael asked.

"About what?"

"The disturbance in the boys' dorm."

Mr. Jarvis looked off to the left, squinting. "Now that you mention it, he kept reaching for the cell phone in his pocket and checking for messages. Sometimes it gets noisy in the echo and you can't hear your phone ring."

"Did he have any messages?" Michael asked.

"If he did, he didn't say."

"Did he go up to the library with you?"

"No."

"Is there anything else you'd like to tell us?"

"No. I'm sorry I couldn't be more helpful." He stood up. "I'd better go. I have assignments to grade."

After Mr. Jarvis had left, Michael said, "Something's not right."

"About what?"

"Mr. Jarvis said Dave had already received the message about a disturbance in the boys' dorm when he met him in the echo."

"So?"

The tiny muscle in his jaw twitched. "If that was Dave's intended destination, he'd have to exit the echo by going upstairs into the girls' dorm, then go outdoors to get to the boys' dorm. Why would he take the echo to get to the boys' dorm? It isn't connected underground."

"He could have taken the echo part of the way as a short cut. Look, Dave already told us he was in the library late that night, and the police have a video that confirms it."

Michael wasn't buying it. "What if the cops asked for Dave's assistance in viewing the video as an excuse to keep him at the station?"

"Do you realize what you're saying?"

He stared hard at me. "It's more about what I'm thinking. And I don't like it one bit."

CHAPTER 13

There was no time to dwell on possibilities. Michael and I decided we'd deal with tangible facts and put aside any doubts about Dave's integrity for now.

An eerie stillness filtered through the echo where shadows danced in silence. The only sound was the thud of our boots against the cement floor. We met the same isolation when we surfaced in the girls' dorm and climbed the stairs to the third floor. No one was around. Then I remembered students were getting instructions regarding the search for the missing food.

"Looks like the water team is working hard." Michael pointed to the bucket of water placed in front of our door and several other doors on our floor.

I noticed a sheet of paper next to our bucket. "They left us another note." My heart thumped faster. Was it another threat? I read it and sighed with relief. "It's a reminder to use the water for flushing the toilet, not for drinking or bathing." I opened the door to our room.

"I bet the water hasn't been inspected in a while, that's why." Michael carried the bucket inside. "One of the things we take for granted in a big city."

Only days had passed since our arrival, but I already missed the conveniences of our home in Montreal. "I can't imagine how people ever managed without clean water, let alone electricity."

"Or less food. I'd give anything to get my hands on whoever ransacked the kitchen." He checked his watch. "Let's go visit Nat's room."

Located on the second floor of the girls' dorm, our next destination was a minute away.

Michael used one of the two keys Sophie had given us to open the outer door and gain access to the small kitchenette she'd shared with Nat. It was furnished with a fridge, two chairs, and a table. A microwave oven claimed more than half of the counter space. Cupboard space wasn't sufficient because dishes were stacked on the counter. The bathroom was on the far left, and the two bedroom doors were adjacent and off the kitchenette.

Using the other key, Michael unlocked the door to Nat's room. My pulse quickened. I felt as if we were trespassing. I reminded myself we were investigating the young girl's death and I had to remain objective.

The décor in the room conveyed softness and youth. Pink curtains matched a pink floral bedspread. A stuffed white poodle sat on the floor by the bed as if it were waiting for Nat to return.

The far left corner of Nat's room reflected her love of Shakespeare and to what extent his writing had influenced her. A poster of the famous author hung on the wall above her small wood desk, not to be outdone by a row of his books on an overhead shelf. I spotted *Macbeth* and *Hamlet*, among others.

It was a pretty room, though sadness washed over me when I spotted the open closet. It still contained Nat's clothes, shoes, and accessories. Her family had driven to Verdell the day after her death but hadn't collected her personal effects because of the ongoing police investigation. I imagined how they'd be waiting for the autopsy results to arrive so they could prepare funeral services for their young daughter. I felt as if Nat's spirit was lingering in this room, guiding us in our search to find the villain who had claimed her life...

"Oh, it's you."

I jumped at the sound of a young female voice. I spun around to see Sophie standing in the doorway.

"I'm sorry. I didn't mean to scare you. I heard a noise and wasn't sure if..." Her voice trailed off.

"I should have knocked at your door," I said, "but I didn't want to disturb you."

Sophie shrugged. "It's okay."

"Can I ask you a few questions?"

She gave Michael a side-glance. "Sure."

"Do you know if Nat's family visited this room after she passed away?"

She nodded. "They were here on Wednesday—the day after. They said hi to me and then they spoke with the police investigator. Nat's mother was crying. I didn't want to intrude, so I shut the door to my room. They left half an hour later."

"Do you know if her parents removed anything from the room?" I asked.

"I don't know," Sophie said.

"And the forensics investigators?"

"I saw them in Nat's room when I went to get water from the fridge. They took away her laptop and cell phone in transparent bags. Other things too, but I couldn't see what they were."

"Did the police speak with you?"

"Yes. I told them what I told you. Except for the part about the intruder and the email they sent. I told Helga about the intruder, though."

I didn't tell her Helga had divulged as much. I wanted to keep her trust in me.

While we'd been chatting, Michael had been inspecting Nat's closet. He stepped forward holding a slim gold bracelet and looked at Sophie. "I found it in the inside pocket of Nat's school blazer."

Sophie flushed. "Oh...I forgot about that. It was a gift from her boyfriend."

He shone his flashlight on it. "The inscription indicates it's real gold. Must be expensive. Strange that she didn't wear it the night she went to meet him."

"I guess she forgot."

A glance from Michael told me he was thinking the same thing: The bracelet could have been one of the reasons the intruder had searched Nat's room the night she died. Not for any monetary need, given the financial standing of most students at Verdell, but to retrieve a gift he'd given his sweetheart.

Michael put the bracelet back in Nat's blazer and extended his search to the drawers in her desk.

"There's something I need to ask you, Sophie." I spoke in a quiet voice. "Do you know anything about students selling drugs at Verdell?"

"Sort of. I've heard rumors." She cast another side-glance in Michael's direction.

"What kind of rumors?"

Sophie put her hands in her pockets, as if that movement grounded her to the spot in the doorway—a neutral place, neither inside nor outside Nat's room. "I'm not sure. I don't want to get anyone in trouble."

Her defensive attitude had become a habit. Somehow this girl had picked up information crucial to our investigation, but she was too afraid to share it. "If drugs had anything to do with Nat's death, it's important that we find out."

She frowned. "Can't you ask somebody else?" Her eyes flitted to Michael who was moving toward her. She stepped aside.

"I'll be back in five or ten minutes." He gave me a perceptive look and walked out.

After the outer door had closed, Sophie let her hands drop to her sides and relaxed a little. She was shy and, for whatever reason, was nervous around Michael.

I took advantage of the moment and approached the drug topic from a different perspective. "We know that Pierre Favreau—the cook who everyone knew as Paul—was a drug dealer in Montreal. We suspect he was selling drugs here too. Did you hear anything that might suggest he did?"

"Some of the rich students might have bought drugs here."

"What kind of drugs?"

"I think it was E."

"Ecstasy?"

"Yes."

"Have you seen these drugs? Can you describe them?"

Sophie's voice fell to a whisper. "The ones I saw were white and had a smiley face on them."

"Where did you see them?"

"A student offered them to Nat and me one night in the echo when we were coming back from the library. We saw another student hand over cash for a tiny packet of pills."

We were taking baby steps but making progress nevertheless. "What did you do?"

"Nat was pretty cool about it. We just walked away. I wanted to tell Mrs. Desmond about the student selling E, but Nat convinced me not to."

"Why not?"

"She said he would be expelled and it would ruin his life. I didn't want to be responsible for that."

"Do you know the name of this student?"

Sophie froze. "I'd rather not say."

"I promise I won't tell anyone."

She hesitated. "It was Greg Talbot. He's a senior here."

I didn't acknowledge he was already on our suspected drug-seller list. "Thanks, Sophie. My lips are sealed."

"Is that all? I can go now?"

"Yes."

She returned to her room.

I walked over to Nat's desk and sat in her chair. I wanted to get a feel for the young girl who had no reservations about proclaiming her love of Shakespeare but kept her relationship with a boyfriend hidden—even from her best friend. Who had she deemed so worthy of her affection and why? Had she seen the simple gift of an expensive bracelet as proof of his love for her?

If I'd expected to get a sudden flash of insight into Nat's killer, I would have been disappointed. All I sensed was unfinished business, confirmation that a young life had ended too soon, and more unanswered questions. The pitter-patter of ice pellets against the window intensified the melancholy mood in the room.

Michael walked in and closed the door behind him. "Are we done here?"

"Yes." I stood up. "Where did you go?"

"To see if they had surveillance cameras in the lobby."

"And?"

"They do. Too bad I hadn't thought about asking my tech friend to access them days ago. They might have showed the comings and goings of the late-night visitor to Nat's room."

I whispered, "Not to mention the cameras in the echo that recorded Greg Talbot selling drugs there."

"Sophie told you about Greg?" he whispered back.

"Yes."

"I had a feeling she'd open up to you once I left the room. If only we had electricity, we could find out who stole the food from the kitchen pantry too."

"There are no surveillance cameras in the corridor off the kitchen pantry," I reminded him.

"Oh...right."

The image of another corridor sprang to mind. "There's someone else we should interview this afternoon."

"Who?"

"The janitor."

Michael's eyes sparkled with interest. "The silent witness."

"Let's hope he's not too silent."

He checked his watch. "Charlie will tell us where we can find him. The staff should be in the kitchen preparing dinner by now."

"Hungry?"

"Always." He smiled. "Let's ask about the menu while we're there."

"First we'll return the spare keys to Sophie and tell her we're leaving."

Our walk through the echo to the main building was more dismal than earlier. Half of the tea lights had been extinguished and shadows stretched up the walls, as if they too were looking for a way to escape the dreary ambience. Without electricity to keep the air ventilation system functioning, the echo had become cold and damp and smelled like wet fur.

The handful of students we passed moved along at a brisk pace. Not speaking, not laughing, not joking. I empathized with the students. They'd suffered not only the loss of three classmates but also their main means of communication. Without warning, their lifeline to the rest of the world had vanished in a second. It was one thing to lose touch with your acquaintances on social media, but not being able to contact family and close friends was pushing the limits of isolation—especially during such a stressful period.

We found Charlie in the kitchen with the rest of the staff. The dinner menu this evening included canned beets, canned peas, and canned peaches. They were reaching the bottom of the barrel.

"How are you doing for supplies?" Michael asked the cook.

"We barely have enough food for a couple more days," Charlie said, keeping his voice low. "I already told Mrs. Desmond. If only we knew where those thieves stashed the rest of it." Sadness filled his eyes. "What I don't get is how it all vanished into thin air so fast."

"Everyone's searching the school," Michael said. "They'll find the supplies eventually."

"Eventually might be too late," Charlie said.

"Would you know where we can find the janitor's quarters?"

He gave us the room number. "Can't miss it. It's the room next to Favreau's. Tell Sam I said hi."

Sam Hill had the sort of face one would be hard pressed to describe, not because it was extraordinary but rather because it wasn't. I imagined that plain features might work in anyone's favor given the right circumstances.

His apartment was as nondescript as his face and contained the same minimal furniture we'd seen in Favreau's room. The main difference was that it was spotless. No décor hung on the walls, except for a picture of the Madonna and Christ child on a wall over the TV. White eyelet curtains were parted to admit the bleak daylight.

Sam invited us to sit at a small table. "Sorry I can't offer you a coffee. You know how it is." He raised the collar of his ski jacket, concealing the wrinkles around his neck.

Michael went right to the point. "Your job covers a lot of territory at Verdell."

Sam nodded. "It's a mighty big place. I work alone. Mostly during odd hours. It's okay. I appreciate the solitude."

"Did you notice anything unusual during your shifts the last few weeks?"

"Unusual? Like how?"

"Like somebody sneaking around."

He grinned, revealing a missing tooth. "At night when I'm washing the floors, sometimes I see a student hurrying back to the dorm after curfew. It's not my business. I pretend I don't see them and continue with my work."

"Do you remember what you were doing last Tuesday evening—the night of the disappearance of the two students?"

Sam didn't hesitate. "I sure do. It was late—about an hour before curfew. I'd finished washing the stairs that go from the lobby of the girls' dorm down to the tunnel. The echo, the kids call it." He grinned, as if he'd exposed a secret.

"Did anything unusual happen on your shift?" I asked.

"Yes, ma'am. I was almost done washing the staircase that goes from the first floor of the dorm down to the lobby. All of a sudden, this young student comes running down the stairs. The girl didn't realize they were still wet. She slipped but managed to grab the railing to break her fall. Otherwise she'd have broken her neck, poor thing."

"Did she see you?"

He nodded. "She sure did. I was standing at the bottom of the stairs. She had to walk by me. She couldn't have missed me, although to some people I'm invisible." He chuckled. "I could say they all look the same to me too, but this girl was different."

"In what way?"

"She spoke to me. Not many students do. She apologized and hoped she hadn't messed up the stairs."

"Messed up the stairs? Why would she say that?"

Sam shrugged. "Because her boots were muddy—like the other times the last couple of months."

My pulse raced. "Other times?"

"Yes, ma'am. Same flight of stairs. Same muddy boots. Same girl. Sometimes she'd be coming in. Sometimes she'd be going out. It made me mad as heck to have to clean the stairs again, but it always puzzled me." He rubbed his chin.

"What?"

"How she could get so much mud on her boots."

My heart beat faster. "Would you be able to identify her?"

He stared at the floor, pondering the question. "She's the young girl they dredged up from the river, poor thing. Natalie Dunn. Yeah. That's her name."

CHAPTER 14

Even the faint light filtering through the ice-frosted windows in the atrium couldn't soften the students' anxious expressions. They stood close together now in small groups to keep themselves warm. But the cold wasn't their sole concern. After the dean's assembly earlier this Sunday afternoon, they had a lot more to talk about.

They weren't the only ones. Our interview with the school janitor minutes ago had provided Michael and me with a clue to Nat's late-night outings. I couldn't wait to bounce my theory off Michael.

We remained silent to prevent curiosity seekers from picking up snippets of our verbal exchange. We'd grown accustomed to walking past two or more individuals who paused in their conversation to listen to ours. Unlike our earlier ventures, students were used to seeing us wandering around by now. They even greeted us by our first name.

Once we were out of earshot, I said to Michael, "I'm positive Nat was leaving the girls' dorm to go meet her boyfriend Tuesday night when the janitor spotted her."

"It's possible." A muscle twitched along his jaw. Something was on his mind.

"What are you thinking?"

"If Nat went to visit her boyfriend, how did she end up in the trunk of a car?" He shook his head. "Too bad I didn't think about it before. I would have asked my techie friend to expand his search to include the boys' residence."

"Don't be so hard on yourself, Michael. Besides, the surveillance system doesn't cover every inch of the campus. We don't know where Nat went that night. We can't even confirm that Nat and Andrew were in the trunk of the car in the first place. The video we watched wasn't clear."

"I'm not giving up on this. We'll have to figure out every path Nat could have taken that evening and who she came in contact with."

I couldn't hide my eagerness. "I think we should explore the infamous ghost tunnel Sophie told us about."

Michael nodded. "We will. We need to interview other people first. I'd like to visit the chapel."

He surprised me. We had no files on personnel connected to the chapel. "Then let's stop by Audrey's office to get the information."

"We should interview her too," he said. "She might be able to help us in areas no one else can."

"Maybe she knows something about that secret passageway," I said.

He opened the door to Audrey's office. The draft caused the candle flames in the room to flicker and project a flurry of silhouettes around the room.

Audrey looked up from a file on her desk. "Oh, hi there. I was about to go looking for you two. Mrs. Desmond would like an update on your investigation before the end of the day. You can find her in the library until five o'clock. She claims the books provide additional insulation against the frigid weather." She adjusted the wool scarf around her neck. "Can I help you with anything?"

"We'd like to ask you a few questions," Michael said.

"Me? Oh...okay." She closed the file. "Have a seat."

We pulled up two wood chairs and sat down.

"Do you know anything about a secret underground passageway on campus?" I asked her.

"Secret passageway?" Audrey shook her head. "The only underground tunnel I know of is the echo. The students and staff use it to get from the main building to the other buildings connected to it on campus."

"Has anyone ever mentioned a *haunted* underground passageway?"

She laughed. "Oh, Megan, believe me, ghosts might be responsible for lots of things disappearing around here, but an underground passageway? I doubt they'd find much to pilfer there."

I appreciated her humor, but it wouldn't stop me from trying to find the passageway.

"Would you know who owns the private property behind the school?" Michael asked.

"Trenton Barratt owns it." She grew pensive. "I think you should know how he acquired the land, mainly because of its connection to the students' deaths."

Her revelation surprised me.

"I ask that you keep our conversation confidential, though." Audrey gave us a pointed look.

"Of course," Michael said.

She leaned back in her chair. "About three years ago, Trenton Barratt paid us a visit. I wasn't in my office when he arrived that afternoon. When I returned, I heard Mrs. Desmond shout 'no' from inside her office. In all my years working for her, I've never heard her sound so adamant. I thought she was in trouble. I was about to open the door to her office when I heard a man say it was the only way to save Verdell from bankruptcy. I'm embarrassed to say I recognized Mr. Barratt's voice and eavesdropped on the rest of the conversation. He said he wanted to purchase a piece of land behind the school. It contains the forest that spans from the edge of the campus east to the river and northward. Mrs. Desmond hesitated over the decision for days but finally agreed to sell it to him."

I didn't know how much Mrs. Desmond had confided in her, so I was careful not to imply the students had been murdered. "You mentioned a connection to the students' deaths."

"I'm referring to the fact their bodies were discovered in the river by Trenton Barratt's property, not on Verdell grounds. It's a technicality, I suppose, but legally the land doesn't belong to Verdell. One more thing. I don't believe in the murder-suicide rumor making the rounds. It's rubbish. I'm open to the notion that Andrew and Natalie were murdered. If so, I'm certain neither one drove the car. Someone else did. Right through Trenton Barratt's forest." She gave us a discerning look.

"What about Pierre Favreau?" Michael asked her.

"What about him?"

"He could be a potential murder suspect, though his motive escapes us."

Audrey raised an eyebrow. "Now that's a new perspective. I hadn't given Favreau a thought in relation to Nat and Andrew, though I don't see a motive either."

"About Mr. Barratt...have the police interrogated him?" I asked her.

"I was getting to that," she said. "Yes, they did. They questioned him at his home in Sherbrooke. Obviously, he knew nothing about the incident. He contacted the school the same day and expressed his condolences to Mrs. Desmond." She took a deep breath. "I suppose the upside for Verdell was that it happened on someone else's property."

I recalled the man's substantial contribution to the school and pursued that line of thought. "How much of Verdell's property was sold to Trenton Barratt?"

"More than half. A huge part of it extends into potential mining areas. Mr. Barratt purchased additional chunks of land from Verdell over the years for that reason. There have been excavations for copper that I'm aware of, but the projects have turned up nothing of value so far." She paused. "We appreciate Mr. Barratt's financial assistance. I have to admit we were in dire need of funds. We still are. However, I feel he took advantage of our precarious financial situation."

"From what you said, it worked out for both parties concerned," I said.

Audrey's expression hardened. "He forced us to sell at a price well below market. He's a narcissistic opportunist. On the other hand, his son Zack is a joy." A smile replaced the shadow on her face. "He's thoughtful and accommodating. Such a fine boy. How two people from the same family could be so different is beyond me." She lowered her voice. "Not that Mr. Barratt made Zack's life any easier. From the day he enrolled his son at Verdell, he expected the moon from him. One doesn't have to question why the boy is such a high achiever."

"What about Zack's mother?"

"She passed away years ago." Audrey tapped her fingers on the desk. "Do you have any other questions?"

"One more," Michael said. "Could you tell me the name of the representative at the chapel?"

"Verdell has a multifaith chapel. In fact, it's a consecrated Roman Catholic space open to all faiths and interests. Our chaplains visit on a rotating basis every month, which keeps things rather interesting." She flipped to a page in her agenda. "Our current guest is Father James Maxwell, a Roman Catholic priest. I'm sure he'll be happy to meet with you. Whether or not he'll tell you anything you want to know is another matter."

CHAPTER 15

Something told me it would be prudent to visit the chapel before popping into the library to see Mrs. Desmond. I was concerned the chapel might hold a mass service later this Sunday afternoon, and we'd miss our chance to interview Father James Maxwell.

"James Maxwell," Michael said as we hurried along the echo to the chapel. "Sounds like a solid name."

"Don't forget to address him as Father," I said. "It's a term of respect. Not that it'll make any difference."

"What do you mean?"

"You won't get any information from him."

He gave me a side-glance. "Talk about a negative attitude."

"It's a fact. That's what Audrey was hinting at. Priests don't give out confidential information."

"Who said anything about confidential information? I'll ask him the usual questions we've been asking everyone else."

I knew Michael so well by now. He could maneuver his way through the most difficult interview sessions. His strategy often entailed not saying more than a few choice words. One way or another, he'd come out of the interview with a wealth of information. Part of his success was due to an unflappable attitude and dauntless tenacity. The rest of it was due to pure luck.

My career path was tame in contrast. Shaped by years of working behind a desk as a ghostwriter, I'd become accustomed to the protection afforded by anonymity. My confrontation with two ex-cons in Montreal last summer reinforced my desire to remain in a protective bubble. I intended to keep it that way.

We entered the chapel, our footsteps intruding on the tranquility in the air.

"The place is empty," I whispered to Michael. "Maybe we should go."

"Why are you whispering?"

"People always whisper in religious institutions. It's a sign of respect. Besides, it creates an echo if you speak too loudly." I pointed to the high ceiling.

"Hello there," a man called out, refuting my argument about whispering.

We turned to see a tall man dressed in black trousers and a multi-striped duffle coat. The trademark stripes told me he'd purchased the wool coat from The Hudson's Bay Company.

"I'm Father Maxwell. How can I help you?" His smile was welcoming. Lines ran across his forehead, though he wore them well under thick white hair.

Michael introduced us. "Do you have a few moments to meet with us? It's about Andrew Boyle and Natalie Dunn."

"Certainly. I was at the assembly when Mrs. Desmond spoke about the internal investigation you were conducting. Please follow me."

He let us through a side door into a small parlor. "We can talk here for a while." He indicated four chairs lined against a wall. He pulled one out so that he sat facing Michael and me. "What would you like to know?"

"Father, I'll be blunt," Michael said. "Have either Andrew or Natalie ever confessed personal problems to you?"

Father Maxwell joined his hands and smiled. "I see what you mean about being blunt." He briefly closed his eyes, giving the impression he was asking for guidance from on high. He looked at Michael. "As a priest, I'm bound by the sacramental seal of secrecy to protect the nature or contents of what someone has confessed to me. As well, I cannot admit that a particular person has come to say their confession to me. Therefore, I'm sorry but I can't help you."

Exactly what I was afraid of.

A negative response didn't deter Michael. "I understand, Father. We're more or less in the same situation, you and I. Informants confide in me and provide me with facts that help put away the bad guys. In turn, I provide my sources with confidentiality."

Father Maxwell nodded. "I can see a certain level of similarity in our work, my son. Nevertheless, it doesn't alter the fact that the seal of the confessional is binding."

"Even after death?"

"Yes."

"Okay. Can we talk hypothetically then?"

"Of course."

Michael leaned forward. "Let's assume that someone comes to you and confesses they've been abused. Would you report it to the authorities?"

Father Maxwell shook his head. "No. I would be bound by the seal of the confessional and therefore prevented from doing so."

"What if the situation was a matter of life and death?"

The priest raised his hands, palms up. "Same response. I cannot reveal what someone confides to me in the confessional."

The sound of ice pellets hitting the window broke the silence in the room. Michael wasn't going to make any headway with Father Maxwell unless he found a way to circumvent the issue of secrecy.

I took a leap of faith. "Father, we've been discussing confessions and the privacy surrounding them. What if someone asked for your advice on a personal matter? Are you bound by the seal of secrecy not to reveal what was discussed?"

"If you're referring to a meeting outside the confessional, no, I am not bound."

"What if this victim had been physically abused, would you advise them to report their complaint to the police?"

"Depending on the circumstances, yes, I might counsel them to go to the authorities."

The sparkle in Michael's eyes told me he understood what I was getting at. He jumped back into the conversation. "Here's my next question, Father Maxwell. Did you ever have occasion to speak with Andrew Boyle outside the confessional?"

"No. I never met the boy."

"Have you ever spoken with Natalie Dunn outside the confessional?"

"Yes, I have."

"What was the nature of your discussion?"

Father Maxwell took a deep breath. "Natalie was a troubled young woman. She came to see me about a personal matter." He hesitated, his eyes scouring our faces for any telltale sign that we knew what he was referring to.

"We know she was pregnant," Michael said.

"I see." The priest joined his hands as if in prayer. "Over the years, students have come to see me for advice. Although Natalie and I spoke for only a few minutes, I had the impression she was a decent person. Now this might seem strange to you, but I'm not here to judge individuals who come to me for help. I'd rather leave that up to a greater power. The point I'm trying to make is that Natalie asked my advice about making a difficult choice: keeping the baby or having an abortion. I'm sure you both know the views of the Catholic Church regarding that subject." He waited until Michael and I nodded in agreement, then continued. "She was happy with her decision to keep the baby, thanked me, and left."

"Did she mention who the father was?" I asked him.

"No, and I didn't ask." He paused. "Any other questions?"

"Yes," Michael said. "Did the police interrogate you about the victims?"

"Yes, they did," Father Maxwell said.

"Did you tell them what you told us?"

"No."

"Why not?"

He smiled. "Because they asked the wrong questions."

Outside the chapel, Michael gave me a quick hug. "I owe you one, Megan."

"For what?" I knew what he meant, but sometimes it felt good to hear him express his gratitude.

"The way you worked out the ambiguity behind the seal of the confessional with Father Maxwell."

"Oh, that's because I'm such a nerd when it comes to words."

"No, it's because you're smart."

"Only smart?"

He stopped and put his hands on my shoulders. "And beautiful." He kissed me on the lips.

"Mmm...nice. You can do it again. The cameras aren't rolling."

Two students ogled us as they passed by.

"I have a better idea," Michael said. "And it's a lot more private."

"It'll have to wait," I said. "We're supposed to meet with Mrs. Desmond in the library, remember?"

"Right." He looked around, then kissed me again. "Okay. That should hold me till later."

We found Mrs. Desmond sitting in a bulky armchair, a wool blanket draped over her legs. Tall frosted windowpanes formed a backdrop to crammed bookshelves in the spacious library. Six glowing candles on a side table next to the dean had since replaced a lamp and fading daylight.

The dean closed her book as we approached and observed us over her spectacles. "Michael, Megan, pull up a couple of chairs." She gestured to wood chairs at a nearby table.

I noticed she'd called us by our first names. Our frequent interactions with her in recent days might have given rise to this familiarity. On the other hand, I recalled she addressed everyone except the teachers by their first names, as if she wanted to keep them at arm's length.

I was uneasy about the privacy aspect of our discussion in a library, but a glance around as we took our seats told me I had nothing to worry about. No one else was here at this late hour of the day. My guess was they were lining up for a meal outside the dining hall.

Michael gave Mrs. Desmond a recap of the day's interviews. She nodded, voicing the occasional word of approval at his findings. She had a different reaction when he brought up the topic of drugs circulating in the school.

"My students know the consequences of breaking the rules," she said. "I refuse to believe that Verdell is a hotspot for drug users."

How did a woman running an institution for teenagers all these years believe that strict school policy meant a drug-free institution? Did she know more than what she was prepared to admit?

"I witnessed an exchange of drugs between two students," Michael said in his defense. "I also know that students have access to rehab programs here."

Mrs. Desmond frowned, her eyes clear and steady. "We recommended drug rehab programs for two students years ago. I've had no reports of drug usage since then. Where would the students be getting these drugs? Do you have a name?"

Michael and I had agreed we wouldn't mention Greg's name to anyone before he delivered the drugs to us. Secrecy was essential to the success of our plan.

"We suspect the drugs are being accessed from outside sources," Michael said. "We'll do our best to dig up more details."

She glanced away for a moment. "I don't tolerate rule breakers, especially when it comes to using illegal drugs. On that note, I owe you an explanation." She took a deep breath. "My husband was killed in a car accident when our only son was sixteen years old. The loss of his father hit Sean hard. He fell into a state of depression. Like most parents, I sought medical advice and believed Sean would soon be on the road to recovery. It didn't happen. Despite the best rehab and repeated efforts by all concerned, Sean took a fatal overdose one night when he was alone in his bedroom. I blamed myself. It took me years to get over the guilt." Her lips quivered but she remained in control of her emotions. "I made a vow that it wouldn't happen again on my watch."

I was stunned by her candor. It would explain her denial that students were still using drugs within the respected halls of Verdell. The school was her "baby" and she didn't want anything to tarnish its growth and reputation.

Unfortunately for Mrs. Desmond, our investigation had already proved otherwise.

And it was just the beginning.

CHAPTER 16

Fewer tea lights were lit in the corridors and covered passageways—a sign that even these supplies were being rationed. To preserve the batteries in our flashlights, Michael and I hadn't used them often. We'd lit a couple of tea lights in our dorm room and the meeting room instead to see our way around after dark. Now we needed our flashlights wherever we went.

From the diminished number of tea lights on the tables in the dining hall, I surmised this room wasn't faring any better. I also suspected that whatever food the students had stashed in their kitchenettes had run out because more students were sitting here than at previous meals. Their strained expressions reminded me of baby birds waiting in the nest for their mother to arrive with food.

As soon as Michael and I were handed our dinner of a peanut butter and jam sandwich, a handful of potato chips, and a sweet pickle, the realization sink in: The kitchen supplies had hit rock bottom. To top if off, we had to share a small bottle of water.

All things considered, we weren't facing the best of circumstances. What with little food and no heat at Verdell, we were fast approaching a desperate situation.

Michael placed his tray on one of the unoccupied tables at the back of the hall. "I didn't dare ask Charlie if breakfast would be available tomorrow morning." He kept his voice low in case students at neighboring tables might hear.

I slid into the chair beside his. "What if there is no breakfast?" I whispered. "Can you imagine the panic it would create?"

"You can bet on it." He took a bite of his sandwich.

"We have to do something."

"Like what?"

"The roads are blocked, so we can't take the car. How about leaving on foot to go get help?"

"No way." Michael frowned. "Did you take a good look at the campus this morning? Live wires are down all over the place. You'd get electrocuted before you crossed the grounds. And if you do make it, a bear might attack you before you completed the forty-mile stretch to town. Food pickings are slim for wild animals too."

The mention of a bear did it. "Okay. Stop. You've convinced me."

He checked his watch. "Six o'clock. Greg will be knocking at our dorm room in an hour."

"I can't wait to see what he delivers." I crunched on a potato chip. "We're almost done with the interviews, right?"

Michael nodded. "I was thinking about interviewing Zack next. He's a student supervisor. He might be able to answer questions about Nat and Andrew and tell us if he's seen or heard about drugs circulating in the boys' dorm."

I happened to glance at the food counter and saw a familiar face heading toward the tables. "There he is now."

Michael stood up. "I'll ask him to join us."

Moments later, they walked back to the table.

Zack set his tray down and sat opposite us, causing the tea lights on the table to dance wildly. "Hi, Megan."

He'd dropped the formality too and used my first name. It didn't bother me, but good thing Mrs. Desmond wasn't around.

Zack sighed with relief. "It's great to sit down. My team just finished the water run. I had to make sure everyone was safe inside before grabbing dinner." He ran a hand over stubble that hadn't been shaved in days.

The gesture drew my eyes to the collar of Zack's jacket. He'd transferred his school pins to the blue winter jacket he was wearing. I also noticed a slit on his sleeve and mentioned it.

"An occupational hazard," he said, waving it off. "I caught the edge of a metal bucket as I was handing it to a team buddy. Not to mention that I'm exhausted, frozen, and would give anything for a hot shower." He flashed a smile in my direction, then took a bite of his sandwich.

"Zack, we hate to intrude on your dinner, but we're trying to wrap things up for Mrs. Desmond," Michael said. "How about answering a few questions?"

Zack swallowed his food before replying. "Sure. Ask away."

"Did you know Andrew Boyle or Natalie Dunn well?"

"Not really. We didn't hang out with the same crowd." He popped a pickle into his mouth.

"Were you ever on the supervisory team for Andrew's dorm?"

"Many times. Admin rotates the student supervisors every week."

"Were you assigned to his dorm the week he died?" Michael asked.

"Yes, I was." Zack reached for a potato chip, snapped it in half, and ate it.

"Did Andrew cause any problems or disturbances in the dorm that you know of?"

"Never. He kept to himself and obeyed dorm rules."

My heart pounded as the intensity of the questions increased, but Michael stayed cool. His expression remained guarded and he kept his eyes on Zack. "Any instances of drugs in the boys' dorm?"

Zack looked down. "I've heard things, so I'd be lying if I said no."

"What things?"

He shrugged. "A couple of guys popping E years back. Nothing major." He eyed Michael. "You think drugs were involved in the car accident here?"

"It's possible. We have it from a reliable source that no school is totally drug free."

Zack drank from his bottle of water. "What happened to Andrew and Nat shocked everyone. Maybe Andrew was using."

Did he know about Andrew's past drug history? Or had he heard that Andrew had returned to his old habits and was using drugs up until that fatal night?

"Do you know that for a fact?" I asked Zack.

He looked at me. "Not really. I was thinking how messed up he must have been to drive a car into the river. That's all." He shook his head. "A tragedy like this…it's going to take time to forget."

He was basing his assumption on the murder-suicide theory circulating the school. "About the relationship between Andrew and Nat," I said, "doesn't Verdell discourage that sort of thing?"

Zack nodded. "It would mean instant suspension if anyone is caught. What student would risk throwing away their future just like that?" He snapped a finger in the air.

"It would be punishment enough," Michael said. "We won't get into the potential repercussions from parents." He raised an eyebrow.

Zack's expression tightened. "Yeah…parents." He blinked. "My dad would kill me."

A student walked by and tapped Zack on the shoulder. "Ready for another round of water buckets tomorrow morning?"

He gazed up at him. "Sure. Let's meet for breakfast and we'll head out together."

The student gave him a nod, looked at Michael and me, and walked away.

"My friends think it's cool you're both doing investigative work here," Zack said. "No one can bring back Nat and Andrew, but it'll be good to get closure." He pushed back his chair. "Any more questions? I'm asking because I'll be chillin'—I mean, relaxing. Slang is taboo here. Mrs. Desmond disapproves of it. What I meant to say was I'll be meeting friends in a while."

"If you hear anything else that can help our investigation, let us know," Michael said.

"I sure will." Zack strolled out.

As had become our habit, Michael and I waited until we'd returned to our dorm room before talking about our latest interview.

Water buckets left in the corridor outside the remaining rooms were proof of the strenuous task Zack and his team had recently completed. I kept thinking how proud Mrs. Desmond must feel to have inspired such camaraderie and support among her students and staff.

Inside our room, I sat on the bed and Michael took the chair. It was discussion time.

"We interviewed Zack and expected he'd have answers to our questions," I said. "At least I did. What did it give us? Zilch."

"Hey, sometimes you win, sometimes you don't," Michael said.

"Do you think Zack knows about Greg's involvement with drugs and is covering for him? After all, they're buddies."

"I don't know. Question is: Would Zack risk his future for Greg or anyone else?"

"When you put it that way, I guess not."

"Either Greg is using and selling drugs on his own, or he's a lackey for someone else. I'll get him to talk. We'll find out the truth soon enough."

Michael stared into space, maybe contemplating what he'd say to Greg when he'd knock at our door.

I grabbed a book and made myself comfortable on the bed.

Half an hour went by, then an hour. Still no sign of Greg.

"He's a no-show." Michael's deep voice broke the tapping of the freezing rain on the window.

I shut the book I'd been reading. "What do you think happened?"

"He got cold feet."

"Or maybe he couldn't get into Favreau's room to get the drugs. You can't be certain unless you go back there and see if Greg tried to break in."

"We'll head out there later." He walked toward me, smiling. "All is not lost, as they say. We have free time on our hands. How about—"

A shrill scream sounded from the corridor.

Michael raced to the door.

I bounded off the bed.

We rushed out to find a young girl standing two doors away, yelling, "Help! Oh my God! Somebody, help!" Tears streamed down her face. When she saw us, she pointed to the bucket of water outside her door.

The tea lights in the corridor gave off a hazy glow, but not so hazy that I couldn't make out what she was pointing at.

I peered closer at the water in her bucket. A finger adorned with a silver ring was floating in it.

Occupants of other dorm rooms had gathered around the student named Lucy who was shaking and sobbing in fear. Two female students were trying to calm her down.

In the meantime, someone had had the presence of mind to go round up Mrs. Desmond. Michael and I made sure no one touched the evidence in the water bucket while we waited for her to arrive.

Mrs. Desmond reached us, out of breath, her crutches tucked under her arms. Michael aimed a flashlight at the bucket while she stared at the digit in the water.

"It's a Verdell student ring," the dean said. "Most students choose to have their name or initials engraved inside it." She gazed up at Michael. "It's the only way we can find out who the ring—and the digit—belongs to."

"Mrs. Desmond," a familiar male voice spoke up. Dr. Finley pushed his way through the crowd. He spoke in a low voice as he reached our side. "I'll take care of this in my office. It's a sterilized environment and will prevent further contamination of the evidence, should it ever come to that."

Mrs. Desmond gave him a troubled look, then motioned for him to proceed.

The doctor pulled out a clear plastic bag. Turning it inside out, he stuck his hand in it and grabbed the digit, then reversed the bag and zipped it closed.

A young girl who had been standing nearby fainted. Other students let out cries of concern and backed away.

"Oh, for heaven's sake." Mrs. Desmond pointed a crutch at two older girls. "Both of you, come here. Help bring this girl to the infirmary." She looked around. "Audrey? Where's Audrey?"

"I'm right here." Audrey materialized.

"Go to the infirmary with them and keep this matter contained.

We don't want a widespread panic." She gestured toward Lucy and said, "Take this young woman with you for observation. She might be in shock."

"Come with me, Lucy." Audrey took the girl by the arm and guided her away.

The dean turned to the group gathered behind us. "Go back to your rooms. There's nothing to be concerned about. Go on now." She watched as they dispersed, then put a hand on Michael's arm and whispered, "Would you mind directing me to your quarters?"

We escorted Mrs. Desmond to our room. She sat in the chair by the desk while I poured water from a new bottle into a paper cup and offered it to her.

She took a few sips. "I didn't want anyone to see me like this." She took a deep breath. "In all the decades I've worked here, I've never witnessed such horrifying events." She handed me the empty cup. "Thank you, Megan." She sat back in the chair and surveyed the room, her eyes falling on the two pieces of luggage on the floor, the unmade bed, and the blankets on the sofa. "I'm not surprised our battle with the ice storm has driven the two of you to share this room."

My parents had taught me to respect the voice of authority, but Mrs. Desmond was out of line. I was about to object when she held up a hand.

"I'm not passing judgment on you or Michael. You're not in my charge, so I have nothing to say about your living arrangements." She stood up. "It's time we visit Dr. Finley to find out who our latest victim is."

We accompanied Mrs. Desmond to the infirmary. The path through the echo seemed even longer because we had to slow down so she could keep pace with us. At one point, she handed Michael her crutches and plodded along without them. The dank odor that permeated the tunnel had worsened. Long stretches of tea lights had burnt out, adding to our grim trek.

We climbed the stairs leading to the atrium. A right turn at the last corridor in the main building meant we were steps from the infirmary.

We found Audrey sitting in the waiting room, her expression anxious.

"No news yet on the student's identity," she said to us. "Lucy is in one of the other rooms. The doctor says she'll be fine."

"What about the student who fainted?" Mrs. Desmond took a seat next to Audrey.

"She has a bruised forehead and a bruised ego. Both are expected to recover." She managed a weak smile.

Dr. Finley stepped out of his office. He was holding the silver ring in a clean plastic bag. "I'm no forensics expert, but I can tell you the finger was severed from a body that was breathing. From the inscription on this ring, I can confirm it belongs to one of our male students." He stared at Mrs. Desmond as if he were requesting her permission to reveal the name.

She paled. "What's his name?"

"Greg Talbot."

CHAPTER 17

Mrs. Desmond informed Michael and me that she was taking over our meeting room to gather a small group there. We collected our files and set them on the floor in a corner and out of the range of inquisitive eyes.

The dean addressed Audrey, Mr. Jarvis, Zack, Michael, and me. "Let's put our heads together and figure out what's going on here. Audrey, any news on Greg Talbot?"

"I contacted supervisory staff and students," Audrey said. "Greg Talbot is nowhere to be found—not in his old dorm room, the gymnasium, or anywhere else. Zack confirmed Greg worked on his water bucket team today."

"We worked together until late this afternoon," Zack said. "It was the last time I saw him."

"Did he appear to be okay?" Mrs. Desmond asked him.

"Yes. He was supposed to join a bunch of us for basketball practice tonight. He never showed up."

"I'd cautioned him about cleaning up his dorm room several times," Mr. Jarvis said. "This evening at six was the deadline. I knocked at his door at six-fifteen. There was no answer. I entered his room and he wasn't there."

I caught my breath. Something horrible had happened to Greg. I was certain his disappearance had everything to do with the drugs he'd promised to deliver to us this evening.

I gave Michael a questioning look.

"Mrs. Desmond, with your permission," Michael said, "I'd like to organize a search for Greg tonight."

"Excellent idea," she said.

"I'd like to help," Zack said, glancing from Michael to Mrs. Desmond. "I can round up other students who know the ins and outs of the grounds like I do. It'll make it easier to move around in the dark with only our flashlights."

"We need to search the well too," Michael said.

"The well?" Zack looked at him. "No one could survive that fall."

"For God's sake, his finger was cut off," I said, causing heads to turn in my direction. "Someone killed him and threw him in the well."

A heavy silence hung in the air.

Zack called on six senior students to help search for Greg. The dark of night combined with falling ice pellets and slippery surfaces didn't offer ideal conditions for a search. Time wasn't on their side either. The temperature was expected to drop with each passing hour.

Mrs. Desmond and Audrey kept each other company in the meeting room. Neither woman wanted to retire for the night until the search was completed, and both had insisted on remaining close at hand.

My comment at the meeting had shaken things up, and Mrs. Desmond was giving me the cold shoulder.

"I'll take a walk to the atrium," I said to the women. "I'll let you know if there's any news on the search."

It was close to curfew. I was surprised to see flickering lights emanating from the glass-walled space. I neared the edge of the corridor and saw Helga and another female student lighting a row of tea lights along the front windows.

"At least Zack and the others will be able to see their way back," Helga said.

"You have a big crush on him, don't you?" the other girl said.

"Who doesn't, Jessie? He's so *boss*. I'll never share him and he knows it."

Helga and Zack? After Zack's argument against dating at Verdell, I doubted these two were a couple. Maybe Helga was staking a claim on Zack to prevent other girls from pursuing him.

They hadn't seen me. I stepped back into the shadows and listened.

"You should have given him a kiss for good luck." Jessie giggled.

"In the atrium?" Helga said. "And risk getting suspended? Or worse?"

"What could be worse? You mean like what happened to Nat?"

"She'd had her eye on Zack and every other rich man's son since she got here. Everyone knows she asked for it."

"Don't talk like that. It gives me the creeps."

"It's true. If Nat hadn't been such a *ho*, she'd still be alive today. And making like she was Mother Teresa to Andrew. As if! That dude was so high, he didn't know what day it was."

Helga's brutal remarks about Nat bothered me and raised a red flag. I made a mental note to ask Audrey for the senior student's file later.

"You believe the rumors about Andrew?" Jessie asked. "That he was jealous and killed Nat?"

"Who cares anyway? Hey, want to hear the latest on Sophie—that "poor me" roommate of hers? She reported her camera was missing. Like, who cares? With Nat out of the way, she's screaming for attention. Such a wannabe."

Jessie laughed.

Helga changed the topic of conversation to how much she missed having access to her phone. "I can't text. I can't tweet. I can't book concert tickets..." And on she went.

I'd heard enough. I traipsed into the atrium and dragged my boots along the floor to announce my arrival. "Hi, Helga. I didn't expect to see anyone here." I glanced at Jessie, who stood glued to the spot, eyes fixed on me.

"Oh...hi, Megan," Helga said. "Jessie and I were worried about the search team. We lit these tea lights. Sort of like a beacon for them."

"Good idea." I checked my watch.

Helga nudged Jessie. "It's late. We'd better go. Bye, Megan." They rushed off.

I paced up and down the atrium, not only to keep warm but also to fight off the jitters about what the search team might find. From time to time, I'd stare out the window, hoping to spot a scattering of flashlights—a sign that the team was approaching. All I saw was a blurry darkness caused by ice buildup.

Footsteps approached from behind me.

I turned around, thinking Helga might have returned for an extended chat.

It was Ann. "See anything out there?" She joined me and gazed out the window.

"No. It's too dark and there's too much ice on the windows."

A long wool scarf enveloped her head and neck. She wrapped the tail end of it around her gloved hands. "My hands are freezing. Damn ice storm."

She was making small talk. I sensed she'd sought me out at this late hour to talk about something more important than the cold. I waited.

"I know the search team is out there looking for Greg," Ann said. "A trusted friend told me."

The only source I could think of was Mr. Jarvis, who'd attended our group meeting with Mrs. Desmond.

"Andrew and Greg were in my math class three years ago," she said. "When I arrived here Thursday, I was shocked to learn Andrew was dead. And now Greg has gone missing." She looked at me. "I think there's a connection between them."

"In what way?" I asked.

"The boys weren't close friends, but they had something in common. They were experimenting with drugs. I caught each of them in the act on an impromptu supervisory visit to their dorm rooms. I reported my findings to Mrs. Desmond."

"What did she do about it?"

"She said she'd look into sending the boys to rehab," Ann said. "Months later, students came to me to report they'd seen Andrew and Greg using and selling drugs. I went back to see Mrs. Desmond.

What she did afterward, I don't know. I quit my job at the end of that school year."

"What about the school board?" I asked. "Didn't they have a say?"

"No. The dean makes the final decision regarding what course of action to take when drugs are involved. Three years have passed since then. Either the boys cleaned up their act or she decided not to expel them."

"Could have been a cover-up to prevent a scandal."

"And to keep sponsor funds rolling in. Though I don't see how she can conceal recent police enquiries into the two students' deaths at Verdell."

"You're referring to Dave?"

Ann nodded. "I'm still upset about the way Mrs. Desmond accused him, as if Dave were responsible because he left his car doors unlocked. If anything bad has happened to Greg, at least she won't be able to blame Dave for it." She shivered. "I'm going back to my room. I hope the team returns with positive news. Good night." She walked away.

I resumed my pacing in the atrium, mulling over what Ann had confided about students using drugs at Verdell. Once more, I perceived Mrs. Desmond as someone who wielded absolute power to suit her own needs.

Half an hour later, two boys from the search team plodded indoors, supporting a third boy between them.

"What happened?" I asked them.

"Ethan slipped on the ice," one boy said. "We think he broke his leg. We're going to the infirmary."

Ethan clenched his teeth in a show of bravery, though silent tears streamed down his face and reflected the pain he was in.

The other boy said, "No sign of Greg Talbot so far. Hope the other guys have better luck." They trudged away.

I hurried to the meeting room to update Mrs. Desmond.

She grimaced when I told her about Ethan, the injured boy. "Go to the infirmary. Have the other two boys alert the team to come back in immediately. We'll resume the search early tomorrow morning."

Michael visited Dr. Finley first thing Monday morning. He said something about wanting to discuss today's search for Greg Talbot and what steps the doctor might recommend he take in the worst case scenario.

I headed for Audrey's office in the meantime and asked for Helga Peterson's student file. Audrey didn't ask why before handing it to me. She gave me the impression she would have provided all the files in her cabinets had I asked for them.

I stopped by the meeting room and reviewed Helga's file. Excellent marks. Super athlete. Overall high achiever. The only bleep on the radar was a notation that Helga had paid her tuition fees through bank loans. According to what Dave had told us, it would put her in the same category as Nat—students who didn't come from wealthy families but managed to pay the exorbitant Verdell fees.

I left the meeting room and headed for the dining hall. It was almost empty. Either the students and staff had already eaten or they'd decided to skip breakfast altogether. While I stood at the food counter, Michael joined me. A paltry serving of cereal, raisins, and water explained why so few people were having breakfast this morning. Complaints about the first meal of the day spread fast.

We sat down at a table. Michael had gone straight to bed after Mrs. Desmond had called off the search last night, so I'd deferred telling him about my rendezvous with Helga and Jessie in the atrium until now.

"Helga and Zack? Interesting." He ate a scoop of cereal.

I mentioned I'd retrieved Helga's student file. "She'd keep every girl at Verdell away from Zack so she can have him to herself. It explains her lack of compassion for Nat."

"Would she be capable of murder, though?"

"Is anyone?" I swallowed a spoonful of cereal. "So what did Dr. Finley have to say?"

"He suggested I tread lightly," Michael said, a smile creeping up on his face. "I wasn't sure if he was referring to my investigation or the campus terrain."

"Maybe both." I smiled. "What else did he say?"

"He suggested we search the immediate grounds and expand outward only if necessary. He suggests we double up—no one searches alone. He's committed to preventing more casualties."

I reached over and squeezed his hand. "Promise me you'll be careful."

He squeezed back. "You bet."

We set off for the atrium where Michael met Zack and the other students. Equipped with a pulley, a metal swivel hook, a bucket, road flares, rope, and a positive outlook, they resumed their task. Half the team would work on the well out back. The other half would search the campus grounds. I watched as they strode down the corridor leading past the gymnasium to the rear exit.

Monday morning also meant a return to classes. With the heat from so many bodies occupying the same space, going to class was a better option than trying to stay warm in one's dorm room.

With no other choice, I'd have to move around to prevent from freezing. While Michael and the team searched for Greg, I'd investigate the mystery of the stolen food supplies from the pantry. Damned if I was going to starve to death in this place.

With little else than logic to go on, I put myself in the thief's shoes. I crossed the covered passageway that connected the main building to the dining hall and turned left at the first corner.

Dark oak wainscoting ran halfway up the walls of the corridor adjacent to the dining hall. The rest of the wall surface up to the stucco ceiling was painted a shade of sand. I wandered along and stopped at the back door to the kitchen. I counted the steps from there to the food pantry at the end of the corridor. The distance was about forty feet.

A short distance, though it didn't explain how the thief could have escaped with a load or two of supplies—even with a cart as Charlie had suggested. He—or she—must have had an accomplice.

Even if more than one thief had been involved in the heist, how could they have transported the supplies out of this corridor without anyone noticing them? They would have had to walk out the front door of the building and down a flight of icy stairs. With a cart? Balancing heavy bags of supplies? Not plausible.

The pantry door was ajar. I peeked inside. Rows of wide shelves spanned the circumference of the room and were bare except for about fifty cans of food. I took note of peas, asparagus, and green beans. Ugh! We were doomed if we couldn't find the stolen food supplies.

I focused on the task at hand. I retraced my steps and surveyed the black and white tile pattern in the linoleum floor. It had suffered the usual wear and tear over the years. I walked ten feet beyond the pantry this time and noticed that the floor was less worn at this end of the corridor.

I took a few more steps and discovered a niche on my left. The far wall inside it contained a dumbwaiter. I walked up to it. A metal panel with two black buttons was installed in the wall beside the dumbwaiter. One arrow indicated up, the other down.

I inspected the walls in the niche for scuffs. Like the rest of the corridor, dark oak wainscoting ran halfway up the wall, paint completing the balance. There were no marks anywhere.

The floor was also less worn in this area, no doubt due to limited foot traffic, which hinted at the possibility the dumbwaiter hadn't been used in years or longer.

Or had it?

My pulse accelerated. I contemplated that maybe, just maybe, I'd discovered the pantry thief's getaway car. What a coup! I couldn't wait to tell Michael.

But wait. I had to test it first. No use tooting my horn if I hadn't proven my hypothesis. I pulled the handle. It wouldn't give. I tried again, harder this time, and ended up slamming my back into the wall as the door swung open.

I gazed inside. The stainless steel cab could easily accommodate an adult in a sitting position. I'd seen a similar model in an old three-story building modified for restaurant use. A commercial dumbwaiter could hold up to several hundred pounds and travel vertically over hundreds of feet. The small pull on the inside of the door baffled me, though.

I was tempted to get in and try it out but decided it was best to tell Michael about my discovery first. Who knew where I'd end up?

And given my claustrophobia, the mere thought of getting into a constricted space was enough to give me palpitations anyway.

My musings were all for naught, as Shakespeare would have said. The dumbwaiter wasn't a manual system but an electric one, I realized as I looked at it more. Even if I tried the buttons, they wouldn't function, what with the power outage. The same principle held true for the day the pantry theft occurred: no electric power. I scolded myself for such shortsightedness.

A dull roar reached my ears. It sounded like a motor running in the distance. Or like the sound a lawnmower makes when a neighbor down the street is cutting his lawn.

I shook my head and shut the door. I was getting paranoid. There was no power in this building and maybe none in the entire province of Quebec. The sound was nothing more than the wind whistling through the cracks in this century-old building.

I noted the double window at the end of the corridor and moved toward it. I was surprised to discover another niche to the left of it that contained a couple of housekeeping carts. Mrs. Desmond had mentioned the water bucket teams would have access to such carts. These carts had to be extras.

Although I'd debunked my theory that the dumbwaiter was the getaway vehicle, I wasn't done yet. I glanced out the window at the ice-covered ground. No tire tracks. I examined the latch on the window. It was an old-fashioned casement latch, the sort you crank by hand to open, and it was rusted. I took out a tissue from my coat pocket. I placed it over the latch and gave it a crank. It broke in my hand. I glanced over my shoulder. No one was around. I placed the latch in a corner on the floor.

Okay. So much for solving the stolen food mystery. Now what?

The notion of a secret underground society hadn't left my mind ever since Sophie had first spoken to me about it. Maybe I could find a hidden door in the echo that would lead to the secret passageway and the equally secret society.

I took the steps down to the echo. I aimed my flashlight at the tunnel walls—even ran my hand across joints that might conceal hidden doorways—but to no avail. I repeated my search twice, back and forth along both sides of the echo. I attracted questioning stares from passing students who might have determined I was a bit ditzy. I smiled at them and they smiled back.

So much for wailing ghosts and secret passageways. Michael was right. I should have known better than to trust unfounded rumors and overactive minds. Only the truth has a loud and clear voice.

That fact was reinforced when Michael and the rest of the search team trudged back into the school an hour later. They didn't return empty-handed.

CHAPTER 18

Michael, Zack, and the other members of the search team joined Mrs. Desmond in the meeting room. The dean asked me to attend, which didn't surprise me, considering she'd included me in other meetings lately.

Zack began. "We spotted an object floating in the well. We attached a road flare to the bucket and dropped it into the well so we could see what was down there. It was Michael's idea." He glanced at Michael with a nod of appreciation, then turned his attention back to Mrs. Desmond. "The flare lit up the bottom of the well and confirmed the presence of a body. We dropped a hook. We tried to heave the body out, but the hook kept getting caught on clothing and—" He choked up but drew a deep breath and forced himself to go on. "After several tries, we managed to heave the body out. It was Greg Talbot." He looked down.

"Where is he now?" Mrs. Desmond stared at Zack, but he kept his head bent and appeared too distraught to answer. "Michael?"

"We left the body at the infirmary," Michael said. "I'd spoken with Dr. Finley earlier this morning and made arrangements—in case. We entered through the back door of the infirmary to avoid running into anyone else."

"Very thoughtful. Thank you." She sighed. "Unfortunately, we have no means by which to contact Greg's family at the moment."

"I should have paid more attention to him, but I was so busy." Zack cleared his throat.

"Zack, you must not take the blame for Greg's death," Mrs.

Desmond said. "No one knows what happened."

Michael met my gaze but broke it, which told me he wasn't prepared to share details about the drug deal we'd set up with Greg.

The dean's gaze encompassed us all. "Please hold back from revealing the gritty details of your search efforts. The last thing we want is more nasty gossip circulating in Verdell. I'll hold an assembly soon to notify everyone of Greg's passing. Thank you for your valiant cooperation today." She gave the group a dismissal nod. "Michael and Megan, please stay. I'd like a word with you."

We remained seated.

Mrs. Desmond waited until the last student had closed the door behind him. "We appear to be in the midst of an Armageddon. The moment I let down my defenses and think that nothing more startling than the last incident can occur, it does." She took in a deep breath. "Michael, I would like your honest opinion about how you think Greg Talbot died."

"It's safe to assume he drowned," Michael said. "After he was attacked."

"Attacked? By whom?"

"We don't know yet, but we believe Greg's death is drug related. We discovered ecstasy pills in Favreau's room. We suspect he was selling to students, including Greg."

Mrs. Desmond's expression mirrored her astonishment. "Why on earth didn't you tell me about this before? How did you get into Pierre Favreau's room?"

Michael leaned forward. "We couldn't tell anyone about our plans," he said, ignoring her second question. "It was part of a sting. I pretended I was a user. I approached Greg because someone informed us he was selling ecstasy at Verdell. Greg said he'd try to get the drugs and deliver them to us after dinner."

"And did he?"

"No. He didn't show up."

"For heaven's sake, someone must have seen him." She held Michael's gaze as if he'd have the answer.

He said nothing.

Mrs. Desmond rubbed her forehead. "Would one of you mind

fetching Audrey for me, please? She's in her office. Ask her to bring painkillers and a bottle of water."

"I'll go," I said.

"Thank you, Megan."

On the way to Audrey's office, I kept thinking how I wouldn't want to trade places with Mrs. Desmond for all the money in the world. The dead students, the food theft, a potential killer on the loose... I imagined the horrendous consequences once everything returned to normal. Not to mention the negative public uproar after articles covering the macabre events hit the news.

I entered Audrey's office to find Dr. Finley waving his hands in the air.

"I won't take no for an answer. I'm telling you, we need a quarantined space or else—" He turned to look at me, his hand hitting a pencil holder on Audrey's desk, causing its contents to tumble to the floor.

I closed the door behind me. "What's going on here?"

Audrey walked around her desk. "Dr. Finley told me fifteen students have caught the flu and ten more are showing symptoms. He wants to isolate them from the rest of the students to avoid an epidemic, but we don't have a room that's large enough." She gathered the pens and pencils and put them back in the holder.

"Why not close off a dorm floor and dedicate it to sick students?" I suggested.

"Boys and girls together?" Audrey raised an eyebrow.

I gave it more thought. "Dedicate a complete floor of the girls' dorm to the sick boys and another one to the sick girls."

"Excellent idea," the doctor said.

"You don't realize what a logistical problem a move like that would create," Audrey said.

"There's another problem, Audrey," Dr. Finley said. "We can't have healthy students remaining in their contaminated rooms or on the same floor as the infected students. As it is now, we're running out of fever and pain medication. We need to curtail the virus as best we can by relocating all the healthy female students."

"Where would we put them?" Audrey asked. "You're talking

about vacating two floors in the girls' dorm. A hundred students. The only other space big enough to contain them is the gymnasium."

The doctor's expression brightened. "Why not? It's a feasible solution to the problem. We can keep the divider curtains drawn. One side for the girls and the other side for the boys. Of course, it would mean an end to basketball and other sports for a while."

"A temporary measure." Audrey frowned. "Suggesting the gymnasium was the easy part. Now I have to convince Mrs. Desmond that her worst nightmare is coming true."

I understood Audrey's reluctance to broach the topic of the gymnasium. Hadn't the dean said she wanted to avoid a giant pajama party at all costs?

"Let me know what she decides." Dr. Finley turned to me. "Has Mrs. Desmond been briefed about Greg Talbot?"

"Yes," I said.

"Good. I'll have an update later." The doctor hurried out the door.

"What's this about Greg?" Audrey gaped at me. "Is he okay?"

"No." I recapped how the search team had discovered his body.

She stared at me in disbelief. "That poor boy. Another death. What on earth is happening here? Mrs. Desmond must be frantic."

"And some." I relayed the dean's request for painkillers and water. "She's in the meeting room."

Audrey opened her desk drawer and took out a bottle of painkillers, then grabbed a bottle of water from a supply by her desk. "To think I have more bad news for her." She opened the office door and looked at me over her shoulder. "Come along, Megan. Part of this wild scheme was your idea. I need all the support I can get."

We joined Mrs. Desmond and Michael in the meeting room and sat down at the table.

"Oh, no," Mrs. Desmond said. "I can tell by the expression on your faces that there's more unpleasant news coming my way."

"You're absolutely right," Audrey said. "Better take these first." She handed her the bottle of water and the pills. She wasted no time in disclosing the flu epidemic and student relocation plans.

"What? Has everyone at Verdell gone mad?" Mrs. Desmond

shook with anger.

Audrey kept her back straight and her expression unwavering. "Dr. Finley recommends the move because the flu is spreading fast. He wants the sick students isolated from the others."

Mrs. Desmond popped two pills into her mouth, then took a gulp of water. She put the cap back on the bottle and seemed to be taking extra time to weigh the consequences. "What do you think, Megan? You're clearly part of this conspiracy."

Once again, I ignored her sarcasm. "It's what hospitals do—they isolate the contagious patients."

Mrs. Desmond nodded. "Fine. Audrey, make the arrangements for relocation. And send word to supervisory staff and students that Greg Talbot's room is off limits." She raised a finger in a cautionary gesture. "But first, call an emergency assembly for this afternoon. I need to tell everyone about our latest victim and other matters. If my announcement doesn't send everyone screaming out the front door, I don't know what will. And get me a whistle."

CHAPTER 19

Mrs. Desmond's prediction wasn't far from the truth. Although the assembly in the chapel on Monday afternoon didn't cause anyone to run screaming from Verdell, it instilled enough angst among staff and students to send them hiding behind locked doors until the end of the ice storm.

First, Mrs. Desmond mentioned the retrieval of Greg Talbot's body from the well. She said Dr. Finley was in the process of examining it to obtain clues regarding the cause of death.

"We heard that someone found Greg's finger in a bucket of water," one student shouted, prompting bellows of support from his peers.

The truth had somehow prevailed. There was no fooling these kids.

"Please, quiet down," Mrs. Desmond said. "I'll answer your questions if I can."

The show of hands was instantaneous.

"Did the ex-con kill Greg and dump his body in the well?"

"Were other fingers missing?"

"Is the killer on campus?"

The ensuing awareness that a vicious murderer might be roaming the school resulted in mounting cries of panic. They were feeding off one another's fears.

Mrs. Desmond reached for the whistle on a chain around her neck and blew, silencing the crowd. "Pay attention. Let me assure you that you are safe. To put your minds at ease, Verdell is creating a buddy system. From now on, no student will travel alone to and from classes and other events within the complex. Please see your supervisory staff about choosing your buddy after assembly."

Exclamations of protest swept across the room, leading to another bombardment of questions for Mrs. Desmond. She was losing control.

She blew her whistle once more. "Silence! I expect more from students who have been schooled to meet world challenges head-on." Her glare, if not her words, subdued the group.

Second, Mrs. Desmond announced that a school search had failed to locate the stolen supplies from the kitchen pantry. "Consequently, the only food remaining on the shelves is in the form of canned goods."

A collective but more restrained gasp emanated from the crowd.

"The canned goods are of the highest quality and will fulfill your nutritional needs for as long as the storm lasts," the dean said. Her tone was as persuasive as that of a military general assuring his regiment that no harm would come to them under his command. Having seen the meager supplies in the kitchen pantry, I knew she was lying to keep everyone calm.

Third, Mrs. Desmond's revelation of the spreading flu epidemic seemed to dash whatever remaining hope the students might have had in maintaining their good health. "There is a feasible solution," the dean said in a firm voice, holding everyone's attention. She explained how students with the flu will be restricted to two floors in the girls' dorm—one for the boys and one for the girls. Healthy female students will be relocated to the gymnasium. "Divider curtains in the gymnasium will be drawn to ensure privacy between the girls and the boys. Girls, please see your supervisory staff who will help you make the necessary arrangements."

Mixed emotions surfaced, transforming into shrieks of delight at one end of the spectrum to uncontrollable tears at the other. It was evident that recent events had driven the more sensitive students close to the breaking point. I reminded myself that these were teenagers who had suffered the loss of three fellow students in recent days. Even well trained law-enforcement officers might have had a hard time dealing with so many gruesome deaths in such a short period of time.

Mrs. Desmond canceled classes the rest of the day so students could prepare to relocate to the gymnasium on Tuesday morning. She invited everyone to attend the memorial service for Greg Talbot in the chapel this evening.

Back in our dorm, I said to Michael, "Mrs. Desmond hit a nerve when she talked about the buddy system."

"What about it?"

"If the system had been in place earlier, Greg might still be alive."

Michael shrugged. "Maybe not. He could have gone outdoors late at night without anyone having seen him. Except for the killer."

"No wonder these kids are freaking out. They realize a murderer could be lurking right under their noses. Maybe I'm biased, but I can't help thinking that Favreau killed Greg."

"There's a definite connection if we can prove Greg bought drugs from him at Verdell. Question is: Where's Favreau?" He stood up and paced around the room. "The sooner we find him, the more answers we'll have. Can't wait for this damn ice storm to let up."

"It won't last forever," I said, trying to lift his spirits—and mine.

"If only the power would be restored," Michael said. "Even the video cameras don't work. There's nothing to stop Favreau—or whoever the killer is. He can choose another victim for whatever crazy reason. Dammit!" He clenched his fists.

"Maybe he's not that far away. Maybe he's hiding close by—like in that secret underground passageway Sophie told us about."

"Like I said before, she dramatizes things."

"She might have exaggerated her fears, but I think she's telling the truth about Nat visiting her boyfriend in a secret place." It was now or never. "I searched the echo."

Michael stared at me. "What?"

"I took a close look at the walls in the echo," I said. "I couldn't find a door opening."

"So much for the secret passageway theory." He gazed at a point in the distance. "On second thought, you could be right. Maybe Favreau pretended to leave Verdell Friday morning, but he's hiding out close by. It was a last-minute decision. He was in a hurry to get out of here. That's why he didn't take the stash of drugs in his room."

"You think he killed Andrew and Nat, don't you?"

He nodded. "He's at the top of my list. He had to be selling drugs to Andrew. Maybe Andrew threatened to tell the authorities about him."

"Why kill Nat? It doesn't make sense."

"Nat was trying to help Andrew. Sometimes innocent people get in the way. Favreau would have covered his tracks and not left any witnesses."

He was right. Favreau had left me tied, blindfolded, and gagged on my client's yacht. Because I hadn't seen Favreau's face when he'd kidnapped me, he'd spared my life. Or was it because he was in a hurry to leave then too?

"Maybe Favreau killed Greg too," he said. "Which means he has to be nearby."

"Did you see the reaction at assembly? The staff and students are petrified."

"Favreau isn't the only problem," Michael said. "Once the food runs out, pandemonium will hit this place. Trust me on this one."

Thinking about food and the kitchen pantry reminded me. "I have something else to tell you. I found the dumbwaiter."

A grin spread across his face. "Who is he?"

"Very funny." I gave him the look. "I can show you where it is. It's wide enough so that an adult can fit into it."

"Tell me you didn't."

"No, I didn't climb into it. It wouldn't work in a power outage anyway. At one point, though, I was sure I heard a motor running, which is impossible, right? It must have been the wind."

"Maybe." Michael's eyes lit up. "We'll wait until everyone's gone to the chapel service tonight and take a closer look at it then."

There was a knock at the door.

I opened it to see Mrs. Desmond standing there, her face paler than earlier and almost swallowed up by the hood of her dark gray coat.

"May I come in?" She flew into the room without waiting for an answer and headed straight for the chair by the desk. She sat down and gazed about the room, as if she'd dropped in for a friendly chat.

"How can we help you, Mrs. Desmond?" I sat on the bed while Michael remained standing.

She looked at me. "I don't know that you can." Her eyes were glassy and void of expression, as if recent catastrophic events had drained all emotions and no new tragedy could ever faze her again.

I waited, bracing myself for whatever she had to say.

"Dr. Finley is not a forensics expert, but he told me that after an inspection of Greg Talbot's body, he hypothesizes the boy was attacked and thrown into the well. He could have hit his head on the stone wall and drowned. The doctor won't say more in view of an impending police investigation." Mrs. Desmond gazed at Michael. "You were right about labeling Greg's death a murder."

"It doesn't always pay to be right," he said.

"Do you plan on telling everyone Greg was attacked?" I asked the dean.

"No," she said. "Since the students already know Greg is dead, Dr. Finley and I agreed there's no need to cause them more stress."

I noticed she hadn't included the staff. "I'm sure they have their doubts about the way he died."

"The less they know, the better." Mrs. Desmond took in a deep breath. "There's another matter. Dr. Finley found a small plastic sleeve containing pills in the pocket of Greg Talbot's jacket. He told me the pills were ecstasy." She looked at Michael. "You were right again."

"Being right doesn't always make it feel better in my line of work," he said.

"I understand. Nevertheless, I'm grateful for your input. I should have given you the benefit of the doubt more often." She made a move to get up but changed her mind. "I suppose it's presumptuous of me to ask if you've made any progress in your investigation into the murders of Andrew Boyle and Natalie Dunn."

"We suspect that Pierre Favreau might have had a hand in killing not only Andrew and Nat but also Greg Talbot," he said.

She gaped at him. "How is that possible? I was told he'd gone to town to purchase groceries and never returned."

"Several factors come into play here: the ice storm, the fact that no one saw Favreau leave Verdell on Friday, and now Greg's death. They indicate a possibility Favreau is hiding on campus."

"Good Lord! Then it's true. Is there no end to this madness? How can we find him? Surely you must have a plan." She studied our faces as if they held the answers.

"We do," Michael said, surprising me. "It's premature to reveal our strategy. What we need right now is the key to Greg's dorm room."

"I can't allow it. I've already cautioned the supervisory staff and students not to enter that room. For all we know, it's a potential crime scene. I assume the police would expect us to bar access to it pending their investigation."

"A police investigation won't happen today or tomorrow. We might find crucial evidence in Greg's room that could help identify the killer. We'll be careful. We'll wear latex gloves so we don't leave our prints."

Mrs. Desmond pondered our request. "Fine. You can pick up a spare key from Audrey. I hope time is on your side. No one is safe at Verdell. The last thing I want to do is declare we're in lockdown with a killer in our midst."

I understood how the recent onslaught of calamities at Verdell had placed such a burden on her. Feeling a sudden sense of communal duty, I asked, "Do you need help moving the girls from their dorm rooms to the gymnasium?"

She waved a hand in the air. "Heavens, no. You're both working on other matters for me already." She stood up. "Let me know if anything develops. I could use good news." She left as swiftly as she'd entered.

I locked the door behind her. "Tell me something, Michael.

What on earth inspired you to say you'd deliver Favreau's head on a platter to Mrs. Desmond?"

He smiled. "*You* inspired me." He walked over and put his arms around me.

"I'm serious. I want an explanation." I looked up at him.

"I'm serious too. When Mrs. Desmond mentioned how Greg died, it convinced me the killer had to be on campus. Our talk about the secret passageway got me thinking you might be right. Favreau could be hiding out in the depths of Verdell. We'll inspect the dumbwaiter later and figure out where it leads."

"Other things still bug me."

"Like what?"

"There are too many loose ends," I said. "We don't know who sent Dave the email from Nat's computer. We don't know who left us the threatening note. We don't know who stole the food supplies and where they're storing them."

"You're right," Michael said. "It's not Favreau's style."

"Style?"

"He's a killer, not a letter writer. I bet he doesn't even know how to use a computer. He must have had inside help at Verdell. We'd better watch our backs."

CHAPTER 12

Michael and I sat across from Helga in the meeting room. The tea lights flickered on the table every time one of us spoke or moved.

"Sophie said she told you about someone breaking into Nat's room," Helga said.

"A break-in?" I repeated.

"My bad." She raised a hand twice the size of mine. "Not a break-in. Whoever it was must have used a key. I don't know who the intruder was, but I think I know who might have supplied the key."

"Who?"

"Me." She leaned back. "Here's what happened. I was watching the guys practice basketball one night. I'm on the girl's basketball team, so I like to watch the guys sometimes. They have awesome moves."

"Like Zack?" I asked.

Helga's face lit up. "Isn't he a cool player?" She smiled and continued. "Thing is, I'm a supervisor of the girls' dorm, so I have a spare set of keys for each room. I'm sure I had the keys with me the same night Sophie mentioned. Anyway, after the practice, I couldn't find them. I looked everywhere. Then I found them in my locker."

"What night are we talking about again?" I had to be sure.

"The night of the accident—when Nat and Andrew went missing."

I noticed the discretion in her choice of words. "I've misplaced things sometimes. Is it possible you'd left the keys in your locker to begin with?"

Helga shook her head. "No way. I keep the keys in one blazer pocket and my phone in the other. Always have. They're part of my daily wardrobe."

"How would the keys have ended up in your locker? Isn't it locked?"

"No. Verdell believes in the honor system where our lockers are concerned. I don't mean to be crude or snooty, but most of the students here don't need to steal from one another."

The message came through loud and clear. "You implied earlier that someone took your keys to get into Nat's room."

"That's right. The timing fits. My keys went missing that night and showed up in my locker the next morning. Since it was the second time it happened, I'm one hundred percent certain that somebody borrowed them from me—again."

"The second time?" I asked.

Helga nodded. "About two weeks ago. I think it was in science class. I checked my pocket and the keys were gone. I found them in my locker."

"Think back," Michael said to her. "In both instances, who was standing or sitting near you?"

"My friends. Classmates. That's what I find so bizarre. We've known one another for years. I can't point to anyone who'd do such a thing." She shook her head.

I offered a plausible alternative. "Maybe someone wanted to play a trick on you and they hid them."

Helga narrowed her eyes. "If you're right, they're in big trouble once I get my hands on them."

I didn't doubt it for a moment.

"Anyway, I solved the problem." She unzipped her jacket and showed us a set of keys suspended on a silver chain around her neck. "It won't happen a third time."

"Is there anything else you wanted to tell us?" I asked.

"No. That covers it." She stood up. "You going to the assembly?"

"Yes…for sure." I'd almost forgotten about the school gathering

CHAPTER 20

Since the search for Greg Talbot and resulting events had prioritized the day's activities, Michael and I hadn't had the time to revisit Pierre Favreau's room until now.

Charlie led the way down the corridor to the staff apartments. "If you need more time—"

"No, it won't take long." Michael took the key from him and inserted it into the lock. He carefully opened the door. The slip of paper he'd placed in the doorjamb glided to the floor. He closed the door and returned the key to Charlie. "Thanks. We're done."

Michael gave me a knowing glance. We'd have time later to discuss theories about the slip of paper in the doorjamb to Favreau's room. The obvious conclusion was that no one had entered the room after we had. The *why* part of it was open to interpretation.

As we headed back to the dining hall with Charlie, I seized the occasion to find out more about a topic of concern. "Charlie, do you or your staff use the dumbwaiter?"

He laughed. "You joking? I don't think anyone's used it in decades."

"Do you know where it leads?"

"They tell me there's a bunch of abandoned mines under the school. They used to manually operate the dumbwaiter to send food down to the miners back then. When Verdell bought the property, they built the school but didn't fill in the shaft. They made renovations to the school, though, including this corridor." He waved a hand to indicate the floor tiles and wainscoting.

I took a chance. "I heard rumors about a secret passageway beneath the school. They told me it was haunted."

"Who told you that?" Charlie gave me a skeptical look.

"A student."

"Figures." He lowered his voice. "You should hear some of the stuff these kids tell me. It comes from being born into money. If you ask me, too much free time breeds vivid imaginations. You know what I mean?" He raised a forefinger and made small circles next to his temple.

I gave Michael a side-glance. His smile told me he'd taken Charlie's joke in stride, which was good, considering that Michael came from a family with oodles of money. The irony of his situation was that he'd chosen to live off his income as investigative reporter rather than make any claim to his inheritance.

"Me, I'm a simple boy, born and raised in the country," Charlie said. "I spent my summers helping out on the family farm in the morning and working at minimum wage during the day to pay for my culinary courses. Working as a cook at Verdell is a dream come true for me. I don't make a fortune, but I put something aside for my old age and the job keeps me sane most of the time." He chuckled.

"Would you know if anyone has ever tried to use the dumbwaiter?"

He shrugged. "What would be the purpose? I doubt it's functional. You're welcome to check it out. Continue down this corridor until you find a niche on the left. It's in there." Charlie stopped at the back entrance to the kitchen. "See you at dinner. The best part is the desert. Chocolate chips." He winked and slipped inside.

Michael and I moved down the corridor to the niche where the dumbwaiter was located.

"Go ahead," I said to him. "Open it."

Michael grabbed the handle and pulled it open. He reached into his pocket for a flashlight and aimed it at the interior of the dumbwaiter. "You're right. I could fit in here." He examined the control buttons on the wall. "This thing won't work without electricity."

"If at all. Charlie did say no one had used it in ages."

"Let's see." Michael hit one button, then the other. Nothing happened. "Figures." He opened the door wider. "The car surface is scratched but clean. There's a small pull on the inside of the door. Weird." He leaned in. "I think I heard something."

My heart raced. "What?"

"I'm not sure."

"Get your head out of there!"

"Don't worry. There's no power." Michael straightened up. "It's like a faraway droning sound." He put away his flashlight.

"That's what I heard. What do you think it is?"

"Could be old plumbing or the wind moving through the tunnels." He shut the door.

"Well, that puts an end to my theory. I thought Mr. Jarvis had given us a good lead when he mentioned he'd overheard those boys talking about having extra food on hand. The dumbwaiter would have made the perfect getaway."

"The architects preserved an interesting feature to this old building. Your idea to check it out wasn't a total loss." Michael hugged me. "Let's go visit Greg's room."

We stopped by the admin office to pick up the spare key to Greg's room. Three supervisory staff members were holding an animated discussion with Audrey about the student relocation to the gymnasium.

Audrey saw us and held out a key for Michael. She smiled at him, then jumped back into a heated conversation about how close to the partition the girls' mattresses should be positioned on the gymnasium floor.

Michael and I took the echo to the girls' dorm, then exited the lobby through the front door. With heads bent against the icy drizzle, we crossed the glassy road to the boys' dorm. Halfway there, I slipped on a patch of ice and would have fallen had Michael not grabbed me in time.

We snapped on latex gloves before entering Greg's room. It had become a habit whenever an investigation had taken us to places connected to a potential victim or crime. The last thing we wanted was to leave our fingerprints in Greg's room and have the police add us to their suspect list. We'd been down that road before when my husband had been murdered and evidence had led the police to suspect our involvement. Michael and I had promised each other we'd take extra precautions to avoid a repetition of similar circumstances.

Unlike the sense of unfinished business I experienced when I'd entered Nat's room, I felt nothing but turmoil in Greg's. Clothes and sports magazines were strewn over the bed and floor. The closet revealed piles of shoes, clothing sloppily hung on a bulging rack, and an overhead shelf supporting a basketball, a soccer ball, and a knapsack under more clothes. A cardboard box on the floor overflowed with high tech gear used in playing video games. Another box held family photos that had remained unhung, owing to the fact that posters of Steve Nash had taken up all available wall space in the room.

In keeping with Verdell policy, rooms were inspected every day and students were required to keep their personal space tidy. Considering the mess in this room, I had to assume that either Greg knew someone on the supervisory team who was negligent in enforcing the rules or he'd paid that person off to bypass his room.

While Michael looked through the closet, I rummaged through Greg's desk for a laptop but didn't find one. Pasted on the wall over the desk was an assortment of stickers in various sizes, each one displaying football or soccer team insignia.

I moved to the bed and sifted through a pile of T-shirts. "Do you think his laptop is somewhere under here?"

Michael glanced my way. "Maybe Mrs. Desmond took it."

"I think she would have told us." I looked under the bed. More T-shirts and sports magazines. I stood up. "No laptop. The killer beat us to it."

Disappointment crossed his face. "He sure knows how to cover his tracks."

"I hope he wasn't thorough and missed something."

A search through Greg's desk drawers produced nothing of significance except a student agenda. I flipped the pages and noticed he'd jotted the meeting times for basketball practice and other sports activities he'd attended at Verdell over the last week or so. On the day he disappeared, he hadn't entered a notation for Zack's basketball practice that same evening. I mentioned it to Michael.

"Maybe he forgot." He glanced at me. "Or he entered it in his cell phone."

"I didn't find a cell phone. Maybe we changed his plans."

"It was only a basketball practice." He shrugged. "Delivering the drugs to us wouldn't have delayed him by more than a few minutes."

I scanned previous pages in Greg's agenda. I noticed a trend: initials with numbers beside them. In one notation, the initials A.B. were written next to the number ten. I showed it to Michael.

"Andrew Boyle," he said. "The number could be the quantity of ecstasy pills."

"Look at this. Greg was selling to all these students." I flipped through the pages to show him a dozen other entries, but none of the initials were familiar to us.

"It goes to prove that Verdell isn't as drug-free as Mrs. Desmond would like to believe. Want to give me a hand here?"

"Sure." I put Greg's agenda back in the desk, then helped Michael comb through the closet. We examined boxes and clothing in case Greg had stashed drugs in them. Assorted tops and pants looked and smelled as if they hadn't been washed in weeks.

Michael got lucky when he checked the pockets of a school blazer suspended on a hook behind the clothing rack. He held up a small pouch of pills. "What do we have here? Let's see. Pink, green, white. Smiley faces, peace symbols, birds. You name it. Ecstasy in every color and theme."

"If Greg had these drugs in his possession, why didn't he make the delivery to us?"

"Two possible reasons. First, because someone killed him before he could make the delivery. Second, somebody planted these pills in his room after the fact."

I was stunned. "How does he do it? How does Favreau—or whoever he's working with—manage to stay one step ahead of us?

Why are they killing these students?"

"Which question do you want me to answer first?"

"It's so frustrating. How can you stay so cool?"

"I have to. It helps me to focus and remain objective." Michael slipped the pills back into Greg's blazer. "Are we done here?"

My eyes flitted about the room. An overflowing wastebasket in the corner had almost escaped my notice. I walked over and opened up several crumpled sheets of paper. "Scribbles about homework, basketball meeting times, and sports scores."

Michael pulled out his share. "A shortlist of girls' names, his mom's birthdate with a note to call her, and a memo about doing laundry."

"I can see why the last one ended up in the wastebasket."

"Now Megan, don't be mean."

"It's a fact. Look around. If this were my kid's room, he'd be in a lot of trouble."

"You bet. I can vouch for that from first-hand experience." His eyes twinkled.

I gave him the look.

"I knew that would get you going." He laughed and kissed me on the cheek.

I smiled. "Okay, let's get serious."

We retrieved the remaining crumpled notes.

The next piece of paper I unfolded revealed a hand-drawn diagram. A narrow horizontal path was punctuated at intervals by capital letters N, A, and P. At the top right were about a dozen crosses. I showed it to Michael. "What you make of this? Could it be a cemetery?"

He studied it. "If I didn't know Greg had been killed, I would have assumed he was depressed and had a death wish. Having easy access to drugs didn't help his condition." He clenched his teeth. "Damn that Favreau."

All of a sudden, I felt sorry for Greg and regretted my earlier comment. Anyone who leaves his room in such disorder lacks self-esteem. I tucked the diagram into my pocket.

"We're done here," Michael said. "Let's go see Audrey."

The disappearance of Greg's computer was a stumbling block in our investigation. We returned to the main building and asked Audrey whether she, rather than the murderer-thief, had removed it from Greg's dorm room.

"No, I didn't take it." Audrey frowned from behind her desk. "Has it gone missing?"

"Yes," I said. "Do you know if anyone on the supervisory teams might have borrowed it?"

She shook her head. "After Greg Talbot's body was discovered, Mrs. Desmond declared his room off limits. I advised the teams accordingly. We can't babysit everyone, so I have to assume they followed directives. That a computer has gone missing or was stolen is a serious violation of Verdell policy. The school owns the laptops. I'll have to notify Mrs. Desmond."

"What about cell phones?" Michael asked. "Are they school property too?"

"No," Audrey said. "They belong to the students."

"Will you let us know if Greg's computer shows up?"

"I certainly will."

Michael suggested we review the personnel files again and look at the big picture. "Since we don't know where Favreau is, we need to find something—or someone—that will lead us to a potential accomplice."

"We've spoken with lots of people at Verdell so far," I said. "We might have come face to face with him—or her—and not even realized it."

"Could be. That's why I'd like to take a second look at the files Audrey pulled from Mrs. Desmond's office."

"Do you have anyone in mind?"

"No, but I'll know it when my gut tells me."

Since Mrs. Desmond had claimed priority over the meeting room, we transported the school files to our dorm room. Michael sat at the desk, the tea lights along the window casting a flickering glow over his face. I removed my boots and slipped under the blankets, coat and hat intact, using the small flashlight from Verdell to light up the file I was reviewing. We spent the rest of Monday afternoon scanning dozens of student and staff files a second time. We shared each file to be doubly sure we hadn't missed anything.

"I can't believe we interviewed all these people." I walked over to Michael and placed the last file in the bin. "Any revelations so far?"

He sat back in the chair and gazed out the window at the darkening landscape. "Greg's finger."

"What about it?"

He looked at me. "It's as if someone cut off his finger and threw it in the well, then decided to dump the rest of him in right after."

"Maybe there was a struggle and the killer cut off Greg's finger," I said. "The doctor did suggest it had been cut before Greg died."

Michael rubbed his chin. "It's possible, but the timing is weird."

"How?"

"For Greg's finger to have gotten into a bucket, it means he was killed while the guys on the team were transporting water from the well to the school. One of them must have seen something."

"Zack told us he made sure everyone was safe inside at the end of the day. Maybe Greg went missing afterward." I caught myself. "On second thought, you're right. His finger was found in the water bucket the team transported into the school. Greg had to have been killed before they completed their shift." I connected the dots. "Do you think Zack lied to us?"

"That's what I intend to find out." He stood up. "Let's go."

CHAPTER 21

Darkness enveloped lengthy portions of the echo. The beams from our flashlights revealed that most of the tea lights had disappeared, no doubt put to good use elsewhere.

The atrium fared no better, its oversized windows encrusted with new layers of ice that incited students to refer to Verdell as "hell frozen over." Despite the bleak ambiance, get-togethers within this glass-framed hub still thrived before the dinner hour. Students and staff held flashlights or tea lights in tiny ceramic pots while chatting in groups and commiserating on the deteriorating situation.

This time of day also marked the completion of the water bucket run. One by one, the team members entered the atrium, heroes to the rest of their classmates. The chatter increased and accolades made the rounds as word spread that it had been yet another successful run with no major injuries.

As soon as Michael saw Zack, he asked him to join us for a short chat away from the crowd. "Zack, we'd like to confirm whose team Greg was on the day he went missing."

"I already told you—mine," Zack said. "What's this all about?"

"You said you were responsible for making sure your team was safely inside at the end of the day," I said. "Why didn't you account for Greg's absence?"

Confusion flickered in Zack's eyes. "His absence?"

"Greg's finger was found in a water bucket. It tells me that he—" I chose my words with care. "He must have ended up in the well before your team's shift ended."

There was a notable hesitation before it dawned on him. "You're right. In all the craziness going on that day, with my team buddies going back and forth, I'd almost forgotten that I lost sight of Greg."

"When?" Michael asked.

"It was close to the end of our shift. I thought Greg had given up and gone inside. He often complained about the cold. I didn't think anything more of it until the discovery of—" Zack blinked.

A student walked by and Michael lowered his voice. "You have spare keys to access the boys' dorm rooms in case of emergency, right?"

"Right."

"Did you enter Greg's room after his body was discovered in the well?"

"No, I didn't. The dean gave the supervisory students and staff clear orders not to enter his room."

That much was true.

"Do you have any other questions?" Zack asked. "I need to wash up for dinner ASAP."

Michael nodded. "One last question. Do you know any students who are using E at Verdell?"

"Like I told you before, some students had been using. They got treatment and are cleaned up or working on it. I won't name names, so please don't ask me. Anything else?"

"No, that's all for now."

Zack walked away.

"What's your gut feeling?" I asked Michael.

"Greg was probably one of the ecstasy users that Zack knew about," he said. "Could be the reason he didn't want to reveal any names."

"It doesn't matter how the pills ended up in Greg's coat or in his dorm room. The boy's death is indirectly linked to his drug usage."

"We can blame Favreau for that."

"The evidence keeps pointing to him, doesn't it?"

"You bet. Dead men don't lie."

"What's next?" I asked.

Michael looked around. "Dinner. I'm starving. I'll go find out what's on the menu and be right back."

I was watching him weave his way through the crowd when I felt a tap on my shoulder.

I turned to see Sophie peering at me from under a wool scarf wrapped around her head. "Can you come to my room right now? Count to twenty before leaving."

"But I—"

She didn't wait for an answer but scurried off like a scared rabbit.

Sophie's request suggested urgency, so I didn't detour to tell Michael where I was going.

I counted to twenty, then hurried down to the echo, using my flashlight to guide me along. I thought I'd see Sophie up ahead but she was nowhere in sight. She must have raced back to the dorm. I increased my pace and flew up the stairs to the girls' dorm. I rushed along the corridor on the second floor to find the outer door to Sophie's dorm suite ajar.

She saw me first. She opened the door wide and waved me inside. "Hurry. I don't want anyone to see you." She closed the door behind us. Using her flashlight to show the way, she ushered me through the kitchenette and into her room.

I looked around. No boxes. No sign that Sophie was getting ready to move out. "Aren't you relocating to the gymnasium tomorrow?"

"No. They're moving the students on the floor above mine first."

The third floor? My floor? I made a mental note to tell Michael about it.

She turned off her flashlight. Several tea lights on the windowsill were the only source of light.

"Why did you want me to come here, Sophie?"

"I have something to show you." She handed me an envelope. "The information in here has to remain confidential. If anyone finds out, I could get in serious trouble."

I opened the envelope. Inside were three photos.

"I'll use my flashlight so you can see better." She clicked it on and aimed it at the photos. "They're pics of the forest behind the school."

The first photo was taken at night in the winter. A glimmer of light shone through leafless trees, but the glow was too small to decipher what the source was.

The second photo was also taken at night in the winter. The bare trees and a light blanket of snow on the ground were giveaways. A larger beam of light appeared through the trees. This time, it emanated from the ground.

The third photo took me by surprise. It too had been taken of the forest one winter night. I could make out the silhouette of a man standing in front of car taillights. I knew they were taillights because they were red.

"How did you get these pictures?" I asked.

"I took them myself," Sophie said. "My room faces the forest. I use the binoculars to spot any animals coming out of the forest at night." She aimed the flashlight at a pair of binoculars on her desk. "If I'm fast enough, I can grab my camera, zoom in, and take their pics. Like these." She aimed the flashlight at a wall where she'd hung photos of deer, raccoons, and birds.

I wasn't surprised. She'd found a connection with living creatures that asked for nothing in return. "They're wonderful shots."

"Thanks."

Even in the dim light, I could tell she was smiling. "Tell me about these pics of the forest." I tapped the photos in my hand.

She aimed the flashlight at them. "It started when I noticed weird lights in the forest. I used my binoculars to get a closer look. I took my camera and zoomed in to take those pics. I thought you'd find them interesting."

Sophie's voice contained a certain level of confidence I hadn't noticed before. She knew she'd latched onto something that could help our investigation into the student deaths at Verdell.

And yet, I didn't know whether to hug her or be angry with her.

"Sophie, why didn't you show me these pics earlier?"

"My printer broke down. I had to use Nat's printer, but after the police found her, I got scared." She glanced away. "I had to wait till it was okay to go into her room."

"You could have kept these pics on your camera and shown them to me."

"That's the problem. My camera was stolen the other day. Good thing I printed these pics before." She smiled with pride.

"If you would have at least alerted Michael and me about the lights in the forest, we could have checked it out."

"Well…it's just that…" Sophie hesitated. "At first I wasn't sure. I knew the forest didn't belong to Verdell. I thought maybe the owner had a flashlight and was taking a walk one night. You know, with his dog."

I doubted Trenton Barratt would drive all the way from his home in Sherbrooke to walk his dog in the forest, but Sophie wouldn't know that. "You've seen the owner and his dog?"

"No, but I heard a dog bark once or twice."

"It could have been a stray dog."

"Maybe."

I studied the photos. "These pics are good but they only capture a moment in time. Can you tell me more about what you saw when you looked through the binoculars?"

"First, I saw the weird light, like in those pics," Sophie said. "It looked as if it was coming out of a hole in the ground. It lasted for maybe fifteen seconds, then everything went dark."

"What about the car?"

"I saw it drive through the parking lot and cross into the forest."

My heart thumped in my chest. "Do you remember when you saw it?"

Sophie nodded. "It was the night before the morning Nat and Andrew were found in the river."

"Did you tell the police?"

"No."

I raised my voice. "You realize it could have been the same car they found in the river the next day, don't you? Why didn't you tell the police?"

"Because...because I was afraid." Sophie's voice trembled.

I flapped my arms in desperation. "Afraid of what?"

"Afraid that he would come after me if I talked."

"Who?"

"The killer."

I took a deep breath and calmed down, knowing too well how fear can often make a person think and act irrationally. I softened my tone. "What about the man standing by the car? What can you tell me about him?"

"Not much," Sophie said. "When I first noticed him, he was putting something big and heavy into the trunk."

"How do you know it was heavy?"

"Because he lost his footing and almost fell into the trunk."

"What happened afterward?"

"He closed the trunk. That's when I grabbed my camera and took the shot."

I prompted her. "And then what happened?"

Sophie gestured toward her desk. "I switched to my binoculars. By then, everything had gone black and the car drove off."

"Did you notice anyone sitting in the passenger seat?"

"No, it was too dark."

"Do you remember what time it was when you took these pics?"

She nodded. "It was after curfew. I usually study till late at night."

"Have you reported the theft of your camera to your supervisor or admin?" Helga had admitted as much, but I had to be sure.

"Yes. Verdell has a strict policy about reporting stolen items. I was afraid, though. I didn't want to draw more attention to myself. Students think I'm trying to steal the spotlight because I shared a dorm with Nat. The opposite is true. I'm trying to stay invisible."

It could explain why she didn't want to be seen speaking with Michael or me. I let it go at that.

I was still holding the photos. "Sophie, can I borrow these pics?"

"Sure. Do you think they can be used as evidence in your investigation?" Her eyes reflected childlike excitement.

With a perpetrator still running around, I didn't want to say anything that might put her life in danger. I answered with caution. "I'd like to show them to Michael first. In the meantime, please keep this between us."

"I haven't told anyone and I won't," Sophie said. "If I see anything else through my binoculars, I'll let you know."

"Thanks, Sophie." I tucked the photos in my pocket.

"Did you find the secret passageway yet?"

"I tried, but I couldn't find a way to get there. Do you know if there's a hidden entrance?"

"No. Nat said only special students were allowed to go there, that it was a secret place on campus." Her eyes widened. "Oh, I remember now. She said it was cold and damp there."

"Cold and damp?"

"Yes," Sophie said. "So if you go looking for the place again, don't forget to wear your boots."

"My boots?"

"Yes. Whenever Nat came back from dates with her boyfriend, her boots were always muddy."

For the second time in her presence, my pulse picked up speed. "Sophie, would you mind letting me into Nat's room again?"

She hesitated. "As long as you make it fast."

"I promise."

As soon as Sophie unlocked the door, I dashed to Nat's closet and slid it open. I aimed my flashlight at the floor. I didn't see any boots and figured Nat must have been wearing them when she died. To be sure, I picked up every pair of shoes and examined the soles for traces of mud. There weren't any.

Much to Sophie's relief, I thanked her and left.

As I moved down the corridor, I had the creepiest feeling I was being followed. I swirled around. I saw the back end of a dark coat slipping through a doorway. Calm down, I told myself, it's probably a student returning to her dorm room.

I took the exit door leading to the stairs. I couldn't wait to catch up to Michael and show him the photos Sophie had taken.

It was too late. Everyone had already vacated the atrium. I headed for the covered passageway that led to the dining hall. I saw Michael in a slow-moving line snaking toward the food counter.

I strolled up to him. "What's on the menu?"

He looked at me. "Artichokes, black olives, and corn. A handful of chocolate chips for dessert."

"Oh, a gourmet meal," I whispered, getting a smile in return.

"Where were you? I went back to the atrium and you weren't there."

"I met a friend." I gave him a discerning look. "What do you say we ask for a doggie bag and head back to our room?"

"Sounds promising."

"More than you can imagine."

CHAPTER 22

Michael retrieved a magnifying glass from his backpack to try to pick up more details in the three photos Sophie had taken. "These pics are incredible."

I sat on the edge of the bed, holding the blanket around me. "Too bad her camera was stolen."

"Yeah, things have a way of disappearing around here. Nat's diary, Greg's laptop, and now Sophie's camera. Tell me this guy isn't hot on our trail."

"What do you think about the weird light in the photos?"

"It originates from a source under the ground."

"I thought so too. The idea of the secret passageway might sound ridiculous, but I'm beginning to believe Sophie is right. The man she saw standing behind the car didn't simply vanish."

Michael looked at me, shadows from the tea lights on the desk skipping across his face. "The opening could be a trapdoor that someone closed, shutting out the light underground."

"Which would prove Sophie's story about a secret passageway that's cold and damp," I said, raising the topic yet again.

"I'm not convinced. I'd have to see it with my own eyes. It could be a sort of man cave. Like the ones you hear about in the news from time to time. Except this one's a potential crime scene."

"What about the taillights? Do you think it's the same car they dredged out of the river?"

"It's hard to tell. The timing is right, though. From what you told me, Sophie could have witnessed a man loading bodies into the car." He paused. "Another thing. It proves at least two people were involved. The guy who loaded the bodies into the trunk and the driver."

"So what do we do next?"

"We'll go check it out," Michael said. "Correction. *I'll* go check it out. Tonight. At midnight."

My heart thumped faster. I wasn't going to stand by and do nothing while he risked his life. As much as I feared the consequences of my decision, I knew I had to take the plunge.

"Do you expect me to wait here while you comb the forest in search of a killer? I'm going with you."

He stood up. "No, you're not. It's too dangerous."

I hopped off the bed. "So it's too dangerous for me but not for you."

"You got it."

"You don't even have a weapon. How are you going to defend yourself against Favreau and his ruthless buddies?"

"I could ask you the same question." Michael folded his arms and stared at me. "You're not going and that's final."

I stormed back to the bed. I wrapped the blanket around me, turned on my flashlight, and pretended to read a book.

I stole glimpses at Michael as he prepared for his venture into the forest. He studied Sophie's photos again and drew a little diagram. Of what, I wouldn't know. He stuffed a compass, a small flashlight, and a piece of rope in his pockets. In a hidden pocket inside his jacket, he placed a Swiss army knife, a lighter, and the diagram he'd drawn.

I got out of bed and pretended I was still upset. "I'm going for a walk."

"Where?" he asked.

"Around. I need to get the blood circulating in my legs."

"Okay."

Michael wouldn't follow me. He trusted that I wouldn't do anything impulsive without telling him first.

I practically ran down the stairs to Sophie's dorm room.

Her surprise changed to apprehension when I explained the

purpose of my visit. "It's only for an hour or so," I said. "I want to make sure Michael stays safe."

"Well...I don't know." Sophie glanced toward the window.

"You won't have to leave your room. I promise I'll be quiet."

"It's not that. I just don't want to get into any trouble."

"I promise, Sophie, nothing bad will happen to you."

She nodded reluctantly. "Okay. See you at midnight."

I hurried back to my room and found Michael napping on the sofa. I didn't say a word, though I'm sure he heard the sound of the door closing. He was a light sleeper. I wrapped a blanket around me and got into bed.

Hours passed before Michael stirred. I heard him gather his keys. He walked toward me, leaned over, and kissed me on the cheek. I pretended I was asleep.

I waited until he'd closed the door behind him, then I tiptoed out of bed. I tucked facial tissues and my peppermint lip gloss in my coat pocket. I dropped my keys and a small pair of scissors in the other. They weren't weapons, but it was the best I could do. Who knew when these items might come in handy? I stuffed each pocket with a mitten.

I peeked out the door to make sure no one was loitering in the corridor. At midnight, no one should be. To lessen the sound of the door closing, I pulled the lever down while I shut it. The last thing I wanted to do was awaken curious students. With a Verdell flashlight in hand, I dashed down the corridor past a sparse row of tea lights, pushed open the exit door leading to the stairs, and hurried down to the second floor.

As before, Sophie was standing inside the outer door to her dorm, peeking through the inch-wide opening at me. She ushered me in, then peered up and down the corridor as I'd seen her do so often.

"I don't think you were followed," she said, by way of confirmation. She led me into her room, lighting the way with her flashlight.

I gravitated to the windowsill. I noticed she'd parted the curtains in anticipation of my visit. The moon was full and shed light on the binoculars on her desk.

I pointed to them. “Do you mind if I use these?”

“Go ahead.”

I focused on the section in the forest where I expected to see Michael. I was disappointed. It was so dark that I couldn’t make out one tree stump from another. I put down the binoculars. “I can’t see a thing. I guess you were lucky that time you spotted the light in the forest.”

She kept her gaze on me and looked as if she wanted to ask me something.

I had a hunch. “By the way, Michael thought your pics were incredible.”

She smiled. “He said that?”

“Yes. That’s why he’s out there tonight.” I gestured toward the window. “He’s investigating the strange light in the forest.” I didn’t mention how he suspected the light came from a so-called man cave, or how it might be the site of a potential murder scene or a safe harbor for an escaped ex-con. Some things were better left unsaid.

Sophie took the first watch, passing me the binoculars after ten minutes. And so it went, back and forth between us, until one o’clock. We hadn’t spotted a thing. The thought hit me that Michael might be in trouble. On a more positive note, maybe Sophie or I had missed seeing him walk out of the forest. After all, it was dark. I dreaded to think he might be waiting in our dorm room all this time. Worse, I imagined what he’d say to me when I walked in at this weird hour of the night, what excuses I’d offer to cover up my tryst.

I was about to call it quits when Sophie put down the binoculars. She excused herself, saying she had to use the bathroom. I lifted the binoculars to my eyes and looked out the window. The freezing rain had stopped, making the view into the forest sharper, though I couldn’t see anything out of the norm. I took the end to the icy drizzle as a good sign. It meant the storm was moving out of the area and power would be restored sooner rather than later.

I heard the sound of a door opening. Sophie was coming out of the bathroom. I sensed movement nearby and placed the binoculars on the desk.

I saw something shiny out of the corner of my eye and felt a stab in my neck. I reached out and clutched a small hard object. The last thing I saw was the full moon fading away.

CHAPTER 23

It was cold and dark.

I didn't know how long I'd been unconscious or where I was.

I raised my arm and hit a smooth metal surface inches above my head. I tried to move and met the same restrictions all around.

Where was I?

In some kind of tomb?

Was I underground, buried alive with rodents and insects?

Who put me here and why?

My lips were parched. I was thirsty. And cold. So cold.

I ran my hands along my coat to the pockets.

Good. My mittens were still there. I slipped them on. Not that it mattered much if I were going to die soon.

No, it couldn't end this way. It *will not* end this way. I refused to entertain another moment of negativity.

What was that noise?

I'd heard it before—that low droning sound.

It couldn't be.

I listened again to be sure.

Oh my God, I was in the dumbwaiter!

Then I remembered. Someone had injected me with who-knows-what in Sophie's room. I couldn't recall a thing, but somehow I'd ended up in the dumbwaiter.

I passed my hands along the walls, looking for a knob or handle that would open the door. Then I remembered the only handle that could open this cubicle was on the outside of the dumbwaiter.

I felt around for the small pull I'd seen when I first discovered the dumbwaiter. It would indicate where the door was. With enough force, I might be able to push it open. I found it and pushed with both hands. The door didn't budge. I tried again. Useless.

My eyes were getting accustomed to the dark. I detected a grilled panel that allowed for air circulation in one of the walls. I wondered how much air was in the shaft. Small spaces triggered claustrophobia. Small spaces with a lack of oxygen doubled the chances of my having a panic attack. If I didn't get out of here soon, it would surely be my coffin.

I banged on the door and started shouting. "Help! Get me out of here! Help!"

I stopped. Who would hear me? I was in a dumbwaiter tucked in a niche at the far end of a corridor that had little to no pedestrian traffic.

I had to stay calm. Conserve oxygen. Someone will come.

Sophie. Yes, Sophie will bring help. She was in the bathroom when they took me. Oh no, did they take her too?

I closed my eyes and tried to slow down my breathing. If I fell asleep, I could conserve oxygen—or die in the process.

No, I mustn't go there. I had to stay awake and think positive thoughts.

It must be almost morning by now. Charlie or one of the kitchen staff would head for the pantry to get supplies. The pantry was ten feet away from me. A short distance. I could bang on the dumbwaiter and call out to them.

On second thought, would I be able to hear their footsteps through the metal walls of the dumbwaiter? Would they be able to hear me banging and calling out?

The droning sound was still there. Was it getting louder or was my mind playing tricks on me?

The dumbwaiter jerked. The car was descending!

How was it possible? There was no electricity in the building, unless someone had a separate source of power. Like a generator. No wonder the up and down buttons on the wall outside the dumbwaiter hadn't functioned. Someone had cut off the wiring to them and bypassed the system.

The dumbwaiter rocked its way down, making a high-pitched screeching noise that sounded like a woman's wail. It explained the rumors about students hearing ghosts howling in the echo.

The car was picking up speed. I had to be prepared for whatever awaited me when it would come to a stop. I took off my mittens and checked my coat pockets. My keys, flashlight, and scissors were still there. I shoved the mittens back in my pockets to hold the other items in place.

I thought about my mortality. If I didn't survive this ordeal, would anyone ever find me?

I couldn't see my watch, but I estimated that ten minutes had passed before the dumbwaiter slowed down.

The car came to a shuddering stop and landed hard. I heard the sound of metal against metal. A door opened on my left. A strong arm yanked me out and I tumbled to the ground, landing face first on a dirt floor.

I wiped the filth from my eyes and mouth, aware that I was now in a damp and low-lit area. I didn't have time to focus on my surroundings before someone injected a syringe into my neck, plunging me into total darkness once more.

I felt groggy and squinted through heavy eyelids. The floor was cold and damp. I was facing a cement wall, hands tied behind my back. At least I wasn't cramped in a small space anymore.

A shockwave flowed through me as I remembered the downward trip in the dumbwaiter and my arrival here. I didn't know how long I'd lost consciousness this time, but it was hard to come out of it. My thinking was fuzzy. Whatever drug had been in that syringe was potent stuff.

Two men were talking nearby, but a droning noise prevented me from hearing most of their conversation. I kept my eyes shut and didn't dare move. I focused on the discussion between the men. I had to figure out what was going on.

"That was your first mistake...what the hell...now two more

captives," one of the men said, then coughed.

His voice had a mature and authoritative tone, but I didn't recognize it. I doubted it was Favreau. The ex-con had a distinctive French-Canadian accent. If only that droning noise would stop, I'd be able to hear what they were saying.

"You told me you were confident I could run this operation on my own." Louder than the other voice, this one belonged to a younger man and was somewhat familiar.

"That was long before you created this bloody mess," the older man said, raising his voice.

"I can take care of it," the younger man said.

"I don't know about that. Your track record leaves a lot to be desired."

"No one's perfect."

"You can't afford to make any more mistakes. You hear me?"

"They weren't mistakes. I had to get rid of them. I took appropriate decisions to protect the operation and handled it as best I could."

The older man chuckled. "You're more coldblooded than I expected. You even surprised Sammy and he's a pro." He coughed. "This place is bad for my asthma."

"You didn't have to come here." The younger man's voice reflected annoyance.

"I was due for a visit. It's been awhile. Besides, it's not as if I walked here. I got Sammy to put chains on the tires so we could drive over. The path was clear of fallen trees. We were lucky."

The younger man remained quiet.

"What's the status on the last order?" the older man asked.

A shuffling of papers. "These are the numbers. My chemist buddies finished production and packaging. The load is ready for delivery."

"Good. We haven't missed any of the angels' deadlines yet. Make sure you stay on top of it."

My pulse picked up speed. Was he referring to the Hells Angels? If so, the end product had to be ecstasy or another drug.

The older man cleared his throat. "Remember what I told you.

Take care of the nosy reporter first, then do the little lady."

I stifled a gasp.

"I'll be at the cabin if you need me. Keep in touch." Footsteps thudded against the ground and stopped when the older man opened a door on the right. He let it slam hard behind him.

Another door clicked open, this time on the left.

A guttural voice said, "We've got the E batch ready for delivery. Wanna check it later?"

"No, Stu. I'll do it now."

More footsteps sounded and the door slammed shut, then silence.

I opened my eyes and craned my neck to look around. I was alone in the corner of a room that measured about thirty feet across by twenty feet deep. Makeshift walls of cement encircled me. The droning noise was coming from a ventilation system of pipes along the walls. A card table and a wood chair sat across the room from me.

I realized I'd been holding my breath all this time. I exhaled. Terror swept over me as I came to grips with the desperate situation. I'd soon discover the identity of the ruthless killer at Verdell. As much as it intrigued me, I knew I couldn't dwell on the subject. If I didn't want to end up on my captor's hit list, I didn't have a second to waste.

I assumed the steel door on the left led to a secret drug lab. The steel door on the right seemed like a better option.

I tried to get up but made the dreadful discovery that I couldn't. My feet were bound, probably with a zip tie handcuff made of sturdy nylon material like the one around my hands.

I remembered the pair of scissors in my coat pocket. It would be futile to try to retrieve them now, what with those men in the next room. I'd have to wait for a better opportunity.

I stared at the wall and thought about Michael. Where was he? And how were they planning to "take care of" us?

I heard the door on the left click open.

"You and Rob can grab a bite to eat after you make the delivery," the same young man said.

"There's lots of of food in the next room," Stu said. "It'll only take a minute. Me and Rob, we can make us a tuna sandwich to go."

"No time. The angels are expecting delivery by six o'clock. You have to meet their deadline."

"The tunnel ain't no superhighway. What if the wagon don't give us enough battery power to get to the warehouse?"

The young man lost his temper. "Look, I don't give a damn if you have to walk there. Do it ASAP."

It was then that I recognized the young man's voice. The way he pronounced ASAP as a word instead of spelling out the letters.

It was Zack!

CHAPTER 24

Verdell's golden boy had triggered an *aha* moment. The pieces of information Michael and I had gathered over the past week fell into place and offered a startling picture.

The mysterious deaths of Nat and Andrew. The Shakespeare evidence that incriminated Dave. The video of the car driving into the forest. It all made sense now. Zack had masterminded everything. Whether he'd used his minions to carry out the deadly deeds had yet to be determined, but it didn't matter in the end.

He'd used his supervisory status at the school—and Helga's keys to the dorms—to get into Nat's room and send the incriminating email to Dave from her computer.

On second thought, maybe Helga was in on it and had lied about how her keys had gone missing to cover her involvement. After all, she despised Nat. I'd heard her say so. But how far would she go to help Zack get rid of a girl she perceived as a competitor?

I thought about Greg's tumble into the well, the drugs found in his jacket, the discovery of ecstasy in Favreau's room. Zack was running a drug-manufacturing operation and supplying users at Verdell. I speculated whether Greg had told Zack he was meeting a new client that evening, namely Michael. I envisioned a scenario where he and Zack might have argued about it during the water bucket task. There could have been a struggle by the well where Zack killed Greg and dumped his body.

What about the drug distribution to the Hells Angels? How had Zack arranged for the transport of drugs to them? Stu and Rob were his minions, but were they more than delivery boys?

How could Zack have fooled so many people with his charm and wit? How could such a promising student throw away his future? To think that Mrs. Desmond and Audrey held him in such high esteem. What would they think of their callous wonder boy now?

I pondered the irony that an innocent college school would be the chosen site for a drug lab—let alone a crime scene where several students had been murdered. My thoughts flashed back to the Columbine High School massacre and other shootings that had occurred in movie theaters and shopping malls. Yes, horrid things did happen in purported safe places more often these days.

I must have dozed off. The sound of footsteps approaching caught me off guard. I glanced up to see a man wearing a full-face respirator. He peered down at me, then removed the respirator and a pair of plastic gloves.

Zack grinned at me. "Well, what do we have here? Sleeping Beauty is awake."

Stu and Rob walked into the room. They wore full-face respirators and plastic gloves too. They were carrying bins that I assumed were filled with packets of ecstasy.

Zack stepped away from me to open the door on the right for them. "Don't forget, Stu," he said. "Collect the payment before you hand over the merchandise."

"Yeah, yeah, we know the drill." Stu grunted. "If you don't trust us to do the job, maybe you should come along and babysit."

"Don't be a smart-ass. I have unfinished business to take care of here." Zack shut the door behind them and uttered, "Morons." He paused, as if to collect his thoughts.

I wished he'd leave. Then I could focus on trying to get out of here and find Michael.

Zack moved toward me, his tall black boots encrusted with dried mud. He bent over me and said, "Too bad you turned out to be even more curious than your boyfriend. We could've had a good thing going, you and me." He reached out and touched my face.

I pulled back.

"Playing hard to get, are we?"

My gaze fell on the school pins adorning his blue jacket. I counted five of them. There was a small slit where the sixth one should have been. A vague memory surfaced, but I couldn't quite grasp it.

Zack straightened up. "That's okay. I like my women feisty. It makes sex all the more interesting."

"Why did you kill Natalie?"

He exaggerated a look of surprise. "Me?"

"How could you do it? She was carrying your child."

"Such a messy problem. Being pregnant, I mean." He shook his head. "We had fun while it lasted. And then...well, I couldn't let the girl ruin my life. You know how a nosy woman can ruin a man's life, don't you, Megan?"

I thought about Michael and fought back the tears. I had to remain strong and not show the least sign of weakness in front of Zack. "Why did you kill Andrew?"

"More questions." Zack sighed. "Okay, I'll tell you why. 'He that dies pays all debts.' That line from Shakespeare's *The Tempest* explains it."

"I don't understand. What debts?"

"Everyone at Verdell knew Andrew had been selling drugs for years," he said with a smirk. "What did him in was the *doing* of it. Mustn't mix business with pleasure." He wagged a finger in the air. "Like Andrew, that other wimp Greg was selling for me. They took money from their sales to pay for their drug habits and other things. I asked for the money—politely, of course. What did those dudes do? They turned on me. They said they'd rat me out. After all I did for them." He shook his head. "Two more messy problems to take care of, but I handled it." He folded his arms and grinned.

I felt sick to my stomach. "How could you?"

He exaggerated a shrug. "Hey, they owed me money. I'm not running a charitable organization here."

"Where's Michael?"

Zack burst out laughing—a disquieting laugh that had me contemplating if he'd recently sampled the merchandise. "I knew you'd mention his name sooner or later. Don't be such a worrywart. Leave the fretting to the old dames like Mrs. Desmond. She's got years of practice on you."

"Where is he?" I shouted.

He exhaled a puff of air in annoyance. "One of my men caught him snooping around and tied him up somewhere. It won't be long before I put him out of his misery. I'll come back here and we can celebrate." He chuckled.

His comment disgusted me—as did the change in his demeanor. He'd gone from Jekyll to Hyde within hours. "Why did you kidnap me?"

"Because."

"What have you done to Sophie?"

"Nothing." He grinned. "Don't you worry, Megan. I have everything under control."

If there was one thing I learned from life so far, it was not to underestimate your adversaries—especially if they were as unstable as Zack. Now I had to worry about Sophie's safety too.

The door on the right opened and a man peeked inside. "We have a problem."

Zack turned to face him. "What is it, Stu?"

"The dude...that reporter guy. He broke free and hit Rob with a rock, then took off. I think he broke Rob's nose."

"How could he break free? Didn't you use the plastic ties?"

"We didn't have any on us. We found some rope in the dude's pocket and used it."

"Can't you morons do anything right?" Zack glared at him. "Get Rob cleaned up. Then head out with the delivery ASAP. I'll take care of the reporter."

Stu nodded and left.

Zack reached inside his jacket and pulled out a long knife. He pointed it at me. "I'm not done with you yet. Don't waste your energy calling out for help. No one can hear you scream from fifty feet underground and through concrete walls." He smirked and rushed out.

Poe's book came to mind. I recalled how Fortunato had been

buried alive behind a wall of stone and mortar. I trembled. I'd be damned if I was going to die in this concrete catacomb.

I struggled to get my hands free, but they were bound too tight. Somehow I had to reach the scissors under my mitten in the right-hand pocket.

I got on my knees for leverage, then pulled the hem of my coat toward the back in an effort to dislodge the mitten. No luck. It—and the scissors—remained wedged in my deep pocket.

I got on my back and swung my feet up on the cement wall. I arched my back in an attempt to draw out the scissors with the help of gravity. It didn't work. My mitten acted like a barrier.

I tried the next best thing. I squeezed my rear end through my clasped hold and succeeded in getting my legs through. With my clasped hands now in front of me, I pulled out my mitten. I arched my back and tried to dislodge the scissors, but the pocket was too deep.

I eyed the door on the left. If I could get inside the lab, I might find a tool I could use to cut the ties around my hands and feet. Stu and Rob had left, and from what Zack had said earlier, his chemist buddies were gone too.

Using the wall for support, I stood up. I hopped over to the door, struggling to maintain my balance and not tip over. I pushed down on the lever type handle and pulled the door open while shuffling out of the way. I looked inside.

The odor of ammonia hit me. I held the door open a few inches with my foot while I put my hands over my nose and mouth. The room was about the size of a two-car garage. Counters were loaded with glass canisters of various shapes, plastic bags, goggles, gloves, cooking utensils, plastic tubing, and trays. Containers on the ground held acetone, hydrochloric acid, and other dangerous chemicals I didn't recognize or couldn't begin to pronounce. I took note of a hi-tech tablet-making machine. Ecstasy tablets in pastel colors were scattered on the floor. The ventilation system was working, yet a film of white powder covered everything.

The door slipped out of my grip and shut with a loud click. Dread flowed over me until I remembered the room had concrete walls. I hoped they muted the sound.

I scanned the floor for a paperclip or anything sharp that I could use to pick the locking mechanism in the plastic ties. As part of my research for Michael, I'd once seen how it was done in a video clip online. It hadn't seemed that difficult. I surveyed the floor but found nothing that could help me—not even a glass shard.

I had a fleeting thought about going back into the lab. I could break an empty glass canister and use a fragment to cut the ties. Then again, why take the chance? The canister might have contained a lethal substance. Zack and his minions had worn respirators and plastic gloves. Even disturbing the film of powder on the surface of an object could have unpredictable consequences. I'd have to find another solution.

My eyes scanned the room and fell on a black coat on the back of the chair by the table. Zack was wearing his blue Verdell jacket. Did the coat on the chair belong to him or someone else?

My attention was diverted when I spotted a large nail protruding through the wall not far from the door to the lab. Perfect!

I pressed my coat pocket against it, piercing the fabric. I'd pushed a little too hard and felt a sharp pain in my thigh. I adjusted my stance and pulled the fabric across the nail with each tug.

Progress was slow. The tiny hole had only spread to half an inch, attesting to the excellent quality of the fabric. Even though I was making small gains by the minute, I sensed that time would run out any second now and the door would burst open.

And it did.

CHAPTER 25

Michael stumbled in, his hands tied behind his back. He had tiny cuts on his face and a trickle of blood ran down his left cheek.

Zack wielded his knife and followed closely behind. "Going somewhere, Megan? Ah, too bad. We were just starting to have fun." He pushed Michael. "Get over there by the wall."

Zack watched as Michael sat down, then he charged toward me. He grabbed me by the arms and dragged me along the ground to where Michael was sitting. I kept hoping he wouldn't notice that my hands were now tied in front of me. From the way he hurried to deposit me, I figured he was more concerned that Michael might take flight.

I looked at Michael. I wanted so badly to wipe the blood from his face and tend to his cuts, but again, Zack might notice my hands. Michael caught the concern in my eyes and gave me a subtle nod to indicate he was okay.

Zack aimed his knife at me and said to Michael, "I'm going to tie your feet. You make a move and she gets it." He placed the knife on the ground next to me. He took a plastic tie from his pocket and bound Michael's feet, then picked up the knife. "I have to go now. I'll deal with both of you later. Parting is such sweet sorrow." He taunted us with a condescending smile, then left.

I had high hopes for an escape plan until I heard a click in the door.

"He locked us in," Michael whispered.

"You don't have to whisper," I said. "These are concrete walls."

"They'd have to be with that noisy ventilation system," he said, motioning toward the duct with his chin.

I rubbed my sleeve against the wall to push back the cuff so I could see my watch. "It's half past six. Zack probably left to go to Verdell."

"Let's give him a few minutes in case he comes back. The guy's unpredictable—aside from being a total lunatic." He frowned. "Are you okay? How did you get here?"

I brought him up to date on my kidnapping and stressed the fact that the dumbwaiter had been functional after all.

Michael nodded. "It makes sense. A remote control flew out of Zack's belt earlier when we were having a go at each other."

"I heard his men talking about lots of food stored in another room. I wouldn't be surprised if Zack used the dumbwaiter to transport stolen supplies down here from the kitchen pantry."

"His remote must have open door and movement controls."

"He probably travels in the dumbwaiter to move between the school and this place," I said.

"Weird that he didn't use it when he left here. It means he's still around."

"How did you get caught, Michael?"

"I was checking out the forest," he said. "I saw this tall gray-haired guy get out of a Mercedes van. He disappeared through a trapdoor in the ground. I approached the door. The next thing I knew, someone clobbered me on the head and I passed out. I regained consciousness in one of the underground tunnels here and managed to escape. I ran into a passageway that turned out to be a dead end. My luck took a turn for the worse when Zack caught up to me."

"That man you saw could be the same one I heard Zack talking to. I had my face to the wall, so I wouldn't be able to identify him. He seems to be keeping an eye on Zack and his drug deliveries." I thought about our current dilemma. "You mentioned underground tunnels. Tell me there's more than one way out of here."

"I think so but this place is like a maze," Michael said. "Just before they caught me, I saw other shafts leading in different directions. When we get out of here, don't take the tunnel on the far left. It has a plate marked number 1 over the entrance."

"What do you mean, when we get out of here? I can get us out of these ties, but how do we get past a locked steel door?" I stared at him.

"Trust me, the door isn't a problem." His confidence reassured me. "What were you saying about getting us out of these handcuffs?"

I told him about the scissors in my pocket.

"The scissors won't work. These plastic ties are thick and rigid. I have a better idea. Unzip me."

"You're kidding, right?"

"Would I joke at a time like this? Unzip my jacket. I hid a Swiss army knife in the inside pocket." Michael's eyes twinkled in amusement. "About what you thought I meant? I'm fast but not that fast."

"Very funny." I leaned forward, unzipped his jacket, and dug out the Swiss army knife. It took me a while to pull out the steel pin from its tight slot. I didn't have much wiggle room to grip the pin between my fingers either. After several attempts, I inserted it in the plastic tie around Michael's hands and pushed the locking mechanism forward. The movement disengaged it from the ridges and freed him.

He took over and unlocked the tie around his feet, then unlocked the restraints around my hands and feet. "We'll hang on to these ties. They might come in handy later." He slipped them into his pocket. He handed me the Swiss army knife. "Here."

"Why don't you keep it?"

"I have a backup."

"Okay." I dropped it in my pocket and pulled out a facial tissue from the other. "Wait. Let me wipe the blood off your face."

"Don't bother," Michael said. "It'll help prove our accusations against Zack when we meet with the dean."

He had a point.

We rose to our feet to tackle the next part of our escape mission.

Michael surprised me by heading in the opposite direction.

"Where are you going?" I asked.

"There might be something useful in here." He opened the door to the lab and stepped inside.

I was right behind him. I stood in the entrance, holding the door open behind me. I watched as he perused the numerous substances in the room. "What are you looking for?"

"Something I could use to produce an explosion. I brought a lighter, in case." He put on his gloves and reached inside a cardboard box. He pulled out a metal container of acetone. "This one hasn't been opened yet." He noticed the startled look on my face and added, "I'll only use it if I have to."

Our focus shifted to the exit door. Anyone would think the steel door might present a formidable challenge, but it didn't seem to trouble Michael. He placed the can of acetone down. He pulled out another tool from his inside pocket—I assumed it was his "backup"—and worked it in the lock. Soon we heard a loud click.

He smiled. "Piece of cake."

"Zack and his men are gone, but someone else could be standing guard out there. Be careful, Michael."

"Always." He winked at me, then grabbed the container of acetone. "Let's go." He slowly opened the steel door and stuck his head out. "It's clear," he whispered. "Stay close to me."

We entered a narrow passageway that extended about forty feet. This area was ventilated too. The lighting was poor but adequate for our needs.

"We have to find the tunnel that heads north," Michael said.

If someone were to ask me in what direction I was heading, I'd be at a total loss. "We're underground. How do you know if we're going north or south or wherever? Do you have a compass?" I knew he did. I'd seen him put it in his jacket before he left the dorm.

"Zack took it."

"Great."

"It doesn't matter. I'm sure I can figure a way out of here."

Which was okay with me. His instincts had a better likelihood of getting us out of this quandary than mine.

Michael put a hand on my arm. "Megan, if we ever get separated down here, promise me you'll keep on going and not come back for me."

I gazed at him. "Why would you say that? We're in this together."

He shrugged. "You never know what could happen."

I refused to entertain the notion and said nothing more.

Up ahead was a junction where the path split into six tunnels. We approached the entrance to tunnel 2. Wood steps sloped downward another thirty feet. The tunnel had a crude rail system, wooden trusses, and ventilation equipment.

"Two of Zack's men left in a battery-operated vehicle to deliver a shipment of ecstasy to the Hells Angels," I said. "I'm sure they took this tunnel."

Michael shrugged. "Then we'll ignore it. And like I said, we'll ignore tunnel 1 on the left. It has descending steps too, but the tunnel is filled with heaps of rocks. It doesn't lead anywhere."

"There are four other tunnels on the right-hand side. Which one do we take?"

He was about to answer when a voice behind us boomed, "Where the hell do you think you're going?"

I froze. I hadn't expected Zack to pop up.

Michael shouted, "Megan, run!"

CHAPTER 26

Adrenaline pumped through my body.

I didn't give Michael's command a second thought. I bolted for the entrance to the nearest tunnel—tunnel 3—and ran for my life.

Everything seemed to move in slow motion. I glanced back and saw Michael swing the canister of acetone at Zack. I heard Zack's groan as it hit him. I saw Zack retaliate against Michael's attack. The punches flew but I didn't dare look back again.

I ran.

I kept on running through the earthen tunnel. Only one thought kept playing in my mind: If I could get out of here and get help, this nightmare would soon be over.

I had no idea how far I'd run before I started gasping for air and had to stop. I looked over my shoulder. The opening to the tunnel had all but disappeared. I couldn't see or hear the men.

Guilt set in. How could I have abandoned Michael?

Part of me wanted to turn back; the other part argued that I had to get help. More than ever, I regretted coming to Verdell. On the other hand, if Michael had come here without me and gone through this ordeal alone, I'd have regretted it all the more.

Ahead of me was darkness. I remembered my small flashlight and dug it out of my coat pocket. I clicked it on and moved forward again, albeit at a slower pace. I directed the beam in a semi-circle from one side of the tunnel to the other. No ventilation pipes. I took it as a sign the tunnel was short. The exit had to be close by.

The ground was strewn with rocks of different sizes. It would be so easy to twist my ankle. I took extra care in surveying the path in front of me and plodded along for five more minutes until I had to stop. I was out of breath. Was I climbing uphill?

I waved the flashlight around. I aimed the beam at the ceiling. It was lower than I thought. Was the tunnel closing in on me?

I stretched my arm upward and could touch the ceiling. It reminded me of a scene in *Alice in Wonderland* where Alice grows to enormous size and has a hard time standing upright in a shrinking room. This certainly wasn't Wonderland, though anyone taking ecstasy might think it was.

I took a few more steps and had to bend my head to avoid hitting the jagged surface above me. The ceiling was dropping, and despite my precautions, my head scraped against protrusions twice. Good thing I'd kept my wool hat on. It cushioned the blows somewhat. I put on my mittens and used my left hand to detect the ceiling extensions instead.

Having to take these extra safeguards slowed me down. I hoped the opening to the outdoors was nearby. It had to be. The air was so cold that my face felt frozen, let alone my fingers inside the mittens.

I heard a melodic chime in the distance—like a cell phone ringing.

Was someone nearby?

I aimed my flashlight in a wide circle. No one.

Had the ringing stopped?

I strained to hear it. Yes, it was still ringing—a sign that the power had been restored. How wonderful!

I increased my pace. The ringing was getting louder.

Then it stopped.

I kept on moving, using my left hand as a guide along the ceiling. I glanced up from time to time anyway to make sure I didn't run into any sharp bulges. A cracked skull wasn't something I needed right now.

I should have been looking down but wasn't. I tripped over something bulky—a mound that had the foulest smell. I jerked back, thinking it was a dead animal.

My flashlight had flown out of my grasp, so I bent over to fetch it. I picked it up and aimed the beam at the object I'd tripped over.

Bulging eyes in a bloated face stared back at me. It was a man!

I screamed and stumbled backwards, clutching the tunnel wall for support.

I wanted to run away, but a spark of curiosity kept me rooted to the spot. I had to know who the man was.

I trembled as I edged closer to the body. I was so much braver when Michael was around.

I directed the beam at the man's face. It was Pierre Favreau!

Oh God, no!

I turned away.

Breathe, I told myself. Stay calm. Stay focused.

I forced myself to take a closer look at Favreau. Damn if I was going to check him for a pulse. He looked as dead as anyone would with a circular wire cutting deep into his bloodstained neck.

How ironic that everyone at Verdell thought he'd gone into town for groceries Friday morning. No wonder no one had seen Favreau leave. He was still on campus—in a way.

Did Zack know Favreau had been murdered? Did he even know Favreau's body was in this tunnel?

My mind wandered to the events of last summer when Faveau had murdered my client Gary Stilt and stolen his Prada portfolio containing thousands of dollars. Favreau was a Hells Angels drug dealer, yet someone with the right connections had referred him to Verdell for the kitchen job—someone whom Mrs. Desmond considered in high regard.

Zack?

I doubted it. The golden boy was a full-time student. How would he have had the time to set up a drug-manufacturing operation, let alone come into contact with notorious criminals? A benefactor must have bankrolled the operation, negotiated deals with the Hell Angels, and handled distribution details.

That mysterious "coughing" visitor who lived in a cabin sounded as if he knew a thing or two about the underground setup at Verdell. Since Zack reported to him, the older man must be higher up in the echelon. Michael and I would have to search out that cabin—once we escaped from here.

The notion that law enforcement officers might be "in" on the drug operation at Verdell crossed my mind. Closing an eye to illegal activities did happen among our men in blue, especially when there were lucrative bribes to be collected. It might explain why the police had arrived to take Dave to the station for questioning instead of hunting for the real killer.

Planted evidence at a crime scene—in this case, the torn page from the Shakespeare book with Dave's blood sprinkled on it—had a tendency to speed things up too. Who else but Zack could have torn the page out and plastered it over Nat's mouth?

Now Favreau's body had been dumped here.

I tried to connect the dots.

Favreau's impromptu demise had to be linked to the drug operation Zack was running under Verdell. The packets of drugs we'd found in Favreau's bedroom, though circumstantial, inferred as much. If Favreau had been working for the Hells Angels, why would Zack—or the coughing man—want to eliminate him? Weren't they playing on the same team? I had to assume there had been a falling out between them—something to do with money. It was always about the money.

Whether Favreau had played a direct role in killing Nat and Andrew had yet to be determined.

Nat.

Andrew.

Pierre.

N. A. P.

I recalled Greg's diagram. The boy had drawn a sketch of a cemetery plot and written the victims' first initials on it. It made sense now.

My mind went off on a tangent and evoked Zack's comment about how a nosy woman can ruin a man's life. Was he referring to the fact I'd recognized Paul the cook as none other than Favreau the ex-con?

Zack's question during my class presentation hinted that he might have known about my dangerous adventure in Montreal.

Maybe Favreau had confided in Zack about how he'd kidnapped me last summer. Maybe he'd shared his qualms that I might have recognized him at Verdell. If I had to put myself in Zack's shoes, I'd say it was an indisputable reason for the cook's immediate removal from the premises.

I envisioned another scenario. I assumed Favreau had grown greedy over time. His weekly trips to town had offered well-timed occasions for drug deliveries to the Hells Angels. Maybe he'd demanded a bigger cut for the risks he was taking. His greed might have cut short his trips in a way he hadn't foreseen.

Whatever the reason behind his disappearance, Favreau had presented a problem for Zack and his underground operation, so he was eliminated. As Michael would say, Favreau's destiny had finally caught up to him.

The ringing started again. I traced it to a pocket in Favreau's jacket. I cringed, knowing I had to reach inside the dead man's bloodstained clothing to get to the phone.

I pulled it out. It was still ringing. I could call for help!

The ringing stopped. I tapped a few keys on the phone but the signal was weak. The screen darkened. Did it die? Some cell phones have enough juice to last for days if they're idle.

I waited, urging the phone to ring again. It didn't. I shut it to preserve the power and slipped it in my pocket, fighting off a feeling of despair.

I continued my journey. It became impossible to walk without bending over. I advanced until an increased dip in the ceiling height forced me to get down on my knees and crawl.

I used my hands and feet to push the weight of my body forward inches at a time. The rocky path soon cut through the fabric of my pants and into my skin. My wool mittens weren't faring too well either. They were getting raggedy.

Was it my imagination or had the tunnel suddenly narrowed? I dismissed it as mounting panic and kept moving. I refused to admit I'd come this far in the tunnel for nothing. I tried to think of something else—anything to allay the panic creeping up on me. There had to be an opening ahead.

My flashlight flickered. I was primed for a full-scale anxiety attack if I didn't see a glimmer of light up ahead. After all, it was morning. Even though the skies were gray, I expected to see a pale light filtering into the tunnel soon.

Something skimmed over my right hand.

I drew a quick breath. Maybe it was a mouse. Definitely not a poisonous spider. My research for a client's science project indicated there weren't any in Quebec, though Black Widow spiders had been known to hitch a ride into the country in bunches of imported fruit, like bananas or grapes.

Food. When was the last time I'd eaten? No wonder I felt faint.

Stop thinking.

Move faster.

Keep going.

A tiny ray of light should be coming through at any moment.

I choked on a bit of earth. I had to rest for a while. Just enough time to catch my breath, what little remained of it.

Okay, enough idling.

Time to go.

Not much further now.

The air was getting thinner. I was having difficulty breathing. My knees stung as if a hundred wasps had attacked them. My hands were numb from the cold.

I couldn't see well because my flashlight kept flickering. It didn't matter. I had to keep moving forward.

What creepy-crawlies was I scraping against? Did I really want to know?

I pushed on, panting for air. I felt lightheaded and wondered if anyone would ever find me if I passed out in the tunnel. Or worse, like Favreau.

I caught one last glimpse of what awaited me before the beam from my flashlight wavered and died.

It was a solid earth wall.

A dead end.

I had no choice.

I had to turn back.

CHAPTER 27

The journey back through the tunnel was faster.

Maybe it was all in my mind. Anticipation accounted for the false perception many people have—that it takes longer to arrive at a destination than to return from it.

I treaded one slow step at a time, my body bent over to avoid hitting the protrusions in the tunnel ceiling. Without a flashlight to guide me, I had to depend on my other senses. I moved along, one hand in front of me, the other feeling the way along the wall.

I was exhausted, but as the space in the tunnel opened up, I felt a sense of relief. Zack hadn't followed me into the tunnel. Then again, maybe he knew it was a dead end and was waiting for me to come out.

As for Michael, I refused to speculate that anything more dreadful had happened to him. I supposed I was in denial about having left him to face Zack alone. He was no match for Zack who was taller and stronger. If the roles had been reversed, Michael would never have abandoned me. Guilty feelings weighed me down, but hope compelled me to keep on going.

I stopped and stretched my hands upward. The ceiling was getting higher.

After I'd tripped over Favreau's body again, I knew I'd passed the halfway mark. It would be less labor-intensive from this point on. The best part was that I could stand up again without hitting my head on the ceiling. The width of the tunnel had broadened and more air was flowing in, so it was easier to breathe too.

The downside was that I was returning to an unpredictable situation. I hated not knowing what would happen next. Dealing with unpredictability was far beyond my comfort zone. The trip to Verdell had put Michael and me in the most precarious of circumstances—one involving life and death. As much as I enjoyed working with Michael on research aspects of his investigative cases, I dreaded coming out of my protective bubble and would have given anything to be sitting in my home office right now.

In the next moment, I reproached myself for being so selfish. I had to go on. For Michael. For everyone at Verdell.

I was nearing the end of the tunnel and could see the overhead lights ahead. I stepped into the junction where the tunnels met and looked around. I noticed the canister of acetone on the ground. There was a smudge of blood on it. Zack must have been too preoccupied with Michael to go back and fetch it. I picked it up.

I approached the steel door leading to the room where Zack had held Michael and me. I put my ear to the door and listened. I didn't hear a sound.

My eyes drifted to the left and down the corridor to two more steel doors I hadn't noticed earlier. I moved up to the first door and listened. Nothing. I tried the handle and opened the door.

The light in the corridor fell upon shelves of food supplies—no doubt stolen from the school pantry. In a corner, a miniature refrigerator hummed. Next to it was a grimy sink. A card table and two chairs squeezed into the remaining floor space. Paper plates and plastic utensils spilled out of a wastebasket. The room reeked of stale leftovers and empty beer bottles.

I moved on to the next door. It was locked. I placed the canister of acetone down and retrieved the Swiss army knife in my pocket. I pulled out a slender tool. After I worked the lock the way Michael had shown me, I heard a click as it gave way.

I opened the door. A vinyl desk held a laptop and a lamp. A flashlight and a pile of papers sat next to the laptop.

I stepped inside and closed the door behind me. I headed for the desk. Afraid I might knock over the lamp, I fumbled to find the flashlight instead, then clicked it on.

The papers turned out to be receipts for supplies purchased at local stores. Nothing unusual, unless one considers the purchase of acetone, distilled water, and Epsom salt in enormous quantities as normal.

The laptop on the desk was flipped open. I tried to power it on but the battery was dead. I looked at the exterior. It was adorned with a row of stickers displaying the school's basketball team insignia. Zack's laptop? Or Greg's?

I moved my search to the three sliding drawers in the desk. The top one contained pens, notepads, and a dozen Verdell flashlights. I dropped two of the latter in my pocket. Zack wouldn't miss them.

The middle drawer stored a ledger book with handwritten quantities and dollar amounts. Entries had been recorded almost daily and included deliveries to coded names in towns and cities in the province of Quebec. Too bad Favreau's cell phone wasn't working. I would have loved to snap a pic.

When I opened the bottom and deepest drawer, my heart picked up speed. Inside was a pink diary. Nat's diary. I flipped through the pages until I found the last entry. Simple words expressed joy at being a future mother and spending the rest of her life with the man she loved—Zack.

I spotted a camera in the drawer. Sophie's? I picked it up and clicked a button to turn it on. Nothing happened. I opened a tiny compartment in it. The memory card was gone.

Beneath these items was a leather portfolio. I pulled it out. On the exterior was a tiny medallion adorned with the Prada logo. I was certain the portfolio belonged to my former client, Gary Stilt. Zack had obviously taken a liking to the expensive piece. Had he stolen it from Favreau before or after he'd killed him? Or had his minions murdered Favreau for him?

I made another connection. Trenton Barratt's company was listed in Gary Stilt's marketing materials. Was the senior Barratt involved in Zack's secret drug operation too? Or did Zack manage it alone, trying to prove his business acumen to a demanding father?

Frustrated by questions that had no immediate answers, I returned the items to their former location and shut the drawer.

I'd found incriminating pieces of evidence that were useless if I couldn't get them to the police. On second thought, I had no intention of interfering with evidence that law enforcement would appreciate seizing and scrutinizing.

Too late I realized I'd left my fingerprints on the items, but I had more imminent problems. I assumed Zack had left to make an appearance at Verdell for one reason or another and would be back soon. I had to find Michael and get us out of this hellhole before the golden boy returned. It was the ultimate challenge, since we had no foolproof escape plan.

Moments after I'd stepped out of Zack's so-called office, I heard a thumping noise from one of the tunnels, like people climbing stairs. Stu and Rob were back!

I swirled around and looked for a place to hide.

There were no more doors.

I grabbed the acetone, ran to the rear section of the junction, and squeezed into a narrow alcove in the wall. There were no overhead lights in this area. My dark coat would blend in with the surroundings.

Heavy footsteps approached.

"All I kept thinking on the way back here was the king-sized sandwich I was gonna make myself," Stu said. "With a bunch of them juicy pickles and olives. Kinda makes your mouth water, eh, Rob?" He snickered.

"We shouldn't have come back here," Rob said.

"How else are we gonna fill our stomachs?"

"That's not what I mean."

"You know what? You worry too much."

"You should be worried too. Coming back here without the dough. That spells big trouble for us."

"Zip it up." Stu lowered his voice. "I'll do the talking. Let's go see if Zack is in."

I heard a steel door click open, then close seconds later.

"Nah," Stu said. "No one's in there except that reporter dude. Zack must've drugged him again. He's out of it." He let out a deep belly laugh. "Let's go eat."

I waited until I heard the kitchen door shut behind Zack's henchmen. I hoped their conversation—and their food preparation—would keep them occupied.

I tiptoed to the next room. I opened the door as quietly as I could and peeked inside.

Michael was sitting on the ground, propped against the wall. As before, his hands and feet were bound with plastic ties. He'd been beaten again. His right eye was swollen and his lip was cut.

I was about to enter the room when a screeching sound filled the air. I recognized it as the dumbwaiter making its descent.

Zack!

I closed the door and rushed back to my hiding place in the niche. My foot tapped against an object, toppling it. The canister of acetone. I hoped no one would notice it.

Rob and Stu rushed out of the kitchen. Standing with their backs to me, the men concealed me without realizing it and discussed how they would deflect Zack's criticism.

"Remember," Stu told Rob, "don't say a word and we'll both live to see tomorrow."

"I don't know about that," Rob said. "You saw what Zack did to that French dude. The angels said Favreau was greedy and got what was coming to him." He made a rasping sound as he ran a forefinger along his neck, pretending to cut it.

"There's a whole lot of difference between him and us," Stu said. "We're not greedy."

Zack exited the other room. "There you are. So? Where's the cash?"

Stu said, "It's a long story."

"Make it short."

"We did what you said. Anyways, them angels, they said it was a misunderstanding. They didn't owe you no money."

"Who told you that?" Zack's tone was cynical.

"I think he was an accountant or something," Stu said. "I didn't get his name."

"Did he say anything else?"

"Yes. He said you're squared off, since you kept the money from the Montreal investment deal last summer."

Zack remained silent.

I would have given anything to see the expression on golden boy's face, but I suppressed the urge to peep.

"He's nuts," Zack blurted. "He's confusing me with someone else."

"I don't think so. He called you by name. Barratt."

Zack paused for a second time. "He's a bloody liar. Go back ASAP and tell him if we don't get payment, he gets no more rush deliveries."

Stu and Rob exchanged glances.

"If we go back beggin' for cash, he's gonna kill us," Stu said.

"I'll kill you both if you don't do as I say," Zack said. "Now move."

"It's a miracle we made it back here," Stu said. "We left the wagon in the tunnel a ways back. The battery's dead."

"Then recharge it. Get going!"

A door slammed.

Stu whispered to Rob, "This is our ticket outta here. I'd rather do time again than work here. They feed us better in jail anyways."

"What about chargin' the battery?" Rob asked.

"You wanna go back and tell the angels they have to pay up?"

"You crazy? We'd be dead meat in a minute."

"That's why we're hightailin' it outta here. I don't know where the other tunnels lead except for the one with the wagon. We'll walk to the warehouse. Make our way to town from there. You with me?"

Rob mumbled in agreement.

There was a rapid movement of feet. I stuck my head out and watched as the two men disappeared into the tunnel.

A dull grinding noise reverberated through the wall. Zack was heading up to Verdell in the dumbwaiter.

I rushed to the steel door and swung it open. Michael was still unconscious.

This time I was ready. I dug out the Swiss Army knife. My hand was shaking. I kept it as steady as I could and worked the locks in the plastic ties. Within seconds, Michael was free.

But the worst wasn't over yet. How was I going to get him out of here? I couldn't carry him.

Then I remembered my lip gloss. I'd once read how a whiff of peppermint oil could bring a person out of a fainting spell. My lip gloss contained peppermint oil, albeit not much, and Michael hadn't fainted—he'd been drugged.

It was worth a try. I took the tube from my pocket, uncapped it, and waved it under Michael's nose.

He groaned and opened his eyes. "Megan?"

"Yes, I'm here. Do you think you can stand up?"

"Huh?" He stared at his feet. "Maybe."

I tucked my shoulder under his and helped him up. His legs gave way and almost caused me to collapse under his weight. I helped him up again and we shuffled to the steel door.

I propped him against the wall while I tried the door. It wasn't locked. Either Zack had forgotten to lock it or he assumed Michael would be knocked out until he returned.

We hobbled out into the corridor.

"Let's walk around a bit," I said. "You're still woozy."

We moved up and down the corridor a few times. Michael gained more control with every step he took.

"I think I can take it from here," he said.

I slipped my shoulder out from under his. "How are you feeling?" I didn't want to mention how battered he looked.

"Not bad, except for where Zack plunged a needle into me." He rubbed the side of his neck. "And that was after he came at me like a bear and punched me in the eye."

"I heard him leave in the dumbwaiter."

"Yeah, the dumbwaiter. Your instincts were right."

"I'm not surprised. I learned from the best." I smiled at him, then took a flashlight from my pocket. "Here. I found a supply in Zack's makeshift office over there." I pointed to the door. "I found souvenirs too. Sophie's diary and Greg's laptop. At least I think it was Greg's. I also found my client's Prada portfolio—the one Favreau stole from my client after he killed him."

"You're kidding." Michael smiled. "Megan, you're surprising me more every day."

"You don't know the half of it." I held back from sharing my adventure in the tunnel with him. There would be time for reminiscing about that ordeal later. "By the way, there's a kitchen behind the other door." I motioned toward it. "We should grab some water before we leave."

We pocketed two bottles of water and fruit bars, then rushed out to the junction of tunnels.

I gazed ahead. "I saw Zack's minions leave through tunnel 2. And you said tunnel 1 was a dead end. Which of the other tunnels leads out of here?"

"Let me see." He pulled out a piece of paper from his inside pocket. "I drew this map earlier. It's a guestimate of old tunnels under the school."

"How did you get that information?"

"I researched abandoned tunnels the first day we arrived here. Remember?"

"Oh...right. The first night you spent alone in your dorm room."

Michael nodded. "Before I left last night to check out the forest, I drew this sketch from memory." He showed me his diagram.

"There are four tunnels in your sketch," I said. "There are six down here."

"I know." He put away the paper.

"We can eliminate tunnels 1, 2, and 3."

"Three?"

"Yes, it's a dead end too. It also happens to be the impromptu burial site for Pierre Favreau." I recapped my trip in the tunnel, including the fact I had Favreau's cell phone in my pocket.

Concern filled his eyes and he held me tightly. "Megan, I'm so sorry you had to go through this alone."

Michael's compassion washed over me. I struggled to hold back feelings of self-pity that threatened to explode and took a deep breath instead. "I'm okay. What do we do now?"

He approached tunnels 4, 5, and 6 and aimed the beam from his flashlight inside each entrance. "Tunnel 4 has no ventilation system. It's probably one of the original tunnels. Tunnels 5 and 6 are level—not steep like the others. They're our best choices."

"How do you know they're not dead ends?" I asked.

"There's ventilation ductwork in them. I have to assume they were built recently."

"How recently?"

"In the last three years or so."

Dread flowed through me as I pondered the most rational solution. "Let's split up. You take tunnel 5 and I'll take tunnel 6. There's a chance one of us will make it out of here."

CHAPTER 28

Michael put up a predictable resistance. "There's no damn way I'm going to let you plod alone through another tunnel again. We don't know what's waiting for us at the other end."

After I appealed to his logic and stressed our time constraints, he gave in. I won the argument, although I wouldn't call treading through a tunnel inhabited by creepy-crawlies a victory. Or worse: a tunnel that might not have an exit.

"There's something I need to tell you before we go, Michael." A lump formed in my throat. "Whatever happens, I want you to know the only reason I hesitated to come to Verdell was because I'd planned a romantic getaway for us this weekend. A special time when we could be alone and do fun stuff together. When we could talk about other things we wanted to do and places we wanted to visit. But I had to put my plans on hold. And now, I don't know what's going to happen to us. I'm so scared because I love you so much." The tears flowed and I couldn't stop them.

Michael wrapped his arms around me and whispered, "You know I can't live without you, Megan." He kissed me, stirring the butterflies inside until I felt as if I were taking flight with them. "Don't cry. We'll make it out of here. You'll see. And we'll have that weekend together."

"Promise?" I wiped away the tears.

"I promise." Michael kissed me one last time.

I watched as he took off down tunnel 5, the container of acetone in his hand.

I inhaled a deep breath of air before entering tunnel 6. I told myself this tunnel would be different. The walls wouldn't close in on me. I wouldn't have to crawl over rocks and insects through a suffocating space, only to find out that...

No, I refused to go there. I blanked it out of my mind.

I moved along at a steady pace to conserve energy, glancing over my shoulder from time to time. I had an eerie feeling that Zack might come up behind me at any moment. Had he gone to check on Sophie? What horrific plan did he have in mind for that poor girl?

The thought of it spurred me on and I sped up.

I aimed my flashlight at the ground to make sure I wouldn't step on anything that might happen across my path, like scorpions or snakes. Who knew what else lurked in these depths?

There was something different about the ground in this tunnel, though. It was more level and less rocky, which established Michael's claim that the excavation was more recent.

Five minutes had gone by but it felt longer. Once in a while, I aimed the beam further ahead in the hope of seeing an opening. I did so now and couldn't believe my eyes. About twenty feet ahead, the tunnel split off in three directions. Three separate passageways.

Oh, hell. Now what?

If there was ever a time when I needed to rely on Michael's instincts, it was now.

I felt tears well up and blinked them away. I refused to feel sorry for myself. I had a life-and-death decision to make. The wrong decision could kill me.

What would Michael do in this situation?

He'd use his senses to guide him, of course.

I approached each entrance to the three paths. I took a few steps inside each one and looked, listened, and sniffed. They were all the same. Each path was rocky, not a sound emanated from any of them, and the odor was damp. Nothing in particular stood out, except for a tiny glint in the tunnel on the left—maybe something reflecting off a piece of metallic rock under the beam of my flashlight.

For no other reason, I chose that path.

I continued along, calculating what the odds were that Zack might follow me into this same tunnel. One out of three? About a thirty percent chance?

I laughed out loud and relaxed a little.

Seconds later I heard a sound above me.

What was that? A bird?

Impossible. Birds don't live in abandoned mines fifty feet below ground.

Clicking sounds.

Crickets?

A beam aimed at the ceiling revealed the source.

Bats in hibernation. Hundreds—maybe thousands—of them bunched on the ceiling and walls.

I lowered my flashlight. I'd once read that bats used a built-in system called echolocation to obtain information about their surroundings. It enabled them to navigate through deep caves in total darkness. They could die if they're accidentally awakened during hibernation.

I hurried away, not wanting to disturb them. If anything, I wanted to avoid getting their stinky droppings on me.

The bats' presence was a positive sign. If these winged creatures found a way to get in, they also had a way to get out. The exit couldn't be too far off.

I was feeling confident about the journey until my flashlight revealed another split up ahead. Michael was right. These underground tunnels formed a veritable maze that could ensnare anyone.

Should I continue along the same path or deviate to this new passageway on the left?

I reached for my bottle of water and took a few sips. After a sleepless night, fatigue was setting in and I was too tired to think.

I looked to the bats for an answer. They'd entered through one or maybe both of these pathways. They'd found a comfort zone that provided safety. They'd also found a cool—but not freezing—environment for hibernation and lots of insects for food. I didn't hear any flapping of wings, which meant they hadn't moved and no doubt wouldn't leave here until spring. They couldn't possibly show me the way out at this point.

The ground was smoother, less rocky, on the path to my left. A sign that it was new or had been used often. Another good sign. I chose it.

I quickened my pace. I was on the final lap of my journey, the homestretch.

I was also out of breath. I stopped. I needed to rest.

Okay. Time to move on.

I shone my flashlight up ahead. I was on the verge of exhaustion, but there it was. A ramp leading up to a wood staircase that would take me to freedom.

With renewed energy, I climbed upward, taking one careful step at a time. Though muddied, the wood planks looked sturdy. The staircase extended about forty feet high.

I'd almost reached the top when I glanced up. A slit in the trapdoor allowed a narrow sliver of light to filter in. I was getting closer to the outside!

Elated, I bounded up the remaining steps.

I waited and listened.

I expected to hear the sound of freezing rain or falling ice hitting the ground, but it was quiet. Was the ice storm finally over?

I slid the flashlight into my pocket and used both hands to push open the trapdoor. It lifted with ease.

I peeked out.

I was in someone's basement!

CHAPTER 29

Cardboard boxes and random pieces of old furniture littered the cement floor—proof that I had indeed entered someone's home.

I tiptoed to the only window in the basement. It was out of reach and had bars on it. I'd need a ladder to reach it. Outside an overcast sky formed the backdrop to soaring ice-laden trees, which meant the home was located in the forest bordering Verdell.

Rather than feeling elated that help might be close at hand, I felt confused and apprehensive. If the house was located on land that belonged to Trenton Barratt, was this his home?

I waved my flashlight around. The basement measured about forty feet by fifty feet. The walls were insulated, so living here would be comfortable all year long. A wood staircase along the far wall led to the main floor. Judging from the numerous cracks in the foundation, the house had probably been built decades ago. Maybe a caretaker lived here.

Aside from a droning sound—possibly a generator outdoors—the house was still. It could be deceiving. Someone might be reading a book or taking a nap upstairs.

I had to rest for a while and think about my next move. I hadn't slept all night and I was hungry. I sat under the staircase on a pile of flattened cardboard boxes. A handful of tall rolled-up carpets stood guard around me. If anyone came down the stairs or through the trapdoor, they wouldn't be able to see me unless they came up close.

I dug out my breakfast—a snack bar and bottle of water—and feasted. The shag rug behind me provided a certain degree of comfort and warmth. It was the coziest I'd felt in days. My eyelids were getting heavy, closing...

A sudden noise startled me.

Someone lifted the trapdoor. I saw the beam from a flashlight. It clicked off and a familiar face surfaced.

Zack rushed across the floor to the staircase. He didn't even look my way but pounded up the stairs and slammed the door behind him.

A dog barked upstairs. A big dog. A man uttered a command and the dog fell silent.

I left my hiding place. I had to find out why Zack was here.

Since a dog's ears are sensitive to sound, I hoped the steps wouldn't creak and give me away. I tested each step by placing the weight of one foot on it, then the other.

A muted conversation drifted my way. I mounted three more steps to hear better but stopped when I noticed shadows beneath the doorframe.

Zack was speaking with another man on the other side of the door.

"How the hell did he escape?" the man asked.

"I don't know," Zack said. "I'd given him a shot and properly secured him. He was unconscious when I left him. I think Megan—his girlfriend—came back for him."

"She knows too?"

"Yes."

"Did anyone see you at Verdell?" The man's voice sounded familiar.

"No, I was careful," Zack said. "Mrs. Desmond was with Michael in her old office. I listened from outside the door. I overheard him telling her about me and the underground drug operation."

"What did the old dame say?"

"Not much. She seemed interested in what he was saying, though."

"He'll want to show her and the entire police force where the tunnels are located."

"She injured her leg and is on crutches. She won't go outdoors in this weather. And the power is still out. No one can reach the cops."

The other man coughed.

I recognized him. He was the same man who'd visited Zack in the underground lab earlier.

"Was Megan with him?" the man asked.

"No," Zack said. "There's no trace of her anywhere."

"She could be lost in one of the passageways. Otherwise she'd be with her reporter friend."

"What if she made it out?"

"I doubt it. Even if she did, how would she call for help or get to town?" The man paused. "You waited too long."

"I had no time. I had to show up at Verdell this morning. My absence would have raised suspicions."

The man spoke louder. "I don't want to hear any excuses. What about the ecstasy delivery? Do you have the payment?"

"No," Zack said. "There was a complication."

"Explain yourself."

"The angels refused to pay. They said they held back payment because I kept the money from the Montreal investment deal last summer. I don't know what the hell they're talking about. Do you?"

Silence hung in the air between them.

I could hear my heart thumping in my chest while I waited for the man's reply.

"Answer me," Zack shouted. "Do you know anything about that money, dammit?" He slapped a hand against the door.

I jumped and grabbed onto the railing to steady myself on the steps. I was afraid the dog might have heard my gasp. It hadn't. Maybe it had trotted off elsewhere in the house.

The man cleared his throat. "Yes, I know about the Montreal incident. I hired Favreau to put a hit on an investment dealer named Gary Stilt. He'd sunk his grubby hands into the pot once too often."

"I don't get it," Zack said. "What does this guy Stilt have to do with the Hell Angels?"

"Stilt handled investments for the angels but he got greedy. He decided he deserved more than his usual commission and started to skim off the top. Favreau and a cellmate had escaped from jail and were hiding out in Montreal. With the angels' blessing, I gave Favreau the order to get rid of Stilt and to bring his portfolio and the money back to me."

"The Prada portfolio? The one you gave me?"

"A small token of my appreciation."

Zack paused. "You never did tell me how Favreau made your hit list."

"Favreau." The man grunted. "Always threatening to blackmail me for a larger cut. Another pig at the trough. When he told me the reporter's girlfriend had recognized him, I knew he had to disappear."

"So Sammy handled it."

"My big brother's always been there for me. It pays to keep the business in the family. You can always trust family."

"Stu and Rob think I killed Favreau."

"I asked Sammy to spread the rumor. It'll keep those two small-time punks in line. Since we agreed you shouldn't tell anyone about the three students you wasted, they needed a reason to respect you."

Zack remained quiet. He probably didn't want to divulge the brazenness Stu and Rob had demonstrated when he'd asked them to go back and get the payment from the Hells Angels. Little did he know the two ex-jailbirds had already flown the coop.

The man coughed. "Don't worry about the payment from the angels. I'll work out an arrangement with them. I'm doing more than my fair share supervising the other underground labs in their network."

"It doesn't solve my immediate problem. What about Mrs. Desmond?"

"Here's what you're going to do. Go back to Verdell. Act as if nothing happened. Visit the old dame. If she questions you in front of Michael, play the game. You know how protective she is of Verdell."

"Yes. Like a lioness with her cubs."

"I'll ask Sammy to get rid of the reporter and his girlfriend right now—before they start blabbing to the cops. Unless you want to take care of it yourself. You think you can handle it?"

"Trust me. I can handle it."

I slid into my hiding place moments before Zack pounded down the stairs. He whizzed by, the back of his black coat smudged with dirt—maybe bat droppings. He was so eager to clear his name and discredit Michael's story that he didn't so much as glance around the basement before exiting through the trapdoor in the floor.

I let out a deep breath.

Michael had succeeded in making it out of tunnel 5 and was now safe at Verdell. Good news.

The bad news: I had no choice but to retrace my steps and take tunnel 5 to join him there.

The horrific news: Michael and I were now on Sammy's hit list too.

I waited a minute to give Zack a head start. The last thing I wanted was to die at his hands in a bat-infested tunnel.

As I stood up, I knocked over one of the rugs. It landed with a loud thud.

I didn't think anything of it until I heard the dog bark. It scratched its paws against the basement door upstairs and kept on barking.

I heard the man's voice. Was he going to open the door and let the dog into the basement?

Oh God, no!

CHAPTER 30

I ran to the trapdoor. I flung it open and let it slam it shut. To hell with the noise.

Then I realized my mistake. What if the owner opened the trapdoor and sent the dog chasing after me?

I slid down the first steps in my panic to escape and grabbed the rail to break my fall. I dug out my flashlight, clicked it on, and hurried down the rest of the staircase.

Hitting the ground, I checked the path before me for stones and ran as fast as I could.

Check and run. Check and run. The routine forced me to tap into physical energy I didn't think I had and I urged myself on.

I heard a noise behind me. Was it the dog? The coughing man?

I swerved around and aimed my flashlight. Assured that no animal or human was on my tail, I slowed down to a brisk walk and caught my breath.

Soon I heard the clicking sound of bats and anticipated their presence. I lowered my flashlight and reduced my speed as I moved past them, then sped up once I'd cleared their resting place.

The light at the juncture of the underground tunnels boosted my spirits, but I remained cautious about the potential danger in the area. I slowed down and stayed within the shadows of the wall in case Zack lurked nearby.

I tiptoed to the edge of the tunnel and peered out. No sign of him or anyone else. No grating sound from the dumbwaiter either. One way or another, Zack must have gone back to Verdell.

I raced into tunnel 5 and darted off.

The journey through this tunnel was much shorter than I'd anticipated. The steps leading to the outside were steep but manageable. With immense relief, I pushed open the trapdoor.

The ice storm was over. The sky was a dull gray, but the wind had died and the drizzle had stopped. I scanned the forest for the coughing man's cabin but didn't see it. It was either well hidden behind a bunch of evergreens or further away than I'd estimated, which meant the river behind the forest was further still.

I looked up. Long spikes of ice dangled from towering tree branches and threatened to fall at any moment. I steered clear and walked along the path between the trees, taking care to avoid shards of ice scattered on the ground.

My thoughts drifted to Nat and her muddy boots. She'd entered the forest along this same path to go meet Zack, the father of her child. According to Sophie, Nat was supposed to see him that evening in their secret place—the underground tunnel—to discuss their future plans. Her terror must have been vivid when she grasped the revulsion in Zack's demeanor and realized her dreadful fate. Zack had ruled a similar fate for Andrew and coordinated their deaths to look like a murder-suicide.

The trapdoor from the tunnel had facilitated the fatal deeds. I recalled Sophie's photos of the car in the forest and the man who'd dumped something heavy in the trunk. It could have been Nat's body. Or Andrew's. The boy's body had been positioned in the driver's seat later to make it look as if he'd driven the car into the river.

I contemplated the convenience of the intruder's access to Nat's dorm room. Once before, I'd questioned Helga's claim that her keys had gone missing. What if she'd lied? What if Helga was working with Zack? What if she'd lent Zack her keys? Better yet, what if *Helga* had entered Nat's room to steal her diary and send Dave the incriminating email?

How lucky Michael and I were to have had Sophie on our side. She'd supplied evidence that proved crucial to our investigation into the students' deaths. What were the chances she'd overhear the intruder in Nat's room late at night when most students were asleep? Or take photos of a mysterious shaft of light in the forest that turned out to be our best clue yet? Yes, it had been pure luck.

Or had it?

What about Sophie? Could she have played a part in Zack's ploy to get rid of Nat? She could have been jealous of Nat and the attention she received from boys. Jealous that Nat had deep secrets and refused to share them with her. So jealous that she pretended to shun the spotlight, when in reality she craved it.

Strange how Sophie had withheld information from the police about the intruder in Nat's room. Convenient that she headed to the bathroom moments before I was kidnapped from her room. Odd how Zack hadn't said anything in the tunnel that threatened Sophie's welfare—I merely assumed she was in danger. Had Sophie known about Zack all along?

I thought again about the photos in the forest that Sophie had shown me. Was she having second thoughts and trying to make up for the wrong she'd done?

Zack, Helga, Sophie—each had their own reasons for wanting Nat to disappear.

A myriad of doubts sent my head spinning.

I took a deep breath and cleared all thoughts. I had to focus on my trek through the forest and across campus. A wrong footing on the icy surface could lead to big trouble, and I had trouble enough waiting for me at Verdell.

My heart soared with joy when I reached the back door to the school. I swung it open and stepped inside.

I rushed down the corridor and stopped at the door to the gymnasium. I glanced inside. The dividing wall was parted. Mattresses filled the boys' side, and a handful of mattresses were lined up in the other half of the floor. Boys and girls mingled in the empty space, many of them wearing backpacks. I didn't do a head count, but I estimated the entire student body was crammed in there.

Audrey was standing inside by the door.

I approached her. "What's happening in the gymnasium?"

She gaped at me from head to toe. "Where have you been?" She sniffed. "You look like you crawled out of a sewer and smell like it too."

"I suppose you could say that. Is Mrs. Desmond holding an assembly here?"

"No, supervisory staff and students started to move the girls and their belongings to the gymnasium."

So that's why Zack kept going back and forth back to Verdell this morning.

"One big pajama party," I said.

Audrey shook her head. "Not quite. I think we've reached a breaking point. Most of the girls have refused to move to the gymnasium. Students are threatening to leave the premises. On a positive note, it looks like the worst of the ice storm is over."

I nodded, knowing that the mother of all storms was about to hit Verdell.

"By the way, people have been looking for you," she said.

"Who?"

"Sophie early this morning. Then Michael and Zack."

"Where are they?"

"Sophie came down with the flu. We moved her to the third floor dorm with the rest of the patients. She was hysterical when she knocked at my office door this morning. She kept saying you'd been kidnapped and carried off. She was warm and sweaty and probably had a high fever. I accompanied her to the doctor's office. She insisted she didn't want to go alone."

"You said Michael was looking for me too," I reminded her.

"That's right," Audrey said. "He looked as if he'd been in an awful fistfight. What happened to him, Megan?"

I ignored her question. "When was this?"

She checked her watch. "About half an hour ago. He was looking for Mrs. Desmond. I helped him track her down."

"Where is he now?"

"In her old office. He wanted to speak with her alone, so I left to tend to other matters. I bumped into Zack on my way back to the gymnasium. He was looking for the dean and asked about you too.

What's going on, Megan?"

"It's a long story. I'll talk to you later."

I rushed down the corridor to the main building. I reached the atrium, turned right, and headed for Mrs. Desmond's office.

I entered the outer office and overheard Michael say, "Mrs. Desmond, I realize you run a tight ship here, but I wouldn't lie about something as serious as a drug-manufacturing operation. This container of acetone is one of the ingredients Zack's team uses in the production of ecstasy that he supplies to the Hells Angels."

"Good Lord!" Mrs. Desmond said. "Zack? What do you have to say about this?"

"Like I said before, he's a liar," Zack said.

"Have you looked in the mirror?" Michael asked. "Being charming and a skilled liar are traits of a psychopath. You fit the bill to a tee."

Zack laughed. "Is that the best you can do?"

"I managed to plant one on you, didn't I? Care to explain your blood on this canister? I'm having it tested for your DNA as soon as I can reach the cops."

"You never give up, do you? I have witnesses who'll vouch that I bruised my face this morning when I was helping to move stuff into the gymnasium."

"It's enough from both of you," Mrs. Desmond said, raising her voice. "I can't begin to understand the animosity between you, but it's inexcusable. Verdell isn't the place to promote verbal and physical confrontation—least of all between two grown men." She paused. "If Zack is involved in a drug-manufacturing operation as you claim, Michael, how is it no one else at Verdell knows what's going on here?"

"Because Zack is clever at covering his tracks," Michael said. "It doesn't end there. We suspect he's implicated in the murder of the three students here too."

She gasped. "Good heavens! Zack?"

"Mrs. Desmond, you've known me since I was a young teen," Zack said. "Have I ever harmed another person in all my years at Verdell?"

"Of course not," she said.

"Haven't my achievements contributed to the success of Verdell?"

"Yes, in many ways."

"Do my school records indicate I ever used or sold drugs at Verdell?"

"Why are you asking me these questions, Zack? You're an exemplary student."

It was my cue. I entered the office and said, "I can vouch for Michael. He's telling the truth."

All heads turned in my direction.

I kept my eyes on Zack. I didn't want to miss the least indication that would betray his guilt. But his expression registered as much emotion as a blank computer screen, though he did put his hands in the pockets of his blue jacket in a defensive gesture. A short-lived memory of Zack wearing a black coat in the cabin basement flashed through my mind. He'd switched coats.

"My dear, you're filthy." Mrs. Desmond gave me a measured look. "Where on earth have you been?"

"In the same maze of underground tunnels as Michael and Zack," I said.

"Me?" Zack laughed. "If I'd have played in the dirt like you and Michael did, my jacket would be filthy too." He motioned toward it. "It's clean."

"You changed coat," I said to him.

Zack turned to Mrs. Desmond. "These two are just trying to make trouble—"

"Quiet!" Mrs. Desmond scowled at him. "I want to hear what Megan has to say."

I hadn't heard the entire conversation earlier, so I winged it. "Mrs. Desmond, everything Michael told you is true. Zack operates a drug-manufacturing setup underground—"

"There's nothing like a loyal accomplice," Zack said. "Mrs. Desmond, this is clearly a joint conspiracy."

"You kidnapped Megan from the dorm, drugged her, and put her in the dumbwaiter," Michael said to him. "It transported her to the underground tunnel."

"It's true," I said.

"The dumbwaiter?" Mrs. Desmond said. "To my knowledge, it hasn't functioned in decades."

"That's correct, Mrs. Desmond," Zack said, then turned to me. "Megan, here's what I don't get." His grin told me he was about to launch a cynical comment. "I consider myself physically fit, yet I doubt I'd be able to carry you through the corridors of Verdell without attracting curiosity."

"Maybe you had help," I said. "And it was late. Not many people walk around Verdell in the middle of the night."

Zack smirked at me. "If I kidnapped you as you claim, how did you manage to escape?"

"Through a tunnel and out a trapdoor in the forest," I said.

Zack laughed. "These stories are getting better by the minute."

I looked at the dean. "Mrs. Desmond, I'd be happy to show you where it is."

Furrows formed along the woman's brow. "Megan, I'm sorry, but I will not venture outdoors in this nasty weather. My ankle is still on the mend."

Defeat had crept in. I glanced at Michael. Fists clenched, he was staring at Zack as if he wanted to pounce on him.

"Can't you send someone else?" I asked Mrs. Desmond.

Before she could answer, Audrey appeared in the doorway. "I'm sorry to interrupt, Mrs. Desmond, but we have an urgent problem in the gymnasium that requires your immediate attention. Zack might be able to help too."

Zack darted out before Mrs. Desmond could say another word.

To Audrey, the dean said, "Go back to the gymnasium. I'll join you soon." She focused on Michael and me, the furrows deepening across her forehead. "It's obvious that you've been beaten, Michael. I'm certain the police will investigate your complaint—and Megan's—as well as your suspicions about the student murders." She drew a long breath. "It shocks me to think that Zack could be involved in such horrific crimes, but I must give your claims due credence based on your journalistic ethics. As for a drug operation under Verdell, I assume the police are quite capable of finding it on their own. Now if you'll excuse me, I have work to do." She took her crutches and shuffled out.

Michael whispered to me, "She put Zack on a pedestal all his life. Now she finds it hard to see him for what he truly is: a murderer and a drug-manufacturing operator."

"I don't think he told her about the murders," I said. "But maybe she knew about the drug operation and was protecting him all along."

He nodded. "She could be getting a cut of the profits. Talk about padding your pockets."

"Now that you mention it..." I briefed Michael on how my trip through the tunnel had led to the coughing man's cabin in the forest. I mentioned how the older man had a direct connection to the Hells Angels, how he'd instructed Zack to kill us before we talked to the police, or else Sammy would. Although I hadn't seen the man, I told Michael about my suspicions regarding his identity.

Michael's eyes went wide. "Megan, you just uncovered the top brass behind Zack's secret setup, if not the whole drug network in the area." Worry tightened his expression. "Stick close. Zack is feeling threatened right now. He'll be looking for the next chance to get rid of us. One at a time."

CHAPTER 31

Michael and I returned to our dorm room. We washed up as best we could, considering we had no access to running water—only what little remained of two bottles of water we'd left under the sink in the bathroom. It wasn't until I'd looked in the mirror that I understood what the remarks had been about. My face was smeared with blotches of dried dirt. I used a damp facecloth to clean it, then wiped the spots of filth off my coat. I threw away my old torn pants and slipped into an extra pair of jeans I'd packed.

Dave's laptop had gone missing in our absence, which wasn't a surprise. We assumed Zack had added it to his trophy collection in the tunnel. Luckily, Michael had kept the flash drive containing the school video and other pertinent information safe in his jacket pocket.

As we hurried to pack up our belongings, I brought Michael up to date on how Zack had switched coats. "I kept wondering how he could have traveled through the same bat-infested tunnel as me and not stink. I caught on when I saw him in the cabin wearing a black coat and then a blue jacket in Mrs. Desmond's office."

"He's cunning," Michael said. "I'll give him that much. Too bad I didn't check out more of the forest earlier. I might have discovered the cabin."

"If you had, they would have killed you on the spot. Or let the dog loose on you."

He shrugged. "Danger comes with the job."

I stared at him. "I'd rather it didn't." I contemplated what Zack or Sammy might have in store for us and started to shake. I was losing it.

Michael noticed and held me close. "I'm so sorry, Megan. You can't imagine how much I regret having dragged you into this mess."

His words couldn't calm my apprehension. "We've seen what Zack is capable of. We were lucky to have escaped from the tunnel, but we're not safe—not even here at Verdell."

He kissed me on the forehead. "I'll keep you safe, I promise." He dug out his key to the room. "We're done here. Let's bring our bags downstairs."

"I want to go see Sophie first. I think she knows more than what she's admitting. I need to get her to talk."

"I'll go with you."

"No. Sophie won't open up to me if you're there."

Michael met my gaze. "It's not safe with Zack looking to hunt us down."

"Class is out. Students and teachers are walking around. I'll be fine."

He hesitated. "Okay. I'll carry our bags to the gymnasium. If you don't meet me there in half an hour, I'll go looking for you."

I donned a protective surgical mask and followed the nurse to the room Sophie occupied with two other patients. Three beds were lined up next to one another, with Sophie's bed by the window. There was limited space to walk between them, so I stood at the foot of her bed. I didn't know what to say but hoped my presence would shock her into admitting her involvement—or not—in my kidnapping.

She bolted up when she saw me. "Megan! You're okay. I was so worried about you."

Sophie's voice was hoarse and her comments attracted the attention of the other two girls. Covered in woolen blankets, they craned their necks to gawk at me.

I forced a laugh. "I'm fine. It was getting late and I was tired, so I left."

The two patients turned away, no doubt disillusioned that I offered nothing more interesting to say.

I looked at Sophie and put a finger to my lips.

She caught on and nodded.

"How are you feeling?" I asked.

"Groggy. They gave me something for the fever." She wiggled forward on the bed and waved me toward her. She whispered, "Someone else was in my room with you last night."

"How do you know?" I whispered back.

"Because I opened the bathroom door and saw him leave." She glanced around to make sure no one was listening. "He left with you."

I was speechless. Sophie could turn out to be the best witness yet, but I had to be sure she was telling the truth. "Who was it?"

She raised an eyebrow. "Zack."

The girl in the next bed rose and headed for the bathroom.

With more distance between the girl in the third bed and us, I felt freer to talk but kept my voice low. "Sophie, tell me everything you saw."

She offered a brief smile. "While I was in the bathroom, I thought I heard the door to my dorm open. At first I thought you'd decided to leave without telling me. Then I heard a thump. I was too afraid to come out of the bathroom. I'm sorry."

"Don't apologize," I said. "You did the right thing. Go on."

Sophie's eyes widened. "It was dark. I opened the bathroom door a little so I could see what was happening. That's when I saw Zack. He was carrying you in his arms."

"How can you be sure it was him?"

"When he opened the outer door, some of the tea lights in the corridor were still lit and I saw his face."

"What happened then?"

She took a deep breath. "I stepped out of the bathroom and listened. I heard more noise in the corridor. I was so afraid. I didn't dare open the outer door until the noise faded away. When it was safe to peek, I opened the door and—"

Sophie stopped talking as her roommate returned from the

bathroom and settled under the covers.

"And?" I was dying to find out.

"He was pushing a housekeeping cart," she whispered. "I think you were inside it. Another boy was walking with him, but I couldn't see who it was."

So that's how he transported me to the dumbwaiter.

"There's something else. I found this on the floor after he left." She reached into her jacket pocket and handed me what looked like a small metal brooch. "It's an Honor Roll pin that Verdell awards to their top students."

I flipped it over. The initials Z. B. were inscribed on the back.

CHAPTER 32

Students grimaced in anger and expressed frustration at the desperate conditions the ice storm had created at Verdell: no food and water, and no access to adequate hygiene facilities. They shouted to be heard and raised their fists in a show of protest.

The chaos in the gymnasium had escalated since my visit minutes ago. Who could have predicted days earlier that well-mannered students attending one of the most prestigious schools in the country would display such animosity?

Mrs. Desmond stood in the bleachers, hands raised, trying to restore order. Her features were strained, and she looked as if she'd aged ten years in the last hours. "Girls and boys, please quiet down. We need to discuss this situation like mature people."

"We're leaving," one male student yelled out. "We're going to starve to death if we stay here."

Outbursts of criticism drowned out Mrs. Desmond's voice. She'd lost the respect of the student body and the ensuing ability to control it. Though not as drastic, the scene reminded me of *Lord of the Flies*, a tale about a group of schoolboys stranded on an uninhabited island who attempt to govern themselves with horrific results.

Audrey stood at her post by the door. She turned to me now, her face ashen. "The team supervisors aren't having much success in calming the students. There's no way we can stop them from leaving. Even some of the staff is on board."

A steady stream of students filed out of the gymnasium, toting their backpacks. They turned right, heading for the main building and out the front door.

Ann walked out. She stopped to talk to Audrey and me. "The students are walking to Sherbrooke. I'm going with them. We'll be safe in a group. We'll probably reach the city by tomorrow, unless we run into live wires and fallen trees."

"Not to mention wild animals," Audrey said.

Ann smiled. "I hope not." To me, she said, "I'll drop by to see Dave, if I can. Take care." She gave me a knowing look, then followed the others down the corridor.

Audrey shook her head. "The media is going to have a field day with this one. I can already envision the backlash from the parents."

I had other things on my mind. "Have you seen Michael?"

"He's in there somewhere." She pointed to the swarm in the gymnasium.

I moved among groups of students who were chatting with eagerness about joining their classmates on the journey to Sherbrooke. Most were ready to leave. Others needed more time to pack up their belongings before taking off.

I stood on my tiptoes and scanned the room for Michael and Zack. Knowing Michael, he'd keep Zack within his line of sight as much as possible.

Many students were taller than me—an impediment that limited my view. On the positive side, I could move among them without attracting too much attention.

At one point I was shocked to discover I was standing right behind Zack. If he'd been wearing a hat, I wouldn't have noticed his blonde hair. I peeked around him. He was having a heated conversation with two other boys and was shouting to be heard over the noise in the room.

"You're the best chemistry students at Verdell," Zack said. "You can't go. You have obligations to me. To the business."

One of the boys said to him, "We quit. Find yourself two other lackeys to do your dirty work."

"Look, Harry, I'll double your pay if you stay." Anxiety ran through Zack's voice.

"Forget it." Harry nudged his friend. "Come on, Wally, let's go."

Zack grabbed Harry's arm. "I filled your bellies with food. You'll regret this."

Harry brusquely shook off his grasp. "What are you going to do, Barratt? Send the cops after us?" The two boys laughed and trailed off.

Students blocked my path, so I couldn't move if I'd wanted to. I held my breath and hoped Zack wouldn't turn around.

I was in luck. A girl rushed up to him and pulled him into a chat with other students. Zack spoke with them, all the while glancing around the room. His eyes narrowed as he stared at someone. He dug out the remote to the dumbwaiter and waved it in the air, grinning and laughing at that person.

I followed his gaze but students blocked my view.

I looked back to see Zack bolt. He collided into other students and tripped over backpacks on the floor in his frenzy to get out of the gymnasium. He got up and ran.

In the midst of a sea of blue streaming toward the doorway, I detected a flash of Michael's brown leather jacket. He was pursuing Zack!

Students fenced me in as they squeezed out of the gymnasium. Despite Mrs. Desmond's pleas to reconsider their decision, they moved with a single conviction. They were embarking on a hazardous trip that—once completed—would at least offer the basic necessities of life.

I thought of Sophie and hoped the three medical staff would stay behind to take care of patients sick with the flu. Good thing Sophie wasn't alone in the dorm room. It could explain why Zack hadn't been able to get to her and harm her.

It seemed like an eternity before I finally pushed my way out of the gymnasium.

Audrey was standing against the wall to avoid the stampede of students. She noticed me. "I can't believe this is happening. I saw most of the faculty heading toward the front door with the students."

"Did you see Michael?" I asked her.

She pointed in the opposite direction. "He went out the back door seconds after Zack did. What on earth is—"

I took off, fear flooding my mind.

I swung open the back door. There was no sign of either Michael or Zack.

Where did they go?

I advanced onto the lot. I stepped on rough patches to get a better grip and avoided flat shiny surfaces. The parking lot spanned to my left. I saw no movement there. To my right was the forest. It was quiet, except for the sporadic crash of icy shards to the ground—a sign that the temperature had risen above freezing and the thawing period was underway.

Zack had taunted Michael out of desperation, using the remote as bait to lure him outdoors. Michael wouldn't risk his life running after him unless there was a chance it could lead to catching a bigger fish.

I heeded my instincts and moved from the campus into the forest, keeping one eye on the treacherous ice and the other for a sign of Michael or Zack. I slipped and almost fell a couple of times but regained my balance and continued along.

I remembered Favreau's phone in my pocket. I dug it out and checked for a signal. There was one but it was weak. I put the phone back in my pocket.

I passed the trapdoor and kept on walking for ten more minutes. The forest was thicker in this area and included more evergreens.

Voices drifted my way.

Argumentative voices.

Voices that reverberated in the frosty air.

Which direction were they coming from?

I took two more steps, then ducked behind a tree.

Michael and Zack were in a face-off about twenty feet to my left. Zack was wielding his knife and slicing the air in front of Michael, forcing him to step backward toward the wide stump of a maple tree.

Partially covered by a clump of evergreens and further back

stood a cabin. I assumed it was the same cabin I'd entered through the underground tunnel. A van was parked in front of it, the license plate visible.

I reached for Favreau's phone. It had power. I chose the video setting and aimed the phone in the direction of the van, zooming in.

"Give it up, Zack," Michael said. "This isn't the path in life you want to take."

"You're wrong," Zack said. "I make loads of money. It beats working my ass off to get a bunch of useless diplomas."

"The cops have evidence against you for the murders. You need to come clean."

"You're just talk."

"They have proof. Witnesses too."

"You're bluffing." Zack lashed out at him with the knife.

Michael jumped back. "Nat's baby has your DNA."

"So what?"

"The cops know you killed her. Like you killed Andrew and Greg."

Zack glowered. "And now I'm going to kill you." He swung his knife in a wide arc, cutting Michael's leather jacket. He swung again, but Michael leaped backward, his body now inches from the tree stump.

A gray-haired man rushed out of the cabin. He had a dog on a leash. A Doberman Pinscher. "Zack! Wait!" The man coughed.

Zack yelled out, "It's okay, Dad. I can handle it."

I drew in a quick breath.

My hand shook as I aimed the phone. It took sheer will power to calm down and record the scene before me.

Another man exited the cabin. He had a beefy build with hair trimmed down to his scalp. He pulled out a revolver. "Let me take care of this, Trenton."

"Careful, Sammy, don't hit my boy," Trenton said. Then to Zack, "Stand back, son."

"No, I can handle this," Zack shouted. "Stay out of it, both of you."

The Doberman broke free from Trenton's grasp.

I watched in horror as it bounded toward Michael, preparing to leap.

Sammy raised his gun and aimed it at Michael but lost his footing on the ice.

A deafening shot rang out.

The dog collapsed on top of Michael, plunging him to the ground.

A loud cracking sound exploded through the forest. Another gunshot?

A massive branch above Zack toppled. Tapered icicles plummeted at rapid speed, piercing his head. Blood splashed in all directions. Zack slumped to the ground, the enormous branch crushing his body.

"Zack!" His father cried out, scrambling over the icy surface to reach him.

"No, Trenton, wait!" Sammy scurried behind his brother.

Trenton slipped and would have tumbled to the ground had Sammy not caught hold of his arm.

"Let me go. I have to help Zack." Trenton yanked his arm out of Sammy's grip and approached his son's lifeless body. Unable to get closer because of the fallen branch, he gawked at the bloodstained scene, shoulders sagging, the tragedy of personal loss etched on his face.

"It's too late, Trenton," Sammy said in a low voice. "He's gone." He put a hand on his brother's shoulder.

Trenton glanced up at me. The look of hatred that spread over his face glued me to the spot.

Sammy steered Trenton to the passenger side of the van, then slid in behind the wheel and sped off.

I rushed over to Michael. My heart beat so hard, I could swear it was echoing through the forest.

I fell to my knees beside him. The Doberman had thrust him clear of the icicles and tree branch, but Michael's eyes were closed. It took all my strength to push the dead dog off him.

I examined Michael's jacket. The animal's blood had splattered over it. Then I noticed a hole in his sleeve.

"Oh, no!" I placed an arm under his head. "Michael, talk to me. Michael!"

He groaned and his eyelids fluttered open. "Megan." He tried to sit up and grimaced in pain.

"Don't move. I'll try to find something to stop the bleeding."

"It's just a flesh wound." His gaze moved to Zack, the young man's blood seeping into the icy fissures around him. "Where are the others?"

"Zack's father and Sammy drove off." I held up Favreau's phone, my hand still shaking. "I caught most of what happened before on video."

"Good work." Michael managed a smile. "You think you can ring up the cops on that thing?"

I looked at the screen. It was lit and indicated a strong signal.

Help was a phone call away.

CHAPTER 33

The ice storm was more widespread than we'd first believed. It had caused massive destruction to trees and electrical infrastructure in southern Quebec and eastern Ontario. The government had declared a state of emergency and deployed thousands of Canadian Armed Forces to help clear roads and restore power even during the catastrophe.

Army patrols cut short the journey of Verdell students and staff to Sherbrooke and arranged for their transportation to the city's emergency shelters. As expected, the media grabbed the occasion to capture photos and videos of the disheveled passengers disembarking. The occasion took a surprising turn when students and staff refused to answer media questions or offer comments. In retaliation, the press used captions like "evasive elites" in their articles the next day.

Unknown to the media, lawyers representing Verdell had sent students and staff cautionary emails. Their advice was to remain tight-lipped about the student deaths at the school until law enforcement officers had completed their investigation. Though not all cell phones were functional, students and staff who had turned off their phones during the ice storm had power to spare. On receipt of the emails, they alerted the others.

Aside from students and staff sick with the flu, everyone received a clean bill of health. Families soon collected their children or made other arrangements for housing them until classes resumed at Verdell.

The license plate number on the video I captured with Favreau's phone helped the police to apprehend Trenton and Sammy Barratt. It had been an easy arrest, since the van registered to the former had careened off an icy road and into a ditch, leaving both men stranded.

As evidence came to light, police discovered the Hells Angels had hired Gary Stilt, my former client, to procure investors for Trenton Barratt's excavation projects. The angels were in a hurry to finance the bogus mining projects so they could use sections of the tunnels for their drug-manufacturing operations.

Police seized toxic chemicals from Zack's underground lab that would have been used to produce 200,000 pills with a street value of a million dollars. A tunnel under Verdell led police along a track to a Hells Angels warehouse. Located miles deeper in the woods, it looked like an abandoned shack, but its basement served as the drop-off point for underground drug labs in the area. Along with the Barratt brothers, twenty other members of the biker group faced charges of possession of illegal drugs, the manufacture and trafficking of illegal drugs, and conspiracy. The arrested members included Stu and Rob.

The police used the video evidence on Favreau's phone to charge the Barratt brothers for an attempt on Michael's life. The men were charged in Favreau's murder too, though there was no evidence to connect them to the murders of students Nat, Andrew, and Greg.

An analysis of Zack's knife, however, did reveal DNA belonging to Greg, which confirmed our suspicions all along. Autopsy reports indicated Nat and Andrew had been drugged and had drowned when the car sank into the river. Police couldn't confirm the identity of the driver, though it was assumed that Zack had acted alone in planning the three murders, which erased any doubts about Helga's implication. My testimony, however, did earn Helga a reprimand and a counseling session in Verdell's Bullying Prevention Program.

Zack's attempts to incriminate Dave Pellegrino fell apart when police reviewed Verdell's surveillance videotapes and Nat's diary. On the night Nat and Andrew were murdered, Zack had lured Dave to the boy's dorm with fake text messages about a disturbance there. The videotape showed Dave exiting the echo through the girl's dorm, raising police suspicions about his alibi. As Dave had already told us, another videotape placed him in the library till late that night—past the time his car had been stolen from the parking lot and driven into the forest. DNA results established Dave wasn't the father of Nat's baby. Zack was.

Our suspicions were confirmed when we learned Mrs. Desmond had played a role in Trenton Barratt's plans to operate drug labs in the tunnels. She'd pleaded ignorance to any knowledge of the drug lab under Verdell at first, but lawyers obtained signed statements from undisclosed sources that corroborated she'd sold off school property to Trenton Barratt in exchange for a percentage of the operation. It explained why she'd kept a close eye on Michael and me and pretended to seek our help, and why she'd protected Zack. Her charade continued until she realized the odds had mounted against her.

I speculated whether Audrey was a police informant and whether she'd made a deal for witness immunity in exchange for her testimony. She wasn't called to the stand to testify and had since left her job at Verdell, so we'd never know for sure. A similar situation might have played out for Zack's chemistry buddies, who were transferred to another private school after they provided their testimony to the police. As for Mrs. Desmond and the Barratt brothers, they'd have a lengthy stay behind bars to atone for their transgressions.

Michael had achieved what he'd set out to do. He published a series of articles covering the Hells Angels and their drug-trafficking operations in the Sherbrooke area, adding a personal spin to his eyewitness account. His articles were nominated for several journalism awards, and I couldn't have been happier for him.

We weren't surprised when the criminal investigation dragged into spring. As often happens with complex cases involving notorious criminals, multiple murders, and drug-trafficking operations, it takes time and resources to get the legal paperwork processed and coordinate courtroom schedules.

We accepted Dave's invitation to visit Verdell after one of our court dates. Sunlight flooded the school atrium and exposed the dust particles floating in the air from recent renovations. Students bustled about, talking and texting on their phones. A new dean had been appointed. Life had returned to normal.

Sophie approached me during our visit. She'd replaced her eyeglasses with contact lenses and had her hair cut short. She made a point to tell me the dumbwaiter had been sealed up and painted over. She also told me about her new boyfriend, then hugged me and wished me well.

I perused Verdell's website from time to time. Students continued to excel and win prestigious awards, thanks to new sponsors who had come forward. I was relieved to see that the school's sterling reputation was still intact and that its "solid learning foundation" would keep generations of scholars moving forward.

The irony of Mrs. Desmond's involvement continued to haunt me. Why would a woman whose son had died from a drug overdose consent to a drug-producing operation deep within Verdell? How could she condone an illegal operation on the one hand while enforcing a stringent code of behavior among her students and staff on the other?

The inevitable answer: easy money. In her mind, Trenton Barratt offered a swift and justifiable means to attain her goal with a convenience she couldn't refuse. Maybe she'd had no choice. After all, she was no match for a coldblooded criminal.

Michael often says that time is a great healer. I wanted to believe that somewhere in a lonely jail cell, Mrs. Desmond was recalling the positive memories of her days at Verdell—memories that would help to ease her guilty conscience and soothe her weary soul.

Michael stood by the front door, holding an overnight bag and staring at my two pieces of luggage. "We're only going away for the weekend."

"I packed a few extra little things. I think you'll like them." I smiled.

"Oh...in that case." He leaned over and kissed me. "You can bring all the luggage you want."

I laughed and picked up my bags. "The clerk at the country resort told me the scenery is spectacular in the spring and worth the three-hour drive. There's a small town nearby with antique shops, delicious restaurants, and a river with waterfalls."

Michael locked the door behind us. "Sounds like the perfect place to unwind and forget about everything else."

Acknowledgments

I wish to acknowledge the special people who have helped me pull this book together. These include my editor, proofreaders, and cover designer. To each of you, my deepest thanks for your support.

A sincere gratitude goes to my husband John, who provided inspiration and encouraged my journey through the pages of this novel.

About the Author

Sandra Nikolai is the author of the Megan Scott/Michael Elliott Mystery series. In addition to her novels, Sandra has published a string of short stories, garnering Honorable Mentions along the way.

A graduate of McGill University in Montreal, Sandra held jobs in sales, finance, and high tech before leaving the corporate world to pursue a career in writing. She likes to think that plotting a whodunit reveals the lighter—yet more mysterious—side of her persona.

To keep up to date with Sandra's latest books and events, visit www.sandranikolai.com where you can read her blog posts and join her Newsletter.

You can also become a fan on Goodreads or Facebook, or follow Sandra on Twitter: @SandraNikolai

Books in the Megan Scott/Michael Elliott Mystery series:

False Impressions

Fatal Whispers

Icy Silence

CPSIA information can be obtained at www.ICGtesting.com
Printed in the USA
LVOW10s1457031016

507207LV00019B/1143/P